COWGIRL CRAZY

The Cowboy Way, Book 2
Ryan's Story

Becky McGraw

Acknowledgements

Thank you to Rob Lang of Rob Lang Photography for the outstanding cowboy photo used on the cover of Cowgirl Crazy. Rob has more amazing photos, including some of the hottest cowboys in America on his website at www.roblangimages.com.

Thank you to both HeatherLynn Portraits and Fitness Model Don Allen for the photo on the back cover. You can find out more about Heather at www.facebook.com/Heatherlynn-portraits or Don Allen at www.facebook.com/DonAllenFitness

I'd also like to thank both my Crazy Cowgirls and my Troublemakers for your amazing support and help with promotion. You guys are both my cheerleaders and my friends. I love and appreciate you all.

Finally, thank you to Carolyn Depew of Write Right Edits for not only your amazing support, but the fantastic job you did with the edit on this book. I'd also like to thank Carolyn's husband, Bob Depew, for providing the hilarious, but true, tampon-up-the-nose-applicator-and-all story that I used for a scene in this book. Life is funnier than fiction sometimes.

This is a work of fiction. Names, characters, places and incidents are products of the author's imagination or are used fictitiously and are not to be construed as real. Any resemblance to actual events, locales, organizations, or persons, living or dead, is entirely coincidental.

COWGIRL CRAZY (Cowboy Way, #2) Copyright © July 2014 by Becky McGraw

Cover image: Copyright © 2014 by Rob Lang Photography
Back Cover image: Copyright © 2014 by HeatherLynn Photography

ISBN-13: 978-1500588076 ISBN-10: 1500588075

All rights reserved. No part of this publication may be reproduced, distributed, or transmitted in any form or by any means, including photocopying, recording, or other electronic or mechanical methods, without the prior written permission of the publisher, except in the case of brief quotations embodied in critical reviews and certain other noncommercial uses permitted by copyright law. For permission requests, write to the publisher, addressed "Attention: Permissions Coordinator," at the address below.

Becky McGraw Books | 13057 SPID, Unit A, Box 189
Corpus Christi, TX 78418 | www.beckymcgraw.com

Ordering Information: Quantity sales. Special discounts are available on quantity purchases by corporations, associations, and others. For details, contact the publisher at the address above. Printed in the United States of America.

Be sure to check out all of the books by Becky McGraw:

Texas Trouble Series:

Book #1 - My Kind of Trouble (Cassie & Luke)

Book #2 - The Trouble With Love (Sabrina & Cole)

Book #3 - Double the Trouble (Karlie & Gabe)

Book #4 - Looking for Trouble (Jess & Wade)

Book #5 - Trouble in Dixie (Katie & Tommy)

Book #6 - Asking for Trouble (Jazzie & Beau)

Book #7 - Chasing Trouble (Jenny & Chase)

Book #8 - Here Comes Trouble (Terri & Joel)

Book #9 - Worth the Trouble (Roxanne & Ethan)

Book #10 - Royal Trouble (Leigh Ann & Wes)

Book #11 - Trouble With the Law (Veronica & Trace)

Book #12 – Borrowing Trouble (Carrie & Dylan)

Coming in 2015 – Book #13 – Trouble Down Under (Zane's Story)

The Cowboy Way

Hope for Christmas (Cord's Story – novella included in Santa Wore Spurs)

Just Shoot Me (#1, Cowboy Way, Dean's story)

Cowgirl Crazy (#2, Cowboy Way, Ryan's story)

COMING SOON – Too Hot to Trot (#3, Cowboy Way, Zack's Story)

New Series – Logan's Lonestar Heroes

Coming in Fall 2014 -- A new western romantic suspense series featuring ex-military, ex-cop, security specialist and private investigator, Dave Logan, from the Texas Trouble series and his hot men.

Look for a novella entitled Hell Bent (Cade's Story) in the Red Hot Treats collection being released on October 15, 2014, which launches the new series. Dave Logan's, book one in the series, will follow shortly thereafter.

CHAPTER ONE

Ryan Easter was worn out, and he hurt like a bitch. That landing on his last ride had jarred more than his teeth. Every bone in his body reminded him he'd abused his body with hard living and hard rides, and at thirty-years-old, he wasn't a young man anymore. But that jarring landing had come after he'd done his eight. He'd won the saddle bronc competition, so every ache was worth it. It might not be next time, if he hurt himself worse, but this time he had a nice paycheck in his pocket for his trouble.

All he wanted right now was a beer, a bath and bed. But it looked like Amber Sue Worth had different plans for him. And she wasn't taking no for an answer. The buckle bunny who seemed to find him every time the rodeo stopped in Tulsa was back again for more.

"Really, Amber, I'm too tired to go out tonight. Go find Zack, he'll go with you." He looked down at her chest and couldn't help but stare at the fabulous rack pushing up and over the low-cut white tank top. His mouth should be watering. Amber was beautiful and very talented with her mouth, but the thought of her left him cold this time.

He really was getting old.

She licked her lips suggestively, leaning in just a little closer so that those beautiful breasts rubbed his arm. "I don't want to go out with Zack. I want you," she said in a low raspy tone. "C'mon, honey.

It's been four months, and you're not gonna be back in town for another five."

The whine in her voice rubbed on his nerves like sandpaper, as much as the fact that she kept up with his schedule.

Her full mouth kicked up at the corner. "We don't have to go out. I'll go get you a beer, you can shower, then we can, ah…cuddle."

Cuddle? Amber knew damned well Ryan wasn't a cuddler. And he knew damned well she had a lot more than that in mind. He was too tired to argue with her though.

"Fine. I'll be in my trailer." She squealed, and Ryan flinched. This was going to be the last time he was with Amber Sue. She needed to find herself another cowboy to entertain her. That's all she was looking for. Free drinks and a fuck.

She bounced off toward the arena and Ryan's eyes locked onto her round ass, then glided down the back of her toned thighs to the top of her cowboy boots. He was sure she wouldn't have a bit of problems finding a willing replacement for him. If he was smart, Ryan would tell her to do that tonight. But she was bringing him a beer. That did make his mouth water. Ryan guessed he needed to get himself together enough to pay for it later.

With a sigh, he shifted his duffle on his shoulder as he walked to his trailer. His steps stuttered then stopped when his eyes fell on Twyla, his best friend's sister, sitting on the steps waiting for him. Twyla and Zack were as close to siblings as he had. They were more than his best friends, they were family, and from the look on her face she was upset about something.

Just what he needed tonight. He really didn't want to know, but he couldn't stop from asking, "What's up, Sissy?"

"Tango was tight tonight," she replied with a frustrated sigh.

"You been rubbing him down like the vet told you to?" Ryan asked setting his heavy bag down beside the steps.

"Yeah, with that smelly ass liniment he gave me." She added a short humorless laugh. "Can't you smell it?"

Now that she mentioned it he did smell a pungent mix of linseed oil and menthol. "I thought that was a new perfume or something," he shot back and grinned.

She laughed and kicked him in the shin. "I don't wear perfume, and you know that."

No, she just wore nature's perfume. Hay and sunshine, often mixed with rich horse. That's what she usually smelled like, and to Ryan it was headier than any bottled scent on earth.

His brain automatically shoved that information to the back of his mind, like it had done for years. Since she grew those proud little breasts and sprouted the longest legs on any woman he'd ever seen. Ryan knew if he ever acknowledged that he noticed those facts Zack would kick his ass. Every cowboy on this circuit knew it too. Zack was as overprotective as they came where his sister was concerned. Besides it would mess up the little family thing they had going on too. Something Ryan needed in his life more than he needed a woman in his bed.

He cleared his throat and shifted his weight from foot to foot. The best thing he could do for her was get her the hell out of here, before Amber came back. For ten years, since she sprouted those perfect little breasts, Twyla thought it was her job to protect him like a mother hen, and she had been his shadow. Hell, his shadow didn't even follow him as closely as Twyla did. And Ryan wasn't blind to the reason why. She wanted more from him than he was willing to give her. His solution was to keep her pissed off at him, so she'd back off. So far it had worked pretty well.

"Yeah, I know. But I don't know what you think I can do to make Tango feel better. Call the vet again. Maybe he has another suggestion."

She looked up at him and pushed her hat back on her head. A long strand of her silky white blond hair fell out to frame her face. The light at the edge of the trailer illuminated her beautiful blue eyes, and she smiled that smile that mule-kicked him in the gut. "You could buy me a beer. Might not make Tango feel better, but it sure would make me feel better."

Out of the corner of his eye, Ryan caught a flash of movement and saw Amber exit the arena with two beers in her hand. Adrenaline shot through him as he grabbed Twyla's shoulders to pull her to her feet. He turned her toward the barn, then with a little push he said, "Not tonight, Twy—I'm tired and you need to go check on your horse." *Right now, this instant, before Amber gets here and we have a catfight that I don't feel like dealing with tonight.*

"Damn, cowboy. You're in a big hurry to get rid of me tonight!" she said with a laugh, and tried to turn around again. He held tight and nudged her forward again. "I need a shower, and I don't have time to talk right now. Just go take care of Tango."

"Alright." With a laugh, she shook off his hands.

She took a few steps toward the barn and Ryan breathed again, but then she turned back toward him. He knew the moment she spotted Amber. Her eyes narrowed, her body tensed and her lips pinched. Her hurt and angry eyes fixed on his. "I forgot we were in Tulsa. No wonder you were in such a hurry to see the back of me. I've never seen a woman chase a man as hard as she chases you."

Piss her off. Get her out of here. "Well, that's pretty much the pot calling the kettle black, isn't it, sweetheart?" he asked meanly, with a snort for emphasis. "You follow me around like a lost puppy. You need to get a life, Twy and stop worrying about mine."

Anger filled her eyes and she put her hands on her hips. "I'm just trying to protect you from women like that one." She notched her chin toward Amber who had stopped beside him.

Amber gasped, and he saw Twyla winding up for a fight. Ryan stepped between them, and put his hands on his hips. "I don't need protecting, Sissy. I told you that so many times, I'm hoarse from it. Just get lost."

Her jaw worked, and he heard a growl rumble in her chest. "And I told you not to call me that!" Her fists clenched at her sides, as she took another step toward him. She pointed at Amber, but her eyes stayed locked on his. "That one isn't good enough for you."

"And who has been in your eyes, Twy?" Ryan asked softly, dangerously. "Who will ever be? And what makes you think you have the right to decide that?"

Twyla huffed out a breath and leaned in closer. Her nose was almost touching his, the heat of her anger enhanced her heady scent, and it surrounded him. "I lo—um, care about you, Ryan. That gives me the right. You're a stupid man and don't see what women like her are up to!" she ground out, pointing at Amber again.

Ryan saw the pulse pounding at her throat, and his tongue tingled to taste it, feel that energy of hers redirected, focused on something different than arguing with him entirely. He inhaled deeply, because he couldn't stop himself, and drank her in through his senses. Twyla Taylor was so damned beautiful when she was angry.

And he didn't need to be fucking noticing that.

He cocked his head to the side and said, "Newsflash, darlin'. You don't have the market cornered on brains, even though you think you do.

And just because you might care about me doesn't give you the right to make my decisions or judge whoever I decide to be with. It's my damned life!" Ryan grabbed her shoulders to turn her around. "Now, carry your ass to the barn, check on your horse, then go back to the trailer and harass Zack for a little while."

He ignored the indignant little grunt, and gave her a gentle push. She staggered a couple of steps, then stiffened her shoulders and stormed off. Good, she was pissed off. Maybe that would buy him a few days peace, he thought, as he turned back toward Amber and took the second beer from her. He tossed his head back and drank it almost down. He smacked his lips together and handed her the bottle. "Thanks for the beer, honey, but I'm not in the mood tonight." He grabbed the strap on his duffle, and hefted it up to his shoulder.

"But—" Amber whined, sticking out her lower lip.

She took a few steps behind him, but Ryan held up his hand. He knew if he let her in his trailer, it would end badly. He really wasn't in the mood now. Not after the fight he'd just had with the woman he really wanted inside his trailer tonight. This little redhead fell way short of Twyla in a lot of areas, and no amount of pretending was going to make that different.

Not this time. Not tonight.

Ryan had been putting it off for a long time, but he knew if he didn't do something about Twyla soon, he was going to go batshit crazy. It was getting harder every day to push her away. Sleeping with buckle bunnies when he wanted her was not the solution. That took the edge off of his hunger for her, and pissed her off enough to keep her away temporarily. But that was just it. It was temporary. The next morning she was in his face, flirting with him, helping him with things he could do on his own, or when she ran out of excuses, she followed him to give him a hard time. Her favorite pastime was giving him a hard time.

And Ryan walked around constantly hard because of it.

No, this permanent solution would have to involve manning up to tell Twyla he would never feel that way about her. Could never feel that way about her. She was family, his surrogate sister, nothing more. He couldn't ever let his feelings for her go beyond that. He hadn't done that before, because he felt like it would hurt her. And that was the last thing he wanted to do. But this was hurting her more, and if he didn't say anything she would end up hurt worse.

The best thing he could do was just tell her he wasn't risking losing the only family he'd ever known, and his best friend, to go there with her. It just wasn't worth it for either of them. Twyla Renee Taylor just needed to back off of his bumper, and he was going to tell her that.

***

Twyla Taylor was done chasing Ryan Easter. She had been chasing the man for ten years, since she was sixteen years old. Enough was enough. Last night had been the final straw.

Ryan had done everything he could to push her away for years, and she was finally taking his not so subtle hints. It was time to get over her infatuation. She just needed to face facts. Her brother, Zack, was never going to let Ryan see her as anything more than an irritating kid sister. Either that or Ryan didn't give a flying rat's ass about her that way.

Her heart squeezed in her chest, as she slammed the door of the tack compartment shut, after stuffing her saddle inside. That was more likely. Hell, the women he was with every night of the week, like the one last night, were a helluva lot better looking than she was. Twyla knew she was tall, gangly and flat-chested, verging on homely in her opinion. She never wore makeup, or did a damned thing to try to be girly. The damned stuff melted off in thirty minutes of practice in the arena, why would she bother?

Because he might have taken you more seriously, looked a little harder, if you'd have taken the time to fix yourself up. If you had spent half as much time trying to be a woman, as you did trying to fit in with the guys.

To hell with that. She was who she was, and Twyla wasn't changing for a man. She was a rough-riding tomboy who didn't give a shit what people thought about her. There had to be a man out there who would appreciate that quality in a woman. One thing was for sure. Ryan Easter would never be that man. She knew that now.

The best thing she could do was just get away from both of them, her overbearing brother and Ryan. Grow up and find a new direction for her life. Hell, get one, just like Ryan had told her to do last night. The anger, hurt and frustration she'd felt last night resurfaced to form a tight knot in her throat. His words had driven right into her heart and branded themselves there. Twyla would never forgive him, but she was going to try damned hard to forget him.

It would take time, because she had been in love with Ryan since she was sixteen years old, and the nineteen-year-old had almost kissed her out by the bonfire at her parent's ranch. Ever since then she'd harbored hope that someday he might finish that kiss. Notice her. Figure out how she felt about him.

But that hope died a painful death last night, and Ryan had just lost the best thing that almost happened to him. She was not going to be held captive by that almost kiss anymore. Twyla was going off to find herself a life, and her friend Heather was going to help her.

She secured Tango's lead rope to the hook inside the trailer, then squeezed out and shut the back door with a little more force than necessary. The loud bang pulled a frightened whinny from Tango. She walked to the window at the side of the trailer, tiptoed and stuck her hand inside to scratch his nose. "I'm sorry, honey. It's not your fault that he's a blind asshole."

He could have his damned buckle bunnies and barflies, and he could have the rodeo. She was going to find something else to do. She'd been barrel racing since she was sixteen too, and she still wasn't winning like she wanted to. Twyla was going to find something she was good at, other than chasing Ryan Easter, other than watching his back to make sure he didn't get roped in by one of those buckle bunnies. He'd called her his wingman before, and it hacked her off every time she heard it. Let her damned brother be his wingman.

Twyla was a woman, and a good one. She was going to find a man who realized that, right after she figured out who she was as a woman. Last night she called her only female friend, Heather, a woman she'd ridden barrels with for a year on the circuit. Heather had invited her to come to stay with her in Dallas. She'd also given Twyla several ideas of things she could try out to see if they fit. Since Heather left the circuit, her friend had gotten involved in a lot of stuff that sounded pretty damned interesting.

And she sounded happy.

That was the feeling that had escaped Twyla for years. It was a feeling she was determined to recapture. With a sigh, she turned away from the trailer, and bumped into a broad chest. Twyla stumbled back, ready to blast whoever was blocking her way. But it was Ryan, and her heart did a fricking somersault in her chest like it always did around him. Damned heart.

Gritting her teeth, she asked, "What do you want?"

"Where are you going?" he asked with his hands on his hips. "We don't pull out until tonight." The damned morning sunlight made the auburn highlights in his beard growth sparkle, and his blue eyes look almost translucent. Twyla was determined not to notice, and she was more than determined not to let the scent of his piney cologne affect her this time.

"*You* don't pull out until tonight. I am pulling out *now*," she ground out, before turning her back to walk around the rear of the truck. Ryan followed closely behind her.

"Where the hell do you think you're going? You have to ride tonight. You're in second place, and can win this time!"

Twyla grabbed the door handle on the truck, but looked back over her shoulder. "I'm always in second place, and I'm tired of it." *With you and in the standings*, she added mentally and fought the damned feminine emotion that tried to choke her. "I told the admin this morning that I'm out. Now, I'm telling you. Pass it on to Zack."

Twyla jerked the handle, but Ryan leaned over her to push the door closed again. "What the hell is wrong with you? You can't just leave! If this is about last night—"

"This is about *every* fricking night!" she shouted, shouldering him away from her. "Now *move*! I've got to get to Dallas."

Twyla swung open the door and managed to hop into the driver's seat, but Ryan blocked the door with his big body so she couldn't shut it. "What the fuck is in Dallas?"

"The life that you told me to get last night," she replied snottily.

His brows furrowed, and his voice became softer, coercing almost. "I'm sorry, Sissy. You can't just leave. Mama will be—"

Anger shot up to her head and it felt like it might explode. It came out of her with a rush of words. "The first thing you need to realize, Ryan Easter, is that I am *not* your sister. And *my* mother knows I'm leaving. I called her last night."

"Zack is gonna be pissed," Ryan said.

It figured that's who Ryan would be worried about. "Zack can get glad the same way he got mad. I'm a grown woman, and it's time both of you recognize that. Now *move*!" She jerked the door, and he backed up, but didn't leave.

She slammed the door, then rolled down the window to get some air. The air conditioning in her old truck had given up the ghost a couple of years ago, and she hadn't had the money to fix it.

"He's going to blame me," Ryan said, tipping his hat back on his head.

"He should blame you, asshole," she replied, angry that her hand shook as she put the keys into the ignition. "But he should blame himself more. I'm done with both of you." Twyla cranked the truck, and put it in drive.

Ryan had no choice but to back up, or have his foot run over by the trailer, as Twyla pulled off. In the side mirror of the truck, she saw him throw up his hands and kick up dust with his boot, before he turned and stomped off toward the arena. She wanted to laugh. If that man felt half of the frustration she was dealing with, had dealt with far too long, he should be good and frustrated. It was about damned time he got some of what he'd been dishing out for ten years.

But Ryan Easter's state-of-mind was the last thing on hers when she pulled out onto the highway. Excitement for the new adventures that waited for her in Dallas built inside of her, as she took the ramp to the interstate heading to Dallas.

Freedom called. Freedom from the oppressive control of her older brother, and freedom from the crush on Ryan Easter that she had nursed for ten years too long.

CHAPTER TWO

"Twyla get up, we're gonna be late!" Heather yelled from the kitchen.

Twyla sniffed, smelled bacon frying mixed with the aroma of rich coffee, and her eyes popped open. God, she could use that coffee. A gallon of it. She hadn't gotten to Heather's apartment yesterday evening until nearly seven o'clock, because she had to meet with the owners at Tango's new barn and get him settled in a stall. She'd been sleeping since then, but still didn't feel fully rested. The bed in Heather's spare bedroom was too soft, a far cry from the pullout in Zack's travel trailer. This whole situation was just strange to her, but Twyla knew she would eventually get used to it. She had to get used to it. This would be her new life.

During the five-hour drive to Dallas, she and Heather talked on the phone nearly the whole time. Her friend had helped her come up with a plan to get her life on a different track. One that didn't include the rodeo, barrel racing, or Ryan Easter.

Rolling over on her side, Twyla covered her head with her pillow. She did not want to go to that salon today with Heather, or shopping. Twyla was not a shopper, and she sure as hell never worried about doing her hair or makeup. But if she wanted the job which was open at the Crazy Cowgirl, she was going to have to suck it up and go along with Heather's plan.

According to her friend, she made nearly a thousand dollars a week working as a waitress there, and Twyla could sure use that money. It would allow her to get the equipment and start training to do what she really wanted to do, enter the Cowboy Mounted Shooting events. Twyla was a good rider and a good shot. She thought maybe she could do better at that than she had at barrel racing. She was at least going to try it. There were a lot of things she was going to try, things that being stuck in the barrel racing circuit for so long had prevented. Twyla felt sure she would eventually hit on something she was good at.

Hopefully she'd get the job at the bar, and be good at waitressing, because the paltry money she had saved from her winnings from barrel racing was going to run out swiftly. All Heather told her about the job was that she would be serving drinks, and maybe doing some dancing. Twyla was as uncoordinated as they came, a tomboy, and Heather knew that. They'd been out together before, and while Heather twirled around the dance floor with a string of men, Twyla managed to step on one cowboy's toes badly enough that word must've gotten around and nobody else asked her to dance.

But Heather was going to teach her. She told Twyla if she could shake her hips, she'd make tips. Twyla thought maybe she could manage that, although she feared her version of hip-shaking might result in someone thinking she was having a seizure and calling 911.

Heather was the performer, a singer and

dancer all her life, and she was good. Making it as a singer was Heather's dream, and Twyla knew she'd eventually make it, because even though Heather was a failure as a barrel racer like Twyla, she had the talent. She'd seen her friend perform and her voice was just amazing.

Twyla knew she had to have some kind of hidden talent too. It was just going to take time and effort to find out what that was. One thing she knew for sure was her talents would never include singing and dancing. She'd leave that to Heather.

Lying in bed wasn't going to help her discover her talents, though. This was the first day of her new start, and she was wasting it. Throwing back the covers, Twyla sat on the side of the bed and got her bearings. With a heavy sigh, she padded across the floor and walked into the small kitchen. "Coffee," she croaked, after unsticking her tongue from the roof of her mouth.

Heather glanced at her, pulled a mug down off the hook below the cabinet then handed it to her. She smiled, as she picked up the spatula again. "You better get a move on, sunshine. We've got dragons to slay today."

"I feel like a damned dragon, so watch out," Twyla grumped as she filled the mug. Primping, shopping and dancing, their to-do list for the day, wasn't going to improve her mood. But if she wanted to be successful at her five-o'clock interview with the manager of the bar, she did need to get a move on. Heather had a miracle to perform in just a few hours.

"I'm probably going to make a fool out of myself in front of your manager."

"Nah, we'll get you whipped into shape," Heather replied with a laugh as she flipped the egg in the bacon grease to cook the other side.

"I'd rather the whipping over trying to dance. You know I'm as clumsy as a stump."

"Stop it!" Heather shouted. "You are going to do fine. Leon isn't looking for professional dancers, he's looking for good-looking women."

"Well, I'm not that either," Twyla said, leaning against the counter to blow the steam from her cup.

Heather looked at her and grinned. "You will be when I get done with you. "

Twyla groaned and took a long hot sip of her coffee which scalded all the way down her throat to her stomach. She welcomed the pain. It couldn't be any worse than the torture she knew was waiting for her at the beauty salon, and then the mall.

Heather elbowed her. "Come on Twy – change your attitude or you won't get the job. You have to feel sexy to be sexy."

"I haven't *ever* felt sexy, and I doubt I ever will. I'm a tomboy. I haven't worn a dress since I was four. Drove my mother crazy."

"Oh, you won't be wearing dresses, darlin'. We're going to find some shorts that will show off those long legs I'd die to have."

"I have bird legs." Long yeah, but skinny as hell. They were toned from all the riding she did, but they weren't something she was proud of. Because she was so tall, Twyla always felt gangly and out of place.

"You have legs up to your chin," Heather countered. "Be proud of them. Own them."

Twyla snorted. "I do own them unfortunately," she replied looking down at the top of her shorter friend's dark head.

Heather tsked, then flipped the egg out of the skillet onto a plate and shoved it at her. "Eat, and for God's sake finish that coffee. You need an attitude adjustment."

"It's gonna take a lot more than a cup of coffee to do that. I'm in a little bit of a funk if you haven't noticed."

"Oh, I've noticed. Now if you want my help, eat your damned breakfast and work on your mood. I'm going to get ready."

Two hours later, Heather shoved her arm through the dressing room door and a silky tank top and a pair of miniscule blue jean shorts dangled from her fingers. Twyla grabbed them, and inspected them. "Holy shit, girl, get the other piece of these shorts off the rack for me will you?"

Twyla held them up and saw they were only about three inches long from the waistband to the ragged hem. And there were wear holes in them that looked like a rat had chewed through the denim. The bottom of the pockets hung past the bottom of the legs.

"Put 'em on Twyla," Heather said firmly.

"We're running out of time!"

Huffing out a breath, Twyla stepped into the shorts, and sucked in to snap them. She jumped from foot to foot and fought the zipper until she finally got it to the top of the track. "Fifteen pounds of feed in a ten pound sack," she grumbled as she turned to look over her shoulder in the mirror. The crease at the bottom of her ass cheeks was on prime display. "I'm not wearing these. Get me a bigger size."

Heather's pretty face appeared through the curtain. Her eyes tracked down Twyla's legs to her toes then flew back up. She grinned. "Those fit you perfect! Turn around!"

All Twyla could figure was her friend must be blind if she thought these shorts fit her. Surely when she saw the back, she'd realize her mistake. Twyla turned her back to the door and folded her arms over her chest waiting for her friend's gasp. Nothing.

"I love the rhinestones on the pockets. That'll sparkle in the lights. Try on the shirt, and I'll get you a few more. There's a pair of boots you need too."

"I can't afford all this, and I don't need a new pair of boots. Mine are perfectly fine."

"Your boots are old, dusty and worn out. They're square-toed men's boots. Riding boots. You need girly boots, and you need this job, remember?"

Twyla's shoulders sank and she unfolded her arms. "I do need this job."

"Then you better start cooperating. Get the shirt on, and I'll get the other stuff. Our appointment at the salon is in fifteen minutes."

Heather disappeared, and Twyla slid the shirt over her head. It swished over her skin feeling like wet silk. When it settled, the material was cold and her nipples hardened. Heather's head poked through the curtain again. "That's too loose. You need something stretchy. Lace maybe. And you need a strapless pushup bra. Take these, and see if they fit better. I'll be right back."

Heather's tone sounded like what Twyla imagined a drill sergeant's would sound like. Authoritative, take no prisoners, your opinion doesn't mean shit. You don't have an opinion if you know what's good for you. So Twyla stifled hers, and changed again. The two shirts fit her just the same, and she knew they weren't going to meet up to Sergeant Heather's expectations either. Twyla was starting to think nothing would, unless she went to that audition naked. Hell, wearing this stuff, she was already halfway there. This whole thing was so not her usual self. Twyla did not wear Daisy Duke shorts, or silky shirts, she never had. Her wardrobe consisted of tank tops, jeans and cotton shirts to cover them.

But look where your usual mode has gotten you. This is a new start for you. You can be anyone you want to be. Nobody here except Heather knows you're a clumsy, dowdy tomboy.

Heather's arm shot through the curtain again and there were two short shirts in her hand. One was a pink checked cotton and the other was sky blue lace. She took them, and Heather handed her a half-bra too. "Hell, I'm flat-chested. I can go without a bra for all that matter," Twyla said looking down in horror at the twenty dollar price tag dangling from the side.

"Make the most of what you have, Twy—that bra will give you the breasts you've always wanted. It has gel inserts."

Holy shit, she was going to have fake boobs. "I don't know, Heather…"

"Just put the damned thing on!" Heather said with frustration.

Her friend really was getting aggravated with her, she could hear it in her tone. Twyla needed her friend's help, so she better get with the program. "Yes, ma'am," she replied with a laugh, sliding the straps of her bra down her shoulders. Reaching behind her, Twyla unfastened the clasp, and dropped her bra to the floor. Quickly, she positioned the new bra and fastened it. When she turned toward the mirror, she gasped. Boobs! She actually had cleavage.

"Holy shit," she whispered in awe.

Heather stuck her head through the curtain, and Twyla saw her broad grin in the mirror. "It's a miracle bra," she said with a laugh.

Twyla's eyes fixed on the mounds of flesh pushing over the top of the cups. "Damn straight it is."

"Try the shirts on and let's get out of here. If we're late to the salon, Sophie will be pissed." Twyla tried on the shirts, and got an approving nod from Heather. They checked out and Twyla thought she might need a second job to pay for the clothes and new boots she'd just bought for her first job. A job she hadn't even gotten yet.

After the trip to the salon for a sixty dollar haircut that didn't amount to much hair being cut at all, a hundred-dollars-worth of makeup, and several cans of hair goop, her debit card was almost melted, and Twyla felt like her face would crack if she smiled. She was definitely going to need a second job, if this one didn't pay off right away, she thought as she got up into the truck with Heather.

"Are we done yet?' she asked plopping the bags down on the floorboard by her feet.

"With shopping yes, but we need to go to Jolie's dance studio for your crash course in the Crazy Cowgirl dance routines. She's our dance coach, and a waitress there too. She owns a dance studio on the side. Between us, I know we can get you up to speed."

Things were already going so fast Twyla's head was spinning. Add any more speed and it might fly off of her shoulders. "Can we reschedule the interview for tomorrow? I'm about worn out from all that!"

Heather laughed. "Girl, you don't know what worn out is. But you're about to find out. You need to work on your stamina, because this job pays well but you have to be able to keep up. When I go home at night, I'm whooped, but my pocketbook is full."

Twyla was starting to have her doubts about how well she was going to fit in at that bar. The job sounded like great money, but she also wondered why she was expected to wear shorts up the crack of her ass, and enough makeup for a clown. Her mother and brother would have a coronary if they saw her. Her daddy would just kill her. She wondered what Ryan would think of how she looked now. She looked a lot like the buckle bunnies she always saw him with.

Stop thinking about him! Who cares what Ryan Easter thinks!

But maybe this job wasn't for her. It was a far cry from rodeoing, or anything else she'd ever done in her life to date. "Maybe I just need to find a regular waitressing job."

"And make eight dollars an hour?" Heather asked with a laugh, as she shoved the truck into gear. "This is the hottest club in town. The job won't be there tomorrow. Girls are waiting in line to work there, because the tips are so good. Leon did me a favor by looking at you first."

Heather was putting her neck on the line to help her. If Twyla backed out, or didn't at least give it her all, her friend would be embarrassed. Maybe lose her own job. Twyla had agreed to do this, told Heather she wanted it. She couldn't let that happen.

"Thank you for asking him," she said.

"I want you to work there too. I think it will be fun. Just like old times."

Not quite. The last time they worked together

had been on the rodeo circuit as barrel racers. This was a whole different ball of wax. "Are you sure I can do this, Heather?"

"I'm positive. Trust me, okay?" her friend said casting her a bright smile.

Famous last words, Twyla thought, as she folded her arms across her newly enhanced bosom and huffed a sigh.

***

"Mama's worried about Twyla. It's your fault she's gone, so go get her," Zack said with a shove to Ryan's shoulder.

"Stop pushing me, dude!" Ryan shouted, as he staggered back into his locker. "Like she told me, your sister is twenty-six-years old and if she wants to leave, she has every right."

Twyla did have every right, but Ryan was damned worried too. He'd tried calling her fifty times since she left two weeks ago to try and talk some sense into her, but she wasn't answering his calls. She evidently wasn't answering her family's calls either. That worried Ryan more.

"My sister belongs here with me so I can watch out for her. You know Twyla gets into trouble on her own."

Twyla did have a habit of getting into trouble. She was stubborn and hardheaded, especially when she was mad. Ryan knew she was madder than a wet hen right now, and he had no idea how to fix it this time, or even if he could. He'd stepped over a line that he'd danced on with her for a very long time.

"Why the hell don't you go after her then?" Ryan countered, as he wound his rigging up to shove it into his duffle bag. "We have a week's break."

"I have to go to see Dean about the rough stock. Remember we promised to help him train the bulls? We can't just dump the stock out there and leave it all to him and Cord. We have a lot of money invested in that herd, and we have contracts."

"I know we have contracts, Zack. Those bulls won't be ready to ride until next year anyway. We have time." Finding his sister should be more important to Zack, and he would probably make a helluva lot more headway convincing her to come back than Ryan could.

"I'm going out there. I promised, and I'm not letting him think we're reneging on our end of the deal. And mama is going to string us both up, if we don't get Twyla back here."

"Twyla is pissed at me. She's not going to listen to a word I have to say. You go after her and let me go out to check on the herd."

Zack cocked his head to the side, and his eyebrow lifted. "You taken up riding bulls now?"

"Um, you know I haven't." Ryan rode broncs, and roped some as a fill-in heeler. He had tried bull riding exactly once and decided it wasn't for him. Zack knew that, and so did he. But Ryan would rather go anywhere than to find Twyla in Dallas. He'd probably even get on the back of a bull and get his ass gored to avoid that. Dealing with her was a lot scarier than getting on the back of a two-thousand pound bull sometimes.

"Then you wouldn't be much help out there, would you?" Zack said sarcastically. He slapped Ryan on the shoulder. "Go find my sister, so I don't have to kick your ass."

Ryan wasn't afraid of Zack, but he didn't want to fight with him either. This man was his brother, almost his salvation. After his father took off with that bimbo when he was fifteen, and his mother took up with the asshole she eventually married, Ryan was going to run away. Zack brought him home to the ranch, and he'd been part of the Taylor family ever since.

He owed the Taylor family a lot. And this situation was his own fault for not addressing the infatuation he knew Twyla nursed for him for so long. The same attraction he'd fought for years. It was time for them to bury the hatchet and make a new start. One that did not include the friction that had been sparking between them for so long. Honesty was the best policy for them to get back on even ground again. It was time for the talk that he'd put off for too long.

He glanced at Zack. "You have any idea where she went?"

"Mama said she's with her friend Heather in Dallas. Remember that hot brunette who used to ride barrels with her?" Zack reached into his shirt pocket and pulled out a piece of paper. He shoved it into Ryan's chest. "Here's the address. Don't come back without her," he growled as he walked away.

Yeah, Ryan remembered that brunette. He remembered her too well. Better than he wanted to remember her. Knowing that Twyla was shacked up with her sent cold chills down his spine. That woman was definitely hot, but she was also wild as they came.

He was as glad to see the back of Heather when she left the circuit, as every other man in their circle was to see her walk in front of them. And for some reason, she and Twyla had connected as friends when she was a rider. The two women couldn't be more different. She had led Twyla into all kind of mischief while she was touring with them. He and Zack had to work double-duty to get the women out of fixes of their own creation. Mostly with disgruntled cowboys who thought they were interested in them.

There was no telling what Twyla had gotten herself into if she was staying with Heather Morrison, but it looked like he was about to find out.

CHAPTER THREE

Ryan stopped his truck at the back of the packed parking lot of the bar. He just sat there a moment staring at the neon sign on the roof. The Crazy Cowgirl, with a curvy blonde cowgirl striking a sexy pose taunted him, making his stomach queasy.

Thank God the maintenance man at the apartment complex knew where Ryan could find Twyla and Heather. The leering smirk on the man's face made Ryan want to knock it off, but he held himself in check, because he realized that man was the only way he was going to find out where the two women were. Once he heard the name of the bar, Ryan knew Twyla really had gone off the deep end. He had driven her to this extreme with his harsh words meant to protect himself. He'd hurt her, even though that had not been his intention.

Now that he saw the place, he was even more convinced that whatever awaited him behind that rough wooden door with the half-moon cutout was going to be bad. Very bad. And he was more than sure Zack was going to kill him—literally—not metaphorically when he found out. If Ryan couldn't convince her to leave this place, he might as well find some place to hide. But he doubted there would be any place he could hide that Zack wouldn't find him.

He had to convince her, before Zack found out.

Ryan pulled the door handle and opened the

truck door. Even at the back of the parking lot, which was the only spot he could find, he was immediately assaulted by loud country music, mixed with loud male whoops and hollers. He shut the door and locked it then walked toward the entrance on leaden feet, his heart sinking lower with every step.

The song playing right then was pretty fucking appropriate, he thought, as he pushed through the crowd outside the door to grab the door handle. "Wild, Wild West," he grumbled in time with the lyrics, as he yanked it open.

This place was as wild as any he'd been in, and that was saying something. The crowd inside was so thick, he had to shoulder his way through. The only open spot was near the wall by the bathroom. He stopped there a moment to breathe and search for Twyla. He had no idea how he would find her. Over the music, and the roar of the crowd, he heard a man shout near the bar on the other side of the room. "Shake it, Daisy—I got a hundred for ya!" the obviously drunk older cowboy slurred.

The woman on the bar whipped her head around. Her layered white blonde hair swished, then settled on her shoulders. A sick knot formed in Ryan's throat, then sank to his stomach as she grinned at the man, before whipping her black hat off of her head. She shook her head and her hair became a wild white mane around her beautiful, but heavily made up face. Turning her ass to the man, the dancer spread her legs wider then bent at the waist to shake her barely covered ass in the man's face. He tilted his head back and stepped closer to get a good look.

The woman extended the hat back to him between her legs, and he dropped a bill into the hat. Before she could move away, he ran his hand up the inside of her calf to her knee. She stumbled away, and spun to put her boot on his forehead, shaking her finger at him. He reached for her calf again, and with a frown she shoved him with her foot. He staggered backward and a chorus of laughter followed.

Some man at the front of the crowd yelled, "Gut Shot!"

Several others joined in the chant, and before he knew what was happening, the dancer gave them a coy look as she tucked the hem of her shirt into her bra. She disappeared beneath the cowboy hats surrounding the bar, and Ryan blindly stumbled that way, hoping like hell that wasn't Twyla. Even though the woman had the exact same willowy build, she certainly didn't look like his best friend's little sister.

The woman on that bar was wearing makeup, and she had bountiful breasts pushing over her low cut top. Twyla had smaller breasts, hated wearing makeup, and wouldn't be caught dead in a getup like that. And Twyla did not dance like that woman was dancing. She was lucky to put one foot in front of the other to walk. It couldn't be her. But he needed a closer look to be sure. He pushed his way to the front row of men around the bar.

"Line up!" a gruff male voice shouted. Ryan leaned around the man in front of him to see the speaker was a musclebound guy who looked to be a bouncer. He crossed his arms over his chest, and eyed the line of men warily. "Have your money ready and no touching!"

Ryan elbowed his way up to the front row and finally got a good view of what was going on. Twyla, he had no doubt it was her now, was laid out on the bar with her knees spread, and Heather was between her knees. The bartender put a shot on her bare belly, right above her navel and Twyla gasped when some of the brown liquor sloshed over onto her stomach. She moaned as it slid down into her navel. Ryan's tongue burned to trace that trail, to sip that fiery liquid from the perfect little indention in her belly.

Heather grinned down at her and tossed her hair over her shoulder, then licked her lips dramatically. Loud pained groans erupted from the men. The bouncer collected bills from the eager men in the front row, counted them then gave her a nod. Excitement buzzed through the crowd like wildfire. Heather shoved Twyla's knees apart forcefully, and loud whoops followed. Twyla's body tensed and she grabbed the edge of the bar, watching the glass intently, as Heather slowly lowered her head toward her stomach.

Heather's lips touched down right above the waistband of her shorts, and Twyla moaned loudly. Her breathing increased as Heather's tongue dragged up from the waistband to her navel, and so did Ryan's. Twyla turned her head to the side arching her back, as Heather circled her navel with her tongue.

She then took a dip inside and flicked her tongue, pulling a shiver and mewl from Twyla. Electricity zipped down his spine right to the end of his dick. Ryan felt that damned tongue on his body, tasted the rich liquid on his own tongue. He was so damned hard, his zipper cut into his flesh. He didn't want to like this, but dammit he did. Just like every other man in this bar. Ryan couldn't help it, he finally had to adjust himself.

This was about the sexiest damned display he'd ever seen in his life. He'd never had two women, but the two putting on the show on that bar could definitely talk him into it. This wasn't Twyla though. He didn't even think she'd had sex before. Zack watched her too closely. Unless she'd had it after she left the rodeo. A lot could've happened in two weeks, a lot had happened, that was obvious. The woman faking an orgasm as Heather licked the trail up from her belly button to the shot glass was definitely not a virgin.

Hell, for all he knew she and Heather could be messing around. From the looks of it, that was entirely possible. His cock got painfully hard, and anger shot through him, disgust at himself, because that thought turned him on. The thought of watching them suck each other, kiss each other would be the ultimate fantasy to him. One he never realized he harbored. He slapped himself mentally though. Every man in this damned bar was having the same fantasy. Because these two women were creating that fantasy. Encouraging it. For money. Disgusting. He had to get her out of here. He needed to get out of here himself and fast.

Heather wrapped her full red-painted lips around the shot glass and tossed back her head, emptying the glass. She moved to her knees to swipe her arm across her mouth. Applause almost deafened him, as the bartender smiled and handed her the fistful of bills. Heather pushed up to her feet then gave Twyla a wink, as she reached a hand down to help her up.

Four other skimpily dressed dancers hopped up onto the bar and converged on them clapping their hands too. A new song started playing and they formed a chorus line of hot flesh, almost naked booties and heaving bosoms. The song choice left him with no doubt that this was about to get worse. *Save A Horse Ride A Cowboy* blared through the speakers behind the bar, as the dancers hopped, their bootheels clicked in tandem on the bar and they spun showing the crowd a line of world-class ass.

Twyla's ass was one of those asses.

If Zack was here, Ryan knew he would already be dead, and Twyla would be over his shoulder being carried out of here. That is what he needed to do, carry her pretty little ass out of this bar and shake some sense into her. But getting to her wasn't going to be easy. She was flanked by the big bouncer, and another mean-looking man who was smaller, but no less fierce. He was surveying the crowd just as intently as the bouncer, while the dancers started their routine of practiced rump shaking and hip twisting.

Twyla, to his surprise, kept up with them in perfect harmony. Ryan had danced with her before out of obligation at her parent's anniversary party a few years back. His toes were just now recovering. It looked to him like she had found her rhythm now though. She was at the center of the group, and the center of attention. Most of the men there were watching her. He knew he sure was. How could any man in his right mind ignore those long legs, that pert little ass, and those perfect breasts pushing over her still tucked-up tank top?

She was the tallest of the group of women, her body the most toned, probably from all the riding she did. As far as Ryan was concerned, Twyla was the sexiest of the bunch by far. And she was definitely working that to her advantage with her exaggerated movements. Heather was good, but Twyla was definitely working it the best. Ryan hadn't ever seen better, even in the many strip clubs he and Zack had frequented while they were on tour. And that pissed him off. Twyla Taylor was not a stripper, she was a fucking cowgirl. She should not be here doing this. He should not be letting her do this, or enjoying it.

That is what his stepfather would be doing, if he was here, and Ryan was definitely not that man. There could be a man just like Clarence James here in this crowd, a predator just waiting for an opening to hurt her. She should have better sense than this.

Ryan shoved the man who had edged his way in front of him aside. He scooted sideways a few feet to the right to stand at the bar in front of where Twyla was dancing. The long fringe on her boots mesmerized him as she stomped them on the bar and wiggled her ass. In his face.

His hands lifted on their own and his fingers flexed, wanting to feel that soft supple skin at the hem of her shorts. The bouncer shot him a hot look and Ryan realized what he was doing. He dropped them to his sides, and heaved a shuddering breath. At least nobody could touch her. That was something. But they could look all they wanted, and it irritated the hell out of him. He would love nothing more than moving down the line of men and punching each one of them in the nose.

He had to find some way to talk to her, or get her out of here. But that damned brute protecting the dancers would kick his ass, and he was sure the rough looking dude a little ways down the bar doing the same would help. Ryan wasn't in the mood to get his ass kicked tonight, and he wasn't going to wind up in jail. The only one he had to call to bail him out would be Zack. And then he'd be dead anyway. They'd both end up in jail because he wasn't going down without a fight. That wouldn't do either of them any good. Twyla would still be here shaking her ass for any man with a dollar in his hand.

The only option Ryan had was to stay here and watch out for her, watch her, until she got off. When the bar closed, she'd have to leave and he could talk to her then. He knew where she lived. She could run, but she couldn't hide. That sounded like as good a plan as any.

Ryan relaxed a little, and refocused on Heather's gyrating ass, so maybe he could get his body under control. She did nothing for him, never had. When she'd been on the circuit, Ryan thought Zack might give her a test-drive though. He had talked about her a lot, but nothing had ever come of it. Then she left the rodeo to come here evidently. This job suited the curvy brunette, as much as it didn't suit Twyla. Suddenly the dancers spun to face the crowd, and he heard a gasp. His eyes flew to Twyla's and her shocked expression quickly faded, replaced by anger. The other dancers were still moving to the music, but she wasn't dancing. Her body practically vibrated with anger as her eyes scorched him.

"C'mon, Daisy! Song's not over--shake your ass!" the drunk guy who'd given her a hundred a few minutes ago shouted. Twyla's gaze bounced to him, then back to Ryan. "What the hell are you doing here?" she leaned forward to growl with her fists clenched at her sides.

He took a step forward and fought the urge to grab her ankles and toss her over his shoulder. "That's damned funny. I was about to ask you the same thing. What the hell are you doing, Sis— Twyla?" He corrected his use of the nickname because he knew if he called her Sissy, as mad as she was, she'd likely kick him in the teeth.

It was Zack's nickname for his sister, and Ryan had adopted it too, to remind himself where he needed to keep things between them when he felt that attraction to her. It also told her where he was keeping things with her. Usually it pissed her off enough that she walked away mad, which meant he didn't have to deal with those feelings. A win-win all the way around. Not this time. He had to keep her from getting to the walk away point, so he could talk to her.

"I'm *working*," she gritted out between her teeth, as she stood back up to put her hands on her hips. When he didn't move, she pointed to the door. "Leave!"

Out of the corner of his eye, Ryan noticed when the bouncer finally noticed him. The man's eyes narrowed as he shoved a couple of men aside to walk over to Ryan. Ryan swallowed hard, and dragged his eyes from Twyla's to meet the man's hard brown eyes. Without looking at Twyla, he demanded, "This asshole bothering you, Daisy?"

Why the fuck was everyone calling her Daisy? It was demeaning, and he figured she earned it from the shorts she was wearing. Anger shot through him, and came out with his words. "Her name is *Twyla*, not Daisy, asshole. And I'm a friend of hers. She's leaving with me."

"I'm not going anywhere, but you sure are, *buddy*," Twyla said smugly, using her nickname for her brother. That told him she hadn't missed his slipup. Crossing her arms over her breasts, she tilted her head to the side. "Teddy, this man is deluded, he's definitely no friend of mine."

Twyla turned her back on him, and shock rocked him as the bouncer grabbed his arm in a painful grip. Ryan swung and then bells went off in his skull when a fist connected with his nose. He heard the sickening crunch, felt the warmth of the blood gushing down his face. "Twyla what the fuck are you doing?" Ryan shouted as he was jerked out of the line.

"Getting a life, just like you told me to," she shouted back, with a dry laugh. She flicked her hair and her hips started moving in time with the other dancers again. "I suggest you do the same once the bruises heal. Try not to kill him, Teddy." The burly bouncer shoved him, then dragged him through the crowd toward the front door.

On his knees outside the front door where the bouncer tossed him, a puddle of blood pooling on the ground in front of him from his probably broken nose, Ryan finally realized exactly how mad Twyla was, and how difficult his task here would be. He no longer had confidence that he could talk her into anything, much less coming back to the circuit with him. His former second-best friend evidently meant it when she said she was done with him. The sad part was Ryan couldn't really blame her.

But even with a broken nose for his trouble of trying to talk sense in her, Ryan knew he couldn't give up. For her own safety, and his sanity, Twyla needed to get out of here before he headed back to the circuit. He had a week, and even if she didn't agree to come back with him, he was going to do whatever it took to get her away from this bar and these men, help her get on another track to finding that life he told her to get.

This wasn't about Zack's anger anymore. This was about Twyla's self-respect. Ryan cared about her. A lot. She was his family, and he couldn't stand by and watch her ruin her life.

Determination filled him as he stood and brushed off his jeans, before pulling his t-shirt over his head to hold it to his steadily bleeding nose. He picked up his hat and slammed it down on his head, before heading toward his truck at the back of the lot.

The bouncer had given him ninety seconds to leave before he called the police. Ryan had used up sixty getting his senses back. He knew the man wasn't kidding, so he double-timed his steps. He couldn't help Twyla if he was in jail. And he wasn't going to be able to drive, unless he got the bleeding stopped from his nose.

Ryan got into the truck and moved the t-shirt from his nose to pinch the bridge and hold his head back for a minute. He turned on the dome light to inspect the damage in the rearview mirror. The bleeding from his right nostril had stopped, but his left poured a steady stream. His left eye was also quickly turning black. It wouldn't surprise him if it was closed shut in the morning. The big bruiser's fist had been almost half as big as Ryan's face.

It had been stupid of him to take a swing at the man, but when the bouncer grabbed him, Ryan's fist flew without thought to the consequences. He only knew he needed to be in that bar to protect Twyla, until he could talk to her. To make damned sure nobody touched her. That man's quick reaction, and brick-like fist convinced Ryan though, that Twyla didn't need his protection. That was the only reason he wasn't charging back inside right now, damn the consequences. Blood dripped onto his chest and he swiped it with his forearm.

Leaning across the truck, he flipped open the glove box, hoping he had some Kleenex in there to pack his nose. He found a half-eaten Twinkie, which had to be Twyla's, and shoved it aside with disgust. He knew she was addicted to Twinkies. He and Zack teased her about it, calling her the Twinkie Queen. Both of them had been forced into late night snack runs when she was upset or feeling bad. That's when she craved them. He pushed a stack of unopened bills to the side and saw a pack of gum, and a cylindrical paper-covered object at the very back. He left the gum, but pulled out the other object and held it up to the dome light.

A tampon, probably left in there by Twyla too. Tampons stopped bleeding, right? The paper was off the end of it, and the cotton was a little brown, but he figured it was better than nothing. He slid the cotton-stuffed cardboard tube out of the wrapper. Leaning close to the mirror, he held his breath and inserted the tip with the cotton end into his nose. He shoved it further up inside and pain shot through his eyeball to the base of his skull.

After a second it subsided, and he looked

back in the mirror and saw the bleeding had lessened, but not stopped. He flinched and shoved it a little farther up inside his nose. Picking up his shirt, he wiped away what he could of the blood on his face and chest. In the process, he accidentally hit the end of the cardboard tube, which sent another shot of pain through his skull, along with a wave of nausea. Across the parking lot, he saw the bar door open, and the big black bouncer step outside.

"Fuck," Ryan groaned, fumbling for his keys in his pocket.

The last thing he needed was round two, he thought, as he shoved the keys into the ignition, cranked the truck and threw it in gear. Twyla would have to come home eventually. And when she did, he'd be at her apartment waiting for her. They were going to talk tonight, whether she wanted to or not.

CHAPTER FOUR

Dog-tired, Twyla picked up the bag of Twinkies she'd made Heather stop for on the way home off of the floorboard. Heather pulled the truck to a stop in their usual spot right by the stairway under the security light, and she opened her door. This secure spot was theirs, because the maintenance man was half in love with Heather. He had even put up a no-parking sign for the spot to make sure it stayed open for them. As many weirdos as they met at the bar, it was necessary for them to take precautions that they weren't followed home at night.

Heather might be wild, but she wasn't crazy or careless with their safety. She looked out for herself pretty damned well. A lot better than Twyla had ever looked out for herself. Sometimes Twyla thought her friend had eyes in the back of her head. She seemed to sense when trouble was about to happen. Maybe as a result of working at the bar, her reflexes were razor-sharp from dodging grabby hands. Twyla hoped she would eventually develop those skills too, or she might not last long at the Crazy Cowgirl.

Tonight, when they left the bar, Heather had taken extra care, even having Teddy walk them to her truck, for a different reason. Ryan had showed up at the bar and she definitely didn't want to see him again tonight. Twyla could only imagine what his face looked like, and how mad he was. She hadn't seen

Teddy hit him, but she'd heard the sickening crunch, and his grunt.

It served him right for coming there, but damn if she wasn't worried sick he was hurt. Tomorrow, she would call him to make sure he was okay and tell him to stay away from her. It was a relief not to see his black truck in the lot when they pulled in. Evidently he didn't know where they lived, or she knew he would be there. All she needed tonight was another confrontation with him.

Twyla wondered what the hell he wanted with her. As far as she was concerned, he could get back in his truck and head back to wherever the hell he came from. But dammit if seeing him hadn't stunned her system, and broke her concentration. Her damned traitorous heart, the one owned by the girl inside of her who had been in love with him for ten years, had melted to her toes because he'd come to find her. There was no other reason he could've been at the bar.

"We have a special date tomorrow night," Heather announced as she reached over to pull her gym bag off of the floor board.

"Date?" Twyla repeated dumbly, as she got out of the truck and shut the door. She walked around the truck and met Heather at the front. Tomorrow was Sunday and in the morning she had a date with Tango and her mounted shooting instructor. Who was pretty good looking, as it turned out.

"What kind of date?"

"One of my regulars, a good guy, wants us to do a—" Heather gasped then her eyes narrowed. "What the hell are you doing here?" She discreetly unzipped her bag, and Twyla turned around, but didn't have to. She knew who was standing behind her.

"Ryan why *are* you here?" she asked with frustration.

"I'm coming to save your crazy ass, but I have no idea why," he growled in a nasally voice, as he grabbed her arm in a tight grip.

On instinct, Twyla threw up her knee, and connected with his crotch. He grunted and staggered back, then bent at the waist with his hands propped on his knees. Heather lunged forward, her arm extended and something squirted out of a black container in her hand. Ryan squealed loudly, staggered back, and his arms flailed as he swiped at his eyes.

"Fuck, fuck, *fuck*," he screamed, all but ripping off his t-shirt to scrub at his face.

Twyla dropped her Twinkie bag and ran over to him. "What did you spray on him, Heather?" she asked as she helped him sit on the curb.

"Just a little asshole repellant," Heather replied with a snort. "He won't die. Come on let's go inside and call the police." She walked up two steps then turned back toward Twyla. Huffing out a breath, she asked, "If you don't want him here, what the hell are you doing, Twy?"

Twyla looked back at Heather. "I didn't want

you to *hurt* him!" Ryan moaned and rested his head on his knees. "Hold your head up, Ryan, so I can see," Twyla said with worry constricting her chest.

"I can't see," he groaned in a voice barely above a whisper. It seemed to Twyla, from her hand on his back, that he was barely breathing. "It burns so bad." Even though he probably deserved this too, the misery in his voice made her insides ache for him.

"Well you can sit out here and play nurse all you want. I'm tired," Heather said with a huffed breath. "I'll be inside. Holler if you need me, and I'll call the police."

"Don't call them," Twyla shouted to her as she walked up the stairs.

"Figures," Heather grumbled shaking her head as she topped the stairs.

"Pepper spray. Need water," Ryan groaned, as he stood up. He stepped into the light and Twyla gasped. His eye was black, and almost swollen shut. His nose was bruised and swollen too. Teddy must've really hit him hard. "You look like you've been mule-kicked! We're going to the emergen—" Twyla stopped to lean in closer to inspect the white string hanging from his nostril. "What the hell is that hanging from your nose?"

"Tampon," he said in a stopped up, nasally voice. "Hurts like hell too. Don't know how y'all stand it."

"I guess so," she said with laughter bubbling in her chest. "You left the applicator in there, nimnut!"

His head swung to hers, and he pried open the slits that covered his fire-red eyes. "Applicator?"

"Yeah, the cardboard comes out then the cotton stops the bleeding," she explained, and a chuckle followed. "I learned that the hard way the first time I used them too." More chuckles bubbled up to her throat, and escaped. His stunned expression melded the chuckles into full-fledged laughter. Twyla held her stomach and staggered back to sit on the first step and let it loose. It felt damned good. She laughed so hard she thought she might crack a rib if she wasn't careful. Tears streamed down her face, as she gulped for breath.

Ryan stomped over to glare down at her, as much as he could glare from his slitted red-rimmed eyes. "Glad to be the comic relief, but my fucking eyes are on fire, and my nuts are up in my throat. Think you could help a poor, dumb bastard out when you're done?"

Twyla sucked in a breath and wiped her eyes with the hem of her tank top. She pushed up to her feet and took his arm to help him as he stepped on the first stair tread. "Sorry, it's not every day a guy sticks a tampon up his nose. Why didn't you just use Kleenex?"

"Didn't have any," he replied angrily.

Laughter tried to consume her again. "But you had a tampon?"

"You left one in the glove box of the truck." He grabbed the stair rail to steady himself, and Twyla carefully led him up to the landing.

At the apartment door, she knocked, because it was shut and locked. After a second of lock flipping, the door swung open, and Heather stood there in only her pushup bra and skimpy panties. Ryan groaned and shut his eyes. Heather shook her head, threw up her hands and walked away. She went inside her bedroom, and slammed the door behind her.

Twyla helped Ryan inside and shut the door behind her, then flipped the deadbolt and door locks. If she didn't, she knew Heather would ream her out in the morning. Ryan staggered toward the couch, but Twyla slid her arm through his and walked him to the tiny bathroom down the hall. Sitting him on the toilet, she got a washrag and wet it in the sink.

When she turned toward him, his head was leaned back on his shoulders and his eyes were closed. She took a long look at his bruised nose and swollen eye. He really should go to the emergency room and get checked out. He had to be in excruciating pain. Her heart tried to bleed for him, but she patched it up mentally. He deserved what he got, she reminded herself.

"You look like ten miles of bad road, cowboy," she said laying the rag on his forehead.

He grunted. "Feel like twenty."

She moved to stand in front of him and one eye, the one not black, popped open. The bright blue iris stood in sharp contrast to the red roadmap that was the white. His hands gripped the toilet, as she bathed his forehead and beard-roughened cheeks, then his chin. "I'm sorry you got hurt, but you should've known better than to come here."

"I'm a dumbass, what can I say?" he said and his one opened eye rolled.

"Why'd you come? I told you I was done."

And Twyla had meant it. Even if she'd had her doubts about her decision since she left, she knew it had been the right one. Moving on, getting over her useless crush on Ryan Easter was what was best for her. Seeing Ryan again though made all those feelings come back, and that made her angry. Dammit, she wanted to be over him as easily as she said those words. Why couldn't it be that easy?

"I came to tell you I'm sorry for saying those things to you," he said, his voice sincere.

That was why. Ryan was a good man, as much as he was as dumb as a box of rocks, and his head as hard as one. "Close your eye," she grumbled, gathering up her determination as she swiped the cloth over his uninjured eye, then gently patted the other. "I appreciate that, Ryan, but you didn't have to come here to tell me that. I didn't want to see you."

Ryan grabbed her wrist, and his eye popped open again. "I wanted to see *you*, Twy. I thought it was right to tell you I'm sorry in person...and I wanted to make sure you were okay. I care about you, Twyla."

Like a sister. She knew it was on the tip of his tongue to add those words. He'd said that to her often enough. Firmly established a line between them she hadn't ever been allowed to cross, one he'd only come close to crossing once with her. That night at the bonfire when she was sixteen. The night of the almost kiss that had captured her heart as surely as if he'd done it.

Ten years of her life she could never get back wanting him to finish that kiss.

Twyla wasn't wasting another minute on him now. When she left the rodeo, left him, she accepted things were never going to change between them. Now she was moving on. He just needed to accept that and leave her the hell alone.

"Don't apologize. You telling me to get a life was the best thing that's ever happened to me. And that's what I'm doing, Ryan." Twyla turned to the sink and rinsed the rag under the tap. "I don't need you to worry about me. You just mind your business, and stay away from me. I'm sure we'll see each other around at *family* gatherings sometimes." *There, put that in your pipe and smoke it, bucko.* She squeezed the water out of the rag, like she wanted to squeeze his neck. *You want to be my brother, buddy? That's exactly what you'll be from here on out.*

She turned back toward him for round two of cleaning up his face, and his fingers closed on her forearm. "Twyla, please listen—"

She put her finger over his lips. "Stop. We've said all we need to say, Ryan. Just let it go. Let me go. I'll be fine."

He mumbled around her finger, "It's obvious you're not fine. You're working at a fricking strip—"

Twyla slapped her palm over his mouth. "It's

not a strip club. I dance and serve drinks, and I'm making damned good money doing it. Who the hell are you to judge me anyway? I've been to those places with you and Zack, remember?"

He mumbled something behind her hand, and Twyla moved it, but she didn't wait for him to repeat himself. She grabbed the string hanging from his nose and yanked. Ryan howled, and grabbed her wrist. "No, wait," he whispered, sucking in a breath. "I'll do it."

"Fine, I'll get the bag of frozen peas from the freezer. That will help the swelling." And it would also give her an excuse to get away from him, from his intoxicating scent which was wearing down her defenses. Twyla spun away and walked down the hall and to the kitchen. She flung open the freezer and shifted stuff around until she found the bag of peas.

Tiredness mixed with depression inside of her as she shut the freezer door and leaned her head against the cool exterior. She needed to get Ryan out of there and on his way back to wherever he was supposed to be. She didn't know how long she was going to be able to pretend she wasn't still nursing feelings for him. They were still there, but she was determined to get rid of them. To exorcise them from her soul. Exorcise him from her thoughts. That was real hard to do with him right here under her feet. But it was nearly three o'clock in the morning. She couldn't in good conscience kick him out. He could sleep on the couch, but she was getting him out of there first thing in the morning, and tell him and her brother to back off.

With a deep sigh, she shoved away and walked back to the bathroom. Walking down the hall, her steps stuttered when she saw the bathroom door was open. Ryan, legs spread, naked except for a small towel wrapped around his lean hips, leaned on the sink examining his nose in the mirror, pressing his long fingers at the bridge. The well-defined muscles in his biceps and back were on prime display, the bottom of his tight ass nearly showing at the hem of the towel.

Twyla's tongue stuck to the roof of her mouth, as she made the last few steps to the door. When she pried it loose, she asked, "Why are you naked?"

He sighed, and patted his fingers gently around the edge of the bruise on his eye. "Seeing if anything is broken. Bleeding didn't start again, thank God."

"That doesn't explain why you've shucked your clothes."

He looked at her, and grinned. "Bothering you, darlin'?" His eyebrow lifted and he flinched. "We're *family*, so it shouldn't matter, right? I'm about to take a shower."

So he hadn't missed her family reference a few minutes ago, and was evidently paying her back. Testing her. Ryan knew how she felt about him. It looked like he also knew she wasn't as over him as she was trying to pretend. Well two could play his game. For some reason he must enjoy having her in the palm of his hand. Panting after him like a school girl. It probably fed his over-inflated ego. Those days were over for her. He needed to know that.

Twyla somehow maintained her cool, even though her palms were itching to see just how soft that light fur on his tightly muscled chest was. To taste the soft skin of his neck where she saw his heart pounding. Clenching her fists at her sides, the peas froze her palm as she inched up her chin. "Doesn't matter a bit. Why bother with the towel?"

Oh please don't bother, her inner woman begged, but she slapped the masochistic bitch, and tossed the peas down on the counter angrily.

"Take your shower, and put those on your eye. Catch a few hours on the couch, then get the hell out of here, Ryan." Her eyes raked him to his toes, then back up. "But Heather is around and she's not *family*, so put some clothes on when you come out." She turned her back, and forced nonchalance into her tone as she finished, "I'll probably be gone when you get up. I have things to do tomorrow. Have a safe trip back to wherever."

She had taken two steps when Ryan drawled, "Twyla?" His deep, now less nasally voice skated along her nerve endings.

Stopping, she slowly turned around and gasped. The towel was now pooled at his feet, and Ryan leaned negligently against the vanity, buck naked, grinning from ear to ear. Because she couldn't stop them, her eyes followed the thin trail of hair that bisected his tight abs downward to his semi-erect penis. It was thick and long, and a vein pulsed from the base along the side to the thick head. Her breathing hitched, moisture gathered between her legs, and a weird throb started at the apex of her thighs. She slammed her eyes shut, wanting to forget what she'd just seen. Wanting to remember just as badly, so she had some point of reference in the future.

"What game are you playing, Ryan? It's not funny. If Zack knew he'd kill you."

"He's probably going to do that anyway. But I'm not leaving here until you come back with me," he said smoothly, then cleared his throat. "Whatever it takes to get you to do that."

Whatever it takes? Her mind quickly put together his naked display with that phrase and came up with his exact meaning. This rodeo Romeo was telling her he was willing to sleep with her to get her to go back with him. He was offering her a sympathy fuck.

Well Twyla might be hard up, because of him and her damned brother, but she wasn't a fucking charity case. Her eyes locked on his dick and she issued a dry, harsh laugh. "Well cowboy, I'm sure that little sprout satisfies those buckle bunnies just fine, but I'm used to um, more mature men." She moved her eyes up to his shocked blue gaze. "But your balls sure are big enough that's for sure."

His face flushed and his hands shot down to cover himself. Twyla threw back her head and laughed loudly. Shaking her head, she turned away, and heard the bathroom door slam shut behind her as she walked to her bedroom. She took one of her pillows and a blanket off of her bed, and walked to the couch to throw them over the back with disgust. If Ryan Easter wasn't out of there tomorrow, she was definitely going to let Heather call the cops to get him out.

His stupidity a moment ago had been the final straw. Twyla Taylor was definitely over Ryan Easter, or she would be as soon as her stupid heart got on board with the plan. She was well on her way to being there now though. If that man ever wanted to find a woman who would put up with his dumb ass, he needed to get over himself. Twyla knew one thing for sure, she wasn't woman enough for the job.

CHAPTER FIVE

Ryan woke up to pans banging loudly and groaned. Every muscle in his body was rubber-band tight, and a spring from the old sofa had almost embedded itself in his hip. He tried to open his eyes and they seemed to be welded shut. Ungluing them, one opened and felt like sandpaper was inside the lid. The other didn't open, then he remembered the bar fight, and the macing he'd gotten from Heather last night. Bright sunlight shot through the crack in the drapes at the front window to pierce his brain. Ryan groaned and flopped his forearm over his eyes.

"I hear you rustling in there, buddy. Get your ass up and on the road," Twyla said loudly from the kitchen, punctuating her demand by slamming a skillet or something down on the stove.

The metallic rattle echoed in his skull. That woman had no mercy at all, no compassion that just last night he'd gotten his ass kicked by not one, but three people. By a man who should be a professional boxer or wrestler, and two fucking wild ass, crazy cowgirls. That last part was pretty embarrassing. A man who had been a professional cowboy since he grew hair on his balls had gotten his ass kicked good by those two women, after the bruiser worked him over.

Maybe he should just load up in his truck and head to Santa Fe, their next stop on the tour. Let Zack come here on their next break to hogtie his sister and haul her back with him. Good luck with that. Ryan was starting to believe neither he or Zack were man enough for the job. But he knew if Zack came here and saw what Twyla was up to, there might not be anything left of her for him to haul home. He would probably just kill her and hide the body to save his parents the disgrace. Ryan knew that's what it would be too. A disgrace.

Mr. and Mrs. Taylor were upright, forthright and straight shooters. They had worked exceptionally hard to give their kids a good upbringing with the right morals. Hell, he knew they'd set a good example for him, something his own family sure as hell hadn't. That's why he knew what he needed to do now. Whatever it took to get Twyla out of here, away from her crazy friend who was leading her down the path to perdition.

If he was lucky, if Twyla was lucky, they'd never find out. Ryan owed it to them to stay and try to talk some sense into their youngest member, and he wasn't leaving before he did that. If he could accomplish that by Wednesday, he'd have enough time for them to make Santa Fe by their first ride on Thursday night.

But it looked like his unfriendly host wasn't going to let him stay here. So that meant he'd be sleeping in his truck tonight, because he wasn't letting her out of his sight. Ryan threw back the light blanket and sat up, biting back a moan when a sharp pain shot through his skull. His nose felt like it was packed, and he knew it wasn't. He'd removed the damned tampon last night, and hadn't repacked it. Gingerly, he reached up and felt the swollen bridge for obvious signs it was broken. Last night, he'd looked and didn't think it was. This morning, it sure *felt* like it was. The bag of peas Twyla had given him had helped some, but they melted.

"You have another bag of peas?" he asked gruffly, his voice rusty and still sounding like he had the head cold from hell.

"No peas, and no room at the inn tonight. Get going, Ryan. We have things to do today. Heather already left to teach her dancing class, and I've got to get out of here too."

Heather was gone. This might be his only opportunity to talk to Twyla alone.

Ryan swung his legs over the edge of the sofa and stood, then raised his arms over his head to work out the kinks in his spine. With a deep sigh he turned toward the kitchen, and found Twyla staring at his crotch through the serving window at the breakfast bar. That meant she had been staring at his ass before he turned around. His morning wood, became California-sized redwood, as her eyes continued to scorch him through his underwear. He covered himself.

Sprout, huh? Now that he wasn't embarrassed and angry, he did see the humor in her comment. Her sharp tongue had always been something Ryan lov—um, liked about Twyla. He enjoyed sparring with her, because he never knew what she was going to come out with.

The only reason he'd done what he had last night was because she'd used that sharp tongue to bait him to drop the towel. He definitely hadn't meant he would have sex with her to get her to come home with him. That's what she thought he meant though. Because it was on her mind. Had been on her mind for a very long time, and his too. There was no way Ryan was giving in to that urge now though. He'd fought it too damned long to give in now. The consequences of doing that were too great. He couldn't do that to his surrogate family.

But he could get a little retribution for her comment. "Thought you weren't interested? You're sure staring like you are," he accused with a wry grin. Her blue eyes swung up to his and she looked surprised, as if she hadn't realized she'd been staring a hole through him.

Twyla wasn't slick like he was. Ryan caught her staring often, and honestly felt bad for her. But not as bad as he felt for himself. That look she got in her eyes ripped at his insides and made it damned tough to keep his hands off of her. Because of that look, every woman Ryan was with wore her face when he closed his eyes. It was just sick. Pathetic.

It had to stop so they could both find peace. If it didn't, they'd end up with hard feelings that could drive a wedge between them forever. Ryan had started that process with his harsh words to push her away the other night. He knew he had pushed too far this time.

That's why she'd left, and was here now. An

honest conversation with her might go a long way to smoothing things between them. But to have it, he would need the balls she accused him of having last night. Ryan wasn't sure at the end of it, that she would understand any better why they needed to remain friends, but he had to try.

Twyla looked down and shifted the skillet to flip the egg she was frying without answering, which told him she was the one embarrassed now.

He sighed heavily. "Twy, we need to talk."

"I have nothing to say to you, Ryan. You just need to leave." Her voice was as flat as the egg in that skillet.

He walked into the kitchen, stood beside her at the stove and crossed his arms over his chest. "I'm sorry for what I said to you the other night. It was wrong, and I only did it to push you away." He swallowed hard and worked up his courage. "What if I told you I want you as much as you want me? Have for years…."

Her breathing hitched, her shoulders tightened, but she still didn't look at him. "That's bullshit and you know it. I'm not buying it, Ryan, and I'm not coming back with you, or sleeping with you if that's what you're after. You had your chance." She shook the skillet extra vigorously over the eye on the stove, sliding the egg around like a hockey puck, showing the level of her agitation. "Give it up and just go back."

"That's not bullshit, Twy. It's the truth," Ryan replied evenly. "And trust me. Saying that to you is not for the purpose of sleeping with you. That's what I am trying to avoid. Going there would be bad for both of us, and for the family. We can work this out, if you'll just talk to me instead of running off." A weight seemed to float off of his shoulders, but plopped back down when she slammed the skillet on the stove and turned her angry blue eyes on him.

Her hand shook as she glanced down at the knob to turn off the burner. "You're a piece of work, you know that?" Twyla growled, shooting him an angry glare as she tried to brush past him.

Ryan grabbed her arm. "We need to work this out, honey. For us, and for the family."

Her angry blue eyes locked on his and the corner of her full lips curled. "*My* family is fine, and I am now too. There's nothing to work out. I hopped off the merry-go-round when I left you in Tulsa. You have nothing to worry about now. It's over, Ryan."

It wasn't over by a long shot. His heart squeezed in his chest and he swallowed hard. "I know it pisses you off, but I think of them as my family too. They *are* my family."

Hell, Ryan had lived with the Taylors since he was a sixteen-year-old runaway. Thank God when his mother found him she had the good sense to just leave him there. Lord knew what would've happened if she'd have forced him to go back and live with her and her new husband. He'd probably be in jail for killing the man.

He almost had when he paid her a visit when

he was eighteen. Ryan hadn't been back since, in twelve years, but he knew they'd moved to a small town outside of Houston. Just far enough from the Taylors' home in Dallas, his home base when he wasn't on the road, for him to keep his distance. The restraining order Clarence James had gotten against him was a sure visit to jail if he couldn't keep that distance.

The irony that the courts had awarded the abuser the restraining order against the person trying to save the abused wasn't lost on Ryan. The system sucked, as far as he was concerned. But until his mother chose to step up and save herself, he couldn't do anything to help her. Somehow he'd managed to stop worrying about her every day a few years ago. That didn't mean he didn't worry though. He just tried not to let it consume him like he had before.

Twyla sighed heavily, and jerked her arm from his grasp. "Fine, they're your family too. I won't be around much, so tell mama I love her when you see her."

She went to turn away, but Ryan grabbed her shoulders and spun her back around. "You are my family too, Twy!"

She shook her shoulders free. "Then you're a perverted son-of-a-bitch, because you just told me you wanted me a minute ago. Make up your mind, Ryan. I'm dizzy from this shit. Enough is enough. Just leave me alone!"

Ryan was just as dizzy as she was from it. He was confused, frustrated and about at the end of his rope here. He wished she'd just talk to him...or at least listen. The problem was, now that he'd admitted the secret he'd kept for ten years, he had no idea what else he wanted to say to her. And Twyla was right, he was a perverted son-of-a-bitch evidently, because he couldn't drag his eyes off of her pert ass as she stomped off toward the bedroom. He reached down to stroke his painful erection, and growled out his frustration as she slammed the bedroom door.

Twyla slammed drawers as she rifled through them to find her riding clothes. She quickly shed her pajama pants, and jerked on her jeans. Ryan Easter was determined to drive her nuts. That's the only explanation she could come up with for his being here at all. For his saying what he'd said to her in the kitchen. The tug of war between them was over, as far as she was concerned. She was trying to put her feelings for him to rest.

Why the hell wouldn't he let her?

She was trying to give him what he wanted. If he'd been struggling that bad for so many years to keep his hands to himself like he said, then why wasn't he happy about it? Was he trying to torture her? Was his fricking ego so big, he couldn't just let sleeping dogs lie? Did he miss her tagging after him like a sad-eyed puppy craving a scrap of his attention?

That had to be it.

The man had been chased by so many buckle bunnies she couldn't count them on both hands and her toes. He seemed to like that chase, rubbed those women in her face often. Twyla had called off the chase, and now he wanted her back in the race.

Not happening.

Even if he taunted her, tortured her, by walking around in those tight, white underwear with his dick the size of a cucumber. Even if he dropped his drawers in front of her like he had last night looking like an ice cream sundae with a Twinkie on top. Twyla wasn't interested. There was nothing the man could do to tempt her do that now.

Absolutely. Fucking. Nothing.

Then why did her hands shake so badly when she picked up her worn t-shirt to pull it over her head. They shook so badly she could barely scrape her hair back into a ponytail. She covered the tangled mess with her ratty straw Stetson, tucked in her t-shirt and somehow managed to slide the supple leather belt with her high school barrel racing award buckle through the loops at her waist. That belt buckle and her saddle were the only awards she'd ever received in the sport. That day had been a shining moment for her, and both Zack and Ryan had been there to watch her ride, and receive her prizes. That night had been the night Ryan had almost kissed her.

Definitely a turning point for her.

The night he told her to get a life was another. Her eyes burned and she rolled them and sucked in a sharp breath, letting it out slowly. She needed to remember that night over the other one so she could keep her resolve. And she would do that.

Ryan Easter needed to leave her the hell

alone.

Twyla straightened her shoulders, grabbed her keys off of the dresser, then opened the bedroom door. Ryan stood there with his hand raised to knock. At least he had on his jeans now.

"What do you want?" she asked gruffly as she brushed past him, and strode across the living room to the door.

"I wanted to see if you wanted to do something tonight. Go somewhere so we can talk?"

Twyla stopped with her hand on the front doorknob and looked back at him. "What part of done don't you understand, Ryan? I have nothing to say to you." Twyla twisted the door knob, and swung it open. "You're the one who needs to get a life. I suggest you get to it," she growled as she walked out and slammed it behind her.

Walking to the top of the stairs, Twyla paused moment to get control of her breathing. Her heart was beating so hard against her ribs, it felt like it would splinter in her chest. Twyla double-timed her steps down the stairs and jogged to her truck. She got inside and fumbled to get the keys into the ignition.

The faster she could get out of here, the better. The emotion building in her chest, and forcing its way up to her throat was never a good sign. It meant she might become a girl at any moment. Something Twyla hated, and refused to give into. Crying was something weak women did. Not rough-and-ready cowgirls. At least not in public. There had been an occasion or two when she had given in, like the night of the almost kiss, but that had been from frustration. She was frustrated right now too, but it was not happening.

Twyla was going out to the barn and she knew riding would soothe her. She threw the truck in reverse, and backed out, then slammed the old truck into drive, before shoving her foot down on the accelerator hard. Tango had always been there for her, she knew he would be today too. Waiting for her, loving her, ready to do whatever she asked him to do. That was the kind of man she needed.

And so was the handsome mounted shooting instructor she'd hired to help her. Randy had been very nice and patient with their lessons so far, and she was making progress. Tango was getting used to the sound of the gunfire, and she was getting used to shifting her focus from Tango to the targets. Once she got pistols of her own, her aim would probably get better. Twyla was a good shot, had always been with a shotgun, but shooting targets while moving at barrel-racer speed was tough. Her first run, she'd missed every target.

Randy hadn't laughed at her, or given up. He'd patiently given her corrections, and told her he had a similar run his first time too. Anticipation at working with him again built inside of her washing away her anger and frustration. She was secretly glad she would get to spend a little time with the man too, even if it was only an hour. Every lesson she had, she was finding more to like about the man. At her last lesson, she had found out he wasn't attached, so that was a plus.

So far there hadn't been any indication that he'd be interested in a gangly, tomboy cowgirl, though. Randy had been totally professional with her, but who knew.

Stranger things had happened.

CHAPTER SIX

Without thinking, Ryan scrubbed his hand over his face. Pain shot up his nasal passages to his brain, and he groaned. "Fuck!" he shouted to the empty apartment.

Jerking his shirt off of the sofa, he picked up his boots and hat then ran out of the apartment to find Twyla's old truck was stopped at the exit of the apartment complex, waiting for traffic to clear so she could pull out. Ryan sprinted down the stairs and hopped into his truck. He tossed his boots and shirt on the floor board then cranked the truck.

He needed to know what other kind of trouble Twyla had gotten herself into. He would have to follow her to find that out, because it was clear she wasn't going to talk to him or listen to anything he had to say. Hopefully, the bar was the worst of it.

If it wasn't, Zack was going to have a stroke.

He saw her turn left out of the driveway and tried to follow, but couldn't make it through the break in the stream of traffic. He watched her turn right as the next intersection, as he sat there waiting for another break.

"Please don't let me lose her," he mumbled as he drummed his fingers impatiently on the steering wheel.

Finally the light at the intersection changed, and he had his chance. Ryan gunned the truck and fishtailed on the loose gravel, before he straightened up and merged to the right lane just in time to hang a left where he'd seen Twyla turn. He didn't see her rattletrap of a truck, so he weaved in and out of traffic, keeping his eyes ahead for any sign of her. About a mile ahead he finally saw her, as she merged onto the interstate. He changed lanes to do the same.

Rush hour traffic had cleared, so Ryan sped up when he merged onto the freeway. He saw Twyla about a mile ahead of him, and decided to hang back a little so she didn't see him. That crazy cowgirl would probably run him off the road, and kick his ass if she saw him. He wouldn't put it past her right now.

Twyla just wasn't in her right mind.

That's all that could explain her attitude and actions, since he'd been there. Maybe after he talked her into coming back with him, or barring that he threw a burlap sack over her head and kidnapped her to take her back home, he'd suggest to her family that they get her some counseling. Lord knew she needed some kind of help. Help that none of them, including her mother, brother or daddy could give her.

Hopefully, they would never hear about what she had been doing since she'd been gone. It would forever damage her family's opinion of her. Hell, he knew it had been an eye opener for him. He had to get her away from Heather as soon as possible. He blamed that woman for most of Twyla's sudden wild behavior.

Ryan followed her for what seemed like forever, but was only about twenty miles outside of town, before Twyla finally turned on her blinker signaling a right turn. Her truck disappeared down the off-ramp, and Ryan hoped he got off in time to see which direction she turned from there. If not, he'd spend hours trying to locate her.

When he got to the bottom of the ramp, she'd already turned, and he was two cars back from the light at the intersection, blocked by the concrete pylons on either side. He slammed his fist on the steering wheel as he waited for the light to change. The two cars in front finally moved, but took their sweet time turning. He'd bet on the left turning lane, and when he eased into the intersection, he saw he lost. He spotted her truck in backed up traffic to the right.

An annoying three minutes later, he made a U-turn and zoomed down the rough road. The traffic from earlier had cleared, so he thought maybe he had a chance of catching up to her. He rounded a curve five minutes later, and saw her truck in the distance, making a left. When he got there, he realized it was a gravel driveway that led up to a horse facility of some kind. That must be where she had Tango boarded, he thought, as he turned. The large parking lot in front of the huge barn in the distance was almost full. Ryan wondered what the heck they did here.

There hadn't been a sign at the gate that told him, and he didn't see any signs by the barn other than the huge one on the side that labeled the ranch as the Rough Cut Ranch. He didn't recognize the two smaller signs that looked like an organization of some kind on either side of the name. He was way too far out. Horses grazed in the pastures flanking the gravel drive, but it wasn't a rough stock herd. These were prissy, expensive horses that English riders rode. Thoroughbreds and Arabians mixed with a few high dollar quarter horses.

In a far off pasture jumps were set up, and several riders practiced out there. Definitely an English Pleasure facility. And he didn't see a barrel in sight. Twyla was definitely not suited to riding English Pleasure. She had about as much grace and finesse as a wrecking ball. He wondered then why she was out here.

Ryan didn't see any sign of Twyla when he hit the parking lot. He slowly passed each row of vehicles, and looked for her truck. When he reached the last row, Ryan was about to believe he'd followed the wrong truck here, but then he saw her. She walked out from between two jacked up trucks with a tall cowboy. The man had his hand on her back while they walked. She was smiling up at him as she talked animatedly with her hands. She turned and the bright sun glinted off of something at her hip.

Ryan leaned across the truck and squinted to make out that Twyla wore a gunbelt that held two shiny silver revolvers. One at each hip. The guy wore a similar rig on his hips too.

What the hell was she up to? A shootout at high noon?

That's sure what it looked like to him. Twyla had rabbit, squirrel and deer hunted with him and Zack plenty of times, but that was with a shotgun.

He'd never seen her use a handgun before. The fact that she had not one, but two in her possession now scared the shit out of him.

Finding an open spot, Ryan pulled in and killed the truck. For a moment, he sat there surveying the area, wondering how he was going to follow her now without being seen. He'd just have to duck and hide, he thought reaching for the door handle. That was total bullshit, but he had to do it if he wanted to find out what she was up to, and who she was with.

That was what Ryan wanted to know, almost more than what she was doing out here at this ranch. They looked awfully familiar with each other, and Ryan needed to know who he was and what he wanted with Twyla. Because of Zack's overprotectiveness, Ryan knew she wasn't all that savvy about men. Zack wasn't here, so it was up to Ryan to make sure that guy wasn't playing her. Or worse, that he wasn't a slimy, abusing bastard like Clarence.

Ryan opened his truck door and slid to the ground, almost crumpling when a sharp piece of gravel dug into his foot. It was only then he realized he wasn't wearing his boots, or shirt. He'd left the apartment half-naked. But he'd been in such a damned hurry to run after Twyla, he was lucky to have on his jeans.

"Damn that woman is gonna be the death of me," he grumbled leaning against the truck to massage his foot.

He reached back into the truck to get his

boots and stomped his feet into them, then pulled the shirt over his head, before slapping his dusty hat on his head with purpose. Screw hiding. He had every right to be here. Zack sent him to find her and drag her ass back with him. That is exactly what he was going to do, he thought, as he strode out into the open aisle between the rows of cars.

Why then did he duck like a goose behind a Mazda pickup when he suddenly caught a flash of blonde hair, and an all too familiar red horse?

Because he was too beat up to get his ass kicked again, and that guy she was with was not small. Stealth would probably be a better plan. He could probably find out more that way anyway. Then he would call her on whatever mischief she was into here, or with that man.

"Twyla, let's just work on the ground with your aim for a little bit," Randy said, as she tied off the lead rope on Tango's halter to the split rail fence near the practice range.

He sat her saddle down by the fence, and laid her bridle gently on top. He'd insisted on carrying her tack for her, even though she told him she had lugged it around herself for years, and could handle it. Randy Hartwell was a gentleman. An added bonus, she rarely found with men on the rodeo circuit. Those guys treated her just like one of the guys. That's what she was used to, not this. It was a welcome change for sure.

"Sounds good," she said turning back to him

with a smile. She was surprised when her face slammed into his broad chest and she bounced back. She hadn't realized he was standing that close. Any other man, she'd have probably bowled over. But Randy was tall. Solid.

His hands closed on her shoulders to steady her. "Whoa there, cowgirl," he said with a laugh. Her eyes met his and there was interest there. Something like a swarm of butterflies fluttered in her stomach, and a warm sensation floated through her.

Twyla was so tall, she rarely found a man as tall as he was. One who she felt small next to, not quite so gangly. She felt like that around Randy and liked it. Ryan was like that too, but not nearly as broad across the chest as Randy.

Randy didn't say anything, he just stared at her for a full second. His lips twitched then he swallowed hard. "Twyla, I've, ah, been meaning to ask you something…'

"Yeah?" she replied dumbly, unable to pull her eyes from his mesmerizing green stare. The air became thick between them and a strange energy buzzed over her shoulders to zip down her spine. Her heart took a couple of strange leaps, then resumed an uneven rhythm.

Was this it? Would this man be her first real date?

"Um, have you ever tried a different saddle on Tango?"

The fog in her mind cleared. "Huh?"

His hands fell from her shoulders to his sides,

and he stepped back. "I have a saddle that's lighter than the one you're using. Your saddle doesn't fit just right across his withers. I'd bet it's pinching him. You could probably get more speed out of him, and he'd have more flex, if you used a different saddle."

Twyla was a little stunned. Her breath came out in a whoosh, and she felt her face heat. Disappointment filled her that she had misinterpreted his signals. She just didn't have the experience to read men, thanks to her brother, her father and Ryan.

Her shoulders slumped. "No, I haven't tried a different saddle. I won that saddle in the only barrel race I ever won, and it's my lucky saddle."

"Not so lucky if you weren't winning," Randy countered with a grin, putting his hands on his trim hips. "It's bulky, and if the damned thing doesn't fit right that could be why you weren't winning. There's nothing wrong with your riding, that's for sure."

Pleasure floated through her at his compliment. "Thank you."

Twyla had always blamed her riding for the reason why she wasn't winning, why Tango wasn't performing up to his potential. This man had given her something else to think about, and more confidence in her riding. Maybe it was her tack. It didn't matter though, she was never going back to the grind of the rodeo. Back to the circus that was her life before, which included the two clowns Zack and Ryan. But that tip might definitely help her with the Cowboy Mounted Shooting competitions.

It also meant more money, if she had to buy a

new saddle. Twyla couldn't use a borrowed saddle forever, or the guns she'd borrowed from Randy. She was going to eventually have to figure out another way to make extra money if she wanted to do this. Ammunition and entry fees, clothing to dress appropriately for the events, wasn't cheap either.

"Okay, let's get started. Tango is pretty set on being gun broken now, so it's time for us to work on your aim. Your run the last time we met told me we need to run the course on foot to get you used to the positioning of the targets. Muscle memory is going to get you where you need to be. Pulling the hammer like it's second nature to you. You need to get comfortable shooting with one hand, crossing over for the targets on the left, and knowing where they are in your mind without thinking. You need to study those configurations for the courses I gave you and know them like the back of your hand. You never know which one you'll draw at the competitions."

She and Randy walked to the beginning of the course, and got into position at the start/finish line. Colored balloons, red and blue, were already tied to the end of flexible poles that marked her path. Randy turned in a slow circle to survey the course, then looked down at her. "Okay we're clear. You have both pistols loaded?"

Twyla nodded, but pulled out the first pistol and checked the loads and repeated an inspection of the second revolver. "Good to go," she said stuffing it back into her gunbelt.

"Okay then…I want you to run this course in

the way you would on your horse. Make sure you hit the targets, Twyla. That's your main focus. If you miss targets in a competition, you lose points. Get used to holstering the first gun as you turn the barrel, and pulling the second. In a level one competition that's not a big deal, but when you move up, if you miss one, drop your pistol or fail to reholster properly you lose. You have to do all those things without thinking. But the first and foremost thing you need to remember is to break the balloons."

Twyla nodded then got set. At his signal, she took off running through the targets. She tried not to hesitate as she took aim and nailed the first three targets perfectly. On the fourth, her arm dropped and she missed which broke her concentration on the fifth blue balloon. Her feet got tripped up, so she stopped and holstered her gun, because she knew she'd just lost if she were actually competing.

"Dammit," she cursed under her breath, staring at the fifth balloon, wondering how in the hell she could be so incompetent at everything.

This was a lot harder than she thought it would be. Maybe she should go to the gun range more. Once she had her own pistols she probably would. She almost had enough money saved up to do that. But that wasn't going to simulate shooting from a horse at breakneck speed. It wasn't her aim that was off, it was her focus. The gun range wasn't going to improve that.

Randy walked up behind her and put his hand on her shoulder to lead her back to the fourth target.

He had her face forward with the balloon at her right. The fifth was catty-corner to her left, on a post a little shorter than the others. He moved behind her and his heat surrounded her, as did the piney scent of his cologne. He put his left hand on her belly and funny flutters danced there. He took her right hand, and his fingers curled around hers to hold her arm out straight, aiming it at the balloon.

She heard him inhale deeply when he leaned close to her ear. His words came out with a slow exhale. "Keep your body square on the horse, Twyla. Keep your balance. Move your eyes and your arm, not your body. You can lean forward and back, but don't turn your body. The best advice I can give you though is to relax."

The thumb on his left hand, which rested on her midriff worked slow circles there and that was definitely not relaxing to her. It was irritating. If he wasn't interested in her, why was he holding her so tight to his body, she wondered. Definitely closer than he needed to be to give her the correction. Or was she imagining things again? Like when she thought he'd been about to ask her out. And was she wishing that he would ask her out, so she could get on her way to forgetting Ryan Easter? Because his touch sure hadn't started the wildfire in her body that she expected. A few pleasant flutters, nothing more. Not good news at all.

She pulled her hand from his, and spun around to face him. Randy looked at her a little strangely, but quickly recovered. "Um, let me get the balloons reset and you can try again."

He turned to walk off, and Twyla couldn't help but admire the view. Randy was definitely a good looking man, and well-mannered. What she couldn't understand though was why his touch hadn't caused the instant lust in her body that Ryan's had done with one almost kiss when she was still a wet-behind-the-ears teenager. That just didn't make sense to her.

She sighed and forced her eyes toward the barn. Movement, as someone dashed into a stall caught her attention. She could've sworn it was Ryan there for a second. But there was no way in hell he was out here. She had left him at the apartment. That again must be wishful thinking on her part. She had to accept that missing that man was going to be a part of her life for a good while to come. He hadn't been gone a few hours and it had already started again.

Damn his black soul for making her want him. If Randy would just finally find his balls and ask her out, at least she'd have a distraction to get on the right track to forgetting him. Who knew maybe eventually she'd feel the same way about Randy. If she focused on him and forgot about Ryan Easter.

It was almost dusk when Randy walked her to her truck. She was tired, but exhilarated too. Their lessons today had really helped her. She made a run on Tango before they quit, and she'd hit every target. Her time hadn't been fantastic, but she'd nailed every fricking target!

Randy said he was proud of her, and that meant a lot coming from him. That man was a Range Master at CMSA events and a level six shooter to boot, with several World Champion titles under his belt. He was also a damned good teacher. It was probably better if they didn't muddy the waters between them by getting involved. She needed to quit hoping for more, and just accept his friendship. Her new career was what was important. Randy was offering her that. It was enough. She'd just deal with missing Ryan like she had since she left, by staying busy earning money to fund her new career and support herself until she got there.

When they reached the truck, Randy opened the truck door for her and stepped back. Twyla tossed her bag inside, then pulled her hat off and tossed it inside too. She slid the rubber band out of her hair and ran her fingers through it, then turned back to him with a smile. "Thanks for being patient with me today, Randy. I know I'm a klutz, and a dullard sometimes," she said with a self-deprecating laugh.

He didn't laugh, Randy frowned and grabbed her chin, tipping her face up to meet her eyes. The air between them got that thick quality again, and he just studied her for a moment. "There is nothing clumsy or dull about you, Twyla. You are a beautiful, talented woman and don't ever let anyone tell you otherwise. You're going to get this, and I know you're going to be good when you do. I don't take on training people I don't have faith in."

Twyla got a melting sensation in the center of her chest and sighed. "I sure hope so."

She was investing a helluva lot of money into this. If it didn't pan out, she had no idea what she was going to do. She knew one thing though, dancing at the Crazy Cowgirl for an extended time wasn't going to happen. That really wasn't her scene. She was going to take that abuse as long as she could though, because it paid well. As long as she knew she would eventually be able to get out of that job, she could take it for now.

"Hope isn't a way to win. You need to have faith in yourself too, honey."

"I lost that about two years into my barrel racing career, when I figured out I'd never be a winner." It was true. It seemed like no matter how hard she tried to be successful at anything, she always failed. At school, barrel racing, love—hell being a woman—she was always mediocre. Twyla was tired of being a middle-of-the-road kind of girl, but how in the hell could she possibly have the faith he wanted her to have that this attempt would be any different?

Randy's fingers tightened on her chin and she felt the tension in his arm. His eyes darkened, and he swallowed hard. "Twyla, I like you," he said suddenly, then let his hand fall from her chin, as he stepped back.

She noticed a tic at the outside corner of his left eye. He seemed like he wanted to say more, but the silence stretched. "Well that's damned good, because I like you too," she said with a laugh. "I appreciate everything you're doing for me." That's when it dawned on her, she hadn't paid him his lesson fee yet, and that's probably why he was so nervous. He didn't want to ask her for his money. "Oh crap, I forgot to pay you! I'm so sorry—just a sec!"

She turned to reach back inside the truck for her duffle, but his hand dropped on her shoulder. "I don't give a damn about the money. You can pay me next week." She lifted back up and met his eyes. "I wanted to ask if you would you go out with me. The bars are closed tonight, or I'd ask you to go have a drink with me…"

Her heart kicked then sped up in her chest. Randy evidently was interested. She hadn't misinterpreted anything. "I've had enough of bars. If I never saw the inside of one again, I'd be a happy girl." And that was the god's honest truth. But Randy didn't know she worked at the Cowgirl, and she wasn't about to tell him. This man would probably think she was loose if he knew that. He'd definitely have a different opinion of her that was for sure.

"The lake is always open," he replied with a shrug and hesitant smile. "You want to pick up a six pack and ride with me out there to talk?"

"That sounds like a perfect date to me," she said with a wide grin. A perfect first date, with a near perfect man. Now, if she could just convince her body of that, she'd be in good shape. "I'd really like that…" Then a thought hit her. She'd promised

Heather that morning that she would be home early this evening. They had a date with one of her regulars tonight. Twyla didn't really want to do it, this was her only night off, but she needed that money.

It was too good to pass up.

"But? You're not interested?" Randy filled in, his face deflating.

Twyla smiled up at him. "Oh, I'm definitely interested. But I have plans with my roommate tonight. Maybe next Sunday? I work all week."

"Aren't you off at night?' he asked taking a step back.

Heat flooded her face, and she stammered. "Um…no, I ah, work nights."

His eyebrows lifted. "What do you do?"

"She's a stripper at the Crazy Cowgirl," a very familiar gruff voice said as Ryan rounded the front of the truck. "So take a hike. She's not your kind of woman."

It *had* been him she'd seen dashing into that stall. He was following her! Spying on her! And now he was lying to Randy to boot.

"What the hell are you doing here, Ryan?" she growled pushing past Randy to shove Ryan's broad chest. "I am not a stripper, and you are not my keeper! Get lost!"

He leaned down to put his nose to hers. "Thank the good Lord for that! You're into so much trouble, even I can't keep up with you. If your brother was here—"

Twyla pushed him again, and he staggered

back. "Well, he's *not* here, and *you* are not my *brother*, Ryan Easter."

"Um, I'll see you next weekend for our lesson, Twyla," Randy said, and Twyla heard a new tone to his voice that sounded very near disgust. It definitely told her that Ryan had succeeded in running him off. Randy would never ask her out again, because Ryan made him think she was a loose woman. Trash. Anger pushed up her throat to fill her skull to the point she thought it might crack open.

Ryan grabbed her shoulders and his fingers dug into her skin. "Well, I'm close enough right now. Zack sent me here to see what kind of mess you'd gotten yourself into and bring you back. Now, you're going to load your pretty ass up in that truck and we're going to your apartment and loading up your stuff!"

He shook her a little to emphasize his words. Twyla narrowed her eyes, and balled her fist. "The only thing I'm loading is my pistol if you don't get your hands off of me."

Ryan evidently realized what he was doing, or he was afraid she would shoot him, which as mad as she was she very well might do just that. His face turned bloodless as his fingers relaxed, and he rubbed her shoulders a second before his hands dropped to his sides.

"I'm sorry, Twy—I didn't mean to grab you."

"You're right you are sorry…a sorry sonofabitch," she spat, as she turned and moved around the truck door to get inside and slam it.

Twyla rolled down her window, and took a deep breath to get a grip on the urge to kill him. "The best thing you can do is get back in your truck and head back to the circuit. I don't want you here. Tell Zack the same."

CHAPTER SEVEN

Ryan stood there a moment, dumbfounded at the way Twyla was acting. He watched her peel out of the parking lot onto the main road. As out-of-control as the tail end of that truck was as it lost traction in the loose gravel when she pulled out is just how out-of-control Twyla was right now too. She had lost traction in her life, was doing things the old Twyla would never have done in a million years. Like threatening to shoot him. The look in her eyes told him she would have if he didn't turn her loose. Like dancing at a bar half-naked for money, and agreeing to go who knew where out in the woods alone with a man she barely knew.

Wild. She was as crazy as a wild mustang right now, and he needed to figure out how to rein her in. One thing was for sure, the tactics he'd used so far weren't working. Ryan was no closer to convincing her to come back with him than he had been the day she left. He had to come up with a different plan of action or she was going to run right off the cliff she was headed toward. And he would lose her for good.

At least he'd been able to run that city-slick, sharpshooting cowboy off. What self-respecting cowboy wore pressed fucking jeans and a button down shirt out to a barn? The chaps he wore definitely hadn't seen any work either. They were as clean and spit-shined as his damned boots. Hiding in that damned hot stall all day watching that man as he watched Twyla had been sheer torture. It had only taken him a few minutes to figure out that guy was after Twyla, working up to asking her out. The way he smiled at her, looked at her, and fucking touched her when he was supposedly giving her a lesson.

Ryan knew what lesson the man was trying to teach her, the same one he'd been fighting himself to keep from teaching her for years, and he wasn't about to let that happen. There was no way he could stay hidden when the man put his arm around her to walk her out to the truck. He knew the moment had arrived, and he wasn't about to stand by and watch it happen.

If not for his interference, they would probably be out by that lake right now making out. The thought turned his blood to ice water in his veins. That's how damned crazy Twyla was right now. She would've gone out to the woods alone with a man she barely knew, maybe gotten raped or who knew what else. No matter what she said, Twyla did need a fucking keeper. She was off her lead now, headed straight toward disaster, if someone didn't jerk her back to reality.

Zack had always been the one with the lead in his hand, but Twyla was a full-grown woman now, could do what she wanted. And Ryan was here, so he guessed he would have to be the one to figure out how to do that.

He'd temporarily turned her by telling Mr. Fancy Pants she was a stripper. At least that had gotten the uptight, obviously rich, asshole off of her scent. His description wasn't that far removed from what Twyla was actually doing at that bar anyway. Flashbacks of her dancing on that bar seized his brain and cold chills zipped down his spine. If Fancy Pants saw what Ryan had seen at that bar he wouldn't be walking away, he'd be running like his ass was on fire. He looked like his typical woman was refined and country-mannered. Twyla was as far removed from that description as a dairy cow in the midst of a herd of beef cattle.

Twyla was more Ryan's type. Rough around the edges, sassy as hell and country beautiful. At least today she was, without all that damned makeup and the sexy clothes she wore at that bar. Today, he thought she was the girl he knew again, the same one who'd been mooning after him for years. The one he'd wanted for ten years too, but run from to keep the peace with her brother. To keep the family he so desperately needed.

Ryan couldn't have been more wrong. He now realized that girl may very well be gone for good. Twyla seemed to be serious. She had finally given up the chase. The coldness in her tone with him told him that this wasn't just about her being angry. She really was done with him and had moved on. *I'm done.*

A sharp pain shot through his heart and he rubbed it. He really believed she meant that now, and this situation was not going to be fixed with a little return flirting or a few smiles. It was like he'd lost every bit of power he'd ever had with her. Twyla was a different girl now. Ryan had to come up with a different way of dealing with her, or he was wasting his time here.

He was gonna lose her. It was time to shit or get off the pot, as his surrogate daddy, Mr. Taylor, was fond of saying. If he didn't fix this soon, he'd have to go back to the rodeo without her, and Zack would not be happy. Ryan wouldn't be either. Because that would mean he'd have to leave her here to the mercy of slick, calculating cowboys and her wild-ass crazy friend's whims.

After that, the odds were he'd never see her again, except at occasional family gatherings. Because he'd be her brother. Just like he'd said he wanted for years. He'd have to watch her date other men like that cowboy, bring them to those gatherings with her, introduce them to her parents. Maybe eventually watch her walk down the aisle to marry one of them, while he sat there wanting to kill them both, eating his heart out, because he didn't have the balls to upset the applecart and tell her how he felt about her.

No, that wasn't happening.

Ryan only had two days left to convince her. But first he had to find her. As fast as she was driving when she left here, she could be halfway to Timbuktu by now. Ryan ran for his truck, and hopped inside and cranked it. He'd check the apartment first. She was dusty and sweaty from her day outside playing shoot-em-up with that cowboy, whatever the purpose of that was. He knew the first thing she'd want before she went anywhere would be a shower.

Even though he knew she wasn't a girly-girl, flowers type of woman, Ryan thought that might be a good start to setting things right between them. He stopped at a grocery store on the way to the apartment and picked up a bunch of spring flowers, and a box of Twinkies. He made it to the apartment complex right at dark, and immediately zoned in on Twyla's beat-up pickup parked beside Heather's newer, black truck. He knew she hadn't had enough time to finish her shower yet, and since Heather was there, if he went up and knocked he'd have her and her damned mace to deal with instead of Twyla.

It was better for him to park and wait a few minutes, he thought, finding an out of the way spot where they wouldn't see him if they looked out the window. He pulled in and settled to wait a few minutes. Sliding down in the seat, he leaned his head back against the seat and closed his eyes. *I have plans with my roommate tonight.*

With those two, and Heather at the helm, there was no telling what those plans were. The possibilities made his stomach curl. Well, whatever the plans were, Ryan planned on canceling them. He and Twyla needed to talk, and that was going to supersede any plans she might have made with Heather. Ryan nodded a couple of times, but then the vibrations from a powerful truck engine woke him up.

He sat up in the seat and leaned forward over the wheel, as a fancy burgundy diesel dually truck pulled into a spot near the stairs. The one directly beside Heather's truck. The door opened and a man in a suit, cowboy hat and shiny black boots hopped down. He reminded Ryan of that man on that show Dukes of Hazzard. What was his name? Oh yeah, Boss Hog.

Short, round and dressed to the nines, the man looked up at the upper floor, before he made his way up the stairs. His arm swung upward and Ryan noticed that he clutched a large bouquet of flowers of some kind. Must have a hot date with the little old lady that Ryan had seen come out of the apartment next door to Heather's. Biting back a laugh, Ryan relaxed back in the seat, until he saw Boss Hog stop at Heather's door to knock.

The door opened and Heather filled the doorway smiling at the man. He shoved the flowers at her, and she buried her nose in the bouquet. From all appearances, it looked like Heather had a hot date with Boss Hog tonight. Somehow that didn't surprise him. She seemed like the type who wouldn't have a problem with finding a sugar daddy. Well, Twyla sure wasn't going to be following her lead there. Ryan would make sure of it. Heather leaned down and gave him a peck on the cheek, then invited him inside. The door shut and Ryan knew he'd have to wait until Heather left to go up there to see Twyla.

He relaxed back against the seat again, but then confusion claimed him as Twyla's words popped back into his head. *I have plans with my roommate tonight.* He sat straight up. If Heather had a date with Boss

Hog, how the hell could Twyla have plans with her? Flashes of her and Heather's 'act' with the shot glass at the bar speared his brain to mix with the fact that Boss Hog was in the apartment with them and Ryan was out of the truck in a hurry.

"Sorry, Boss, ain't happening," Ryan mumbled as he slammed the truck door and strode toward the stairs. By the time he reached the landing he could hear his heart pounding in his ears. Just as he rounded the railing, the front door swung open and Heather walked out dressed in her *dancing* clothes, followed by Twyla, then Boss Hog. Twyla stood beside Boss, looking nervous while she watched Heather fish for her keys in the bag on her shoulder.

Ryan grabbed her arm. "Twy—what the hell do you think you're doing?"

Her eyebrows lifted, then fell over her angry blue eyes. She jerked her arm from his grasp and stepped closer to Boss Hog. "I'm *working*," she grated through her teeth, then glared at him. "And you're about to go to jail!"

"*Working!?!*" Ryan screeched, waving his hands at her half-naked body. "Is this what you do for a living now? If it is, I sure wouldn't be calling the cops if I were you."

Boss Hog grunted and took a step toward him, but Ryan pinned him with a hot look. He lifted his hands and backed up, which was a damned good thing. Ryan's hands fisted at his sides as his gaze swung back to Twyla. "How much is he paying you and what for?" he demanded, angrier and more disgusted than he'd ever been in his life. He definitely didn't know the woman standing there dressed like a whore with half-a-pound of makeup caked on her face, the one who obviously was half of the main course on Boss Hog's menu tonight.

"A thousand dollars, and you're not about to make us lose that," Heather said giving Ryan's shoulder a push. Her other hand flew up out of her purse, but this time he was ready for it. He grabbed her wrist and shoved her hand aside, just as a stream of liquid shot out of the end. He inhaled a little of the mist and coughed, his eyes burned too, but at least he didn't get the full brunt of the spray like he had the other night.

Ryan squeezed Heather's wrist until her hand opened and the canister clattered to the ground. He kicked it over the edge of the balcony with his boot, then let her hand go to wipe his on his jeans. Pinning her with a glare, he grated through his teeth, "Lady, that's the last time you're going to spray me with that stuff, or I'll be the one calling the cops. Now, you go do whatever you were going to do with Boss Hog here, but Twyla is staying here with me."

"I'll go where I damn well—" Twyla started, but Ryan shut her up with a glare.

Heather took a step back and rubbed her wrist. "He paid us both, and she agreed to go."

"Well, she's not going," Ryan said flatly, then nodded at Twyla. "Give him the money back, Twyla."

Twyla folded her arms over her barely

covered breasts. A damned sports bra with pushup pads was not outerwear, but Twyla Taylor didn't seem to know that. She was about to find out, because this crazy cowgirl and him were about to come to a meeting of the minds, even though it was obvious she'd lost hers.

"Heather has a check."

"Then tear it up, and write her another one," he said to Boss Hog who didn't seem to be inclined to get in the middle of this situation. A very smart move on his part considering Ryan's mood.

Twyla unfolded her arms, and stomped her boot. "I need that damned money, Ryan! I'm going! We're just dancing, it's not like we're…um.…"

"Having a threesome?" Heather supplied with a lifted brow and a smug smile for Ryan. Twyla didn't know the term, but Heather sure did. That woman was experienced. She knew exactly what Ryan had been thinking. And that made it even worse that Twyla was staying with her, being influenced. The sly look in Heather's cat green eyes said this woman had been there and done a lot of things in her lifetime. She could probably teach Ryan a trick or two.

Boss Hog cleared his throat, then stepped around Heather. "I'll be in the truck. Y'all decide what you're going to do." He eyed Ryan warily as he sidestepped him, then his boot heels echoed as they struck the concrete on his way to the stairs.

"You going or stayin?" Heather asked Twyla.

Her eyes slid to Ryan then back to Heather. "I need the money."

Twyla took one step toward the stairs, but Ryan grabbed her arm. Desperate and beyond angry at her, Ryan said, "I'll pay you twice the money to stay here with me." He had that much in his wallet and couldn't think of a better way to spend it.

Twyla snorted, and with a challenging look said, "Since when do you have a thousand bucks in your wallet?"

"Since I won and left after my last ride to come here and save your crazy ass. I haven't had a chance to go to the bank."

Twyla lifted that stubborn chin of hers. The one with the little notch in the center that always made him want to lick it. Her eyebrow lifted, over her heavily made up eyes. "I don't need saving. I'm perfectly fine...and I don't want your money."

"Well that's too damned bad, sugar, because you're getting it." Ryan grabbed her wrist and pulled her toward the door as she dug in her heels trying to stop. He twisted the knob and flung open the door. "My money is as green as his, and I'm a lot better looking. Should be easier on you fucking me than him."

Heather laughed loudly, but Twyla fought harder, pulling against his grasp with all her might. Ryan grabbed her around the waist and dragged her inside. As he slammed the door, he heard Heather say, "Y'all have fun, I may not be home tonight,"

He rounded on Twyla, who was standing near the sofa looking like a mad, wet hen. Shoving his hand into his back pocket, he pulled out his wallet and rifled through it. He pulled out ten, crisp hundred dollar bills and tossed them on the floor at her feet. Ryan was about to teach Twyla a valuable lesson. One he hoped she remembered for a very long time.

Twyla wanted to be that kind of woman? Well, he was going to show her what that really meant. What she would have faced if she had gotten in the truck with that asshole. If she chose to live this kind of lifestyle. At least he was a safer way for her to learn that lesson. Considering his mood though, that might not be the case.

"Get naked," he grated coldly as he flipped the locks on the door.

"I'm not getting naked," she said indignantly, as she stomped toward the front door. I'm leaving."

Ryan grabbed her around the waist and carried her back toward the sofa. He set her on her feet then sat on the sofa. "I paid you the thousand bucks, remember? Now you're going to give me my money's worth." He took off his hat and tossed it on the side table, then unbuttoned his jeans and stroked himself. "You want to dance? Do it. For a thousand bucks, you're going to do that naked. I want to see what I paid for."

Twyla stood there still as a statue, her eyes as wide as saucers.

"What's wrong, *Daisy*?" Ryan asked snidely, as he unzipped his jeans. "You feel cheap?" Her eyes got wider, and her lower lip trembled, but he was determined not to let it affect him.

Twyla needed this lesson, and he needed some fucking stress relief. This woman had him tied in knots for ten years. He'd just paid her a thousand bucks to work out some of those knots. "Trust me when I tell you you're not. I've been here and done this many times, and you are about as expensive as I've ever had. Now get to it."

CHAPTER EIGHT

Ryan notched his chin at the bills. "Pick 'em up—they're yours."

Her eyes dropped to the bills and seemed to be fixed there. "I don't want your money, Ryan," she said in a deflated voice.

"You wanted Boss Hog's...you said you *needed* it," he growled. "Show me how bad you need it, Twyla. Pick 'em up, and get undressed. Earn your money. I'm getting tired of waiting."

He knew he was being rough and cold with her, and doing it made him sick at his stomach. Treating her like the dancers he'd paid at those strip clubs he visited on the road, made him sick. But that was the only way he was going to get through to her. To treat her exactly how she was acting. His heart wasn't in it, but his body damned sure was. The thought of having her hover over him, her heat teasing him, made his dick grow thick under his palm.

Excitement buzzed along his nerve endings as he stroked himself, waiting for her to move. Her eyes shot up to his and there was fear there now. Her face was a mask of embarrassed shock. Good, she needed to be ashamed. Maybe Twyla finally realized exactly what she'd been doing by dancing at that bar, the life she was buying into. There was no way Ryan was letting her off the hook that easily though. He wanted to make damned sure she didn't forget this lesson tomorrow morning.

She gnawed her lower lip, then finally bent to gather up the money. She stuffed the bills into the pocket of her almost non-existent shorts, then stood. Spearing him with her eyes, she folded her arms over her chest, and the corner of her mouth kicked up smugly. "That should be insurance enough that I don't tell Zack about this and get your ass kicked."

Blackmail? Well, two could play her game. She had more to lose than he did, really. "And I'm paying you for something I could get for free if I threatened to tell your folks what you're up to…to tell Zack," he challenged with a lifted brow. "If I were you, sugar, I'd be thankful. I'd also get undressed and start dancing, before I change my mind and make that call."

Twyla didn't move, but her body tensed as she thought about it. It looked like he needed to up the ante some, and Ryan knew just what button to push. "And then there's always Grandma Sibley. I'm sure she'd be extremely interested in what her precious granddaughter is up to here in the big city."

Twyla gasped and her face went chalk white. "You wouldn't…"

"Oh, yes I would. All of the above," he said calmly, with a smug smile of his own.

Twyla wasn't smiling now. Her hands trembled as she fumbled with the button on her shorts. She shot him an angry glare as she jerked the two inch zipper to the bottom then shoved her shorts over her hips. His eyes followed the worn denim down her long legs until they reached her ankles.

Slowly his gaze glided upward until he met her hurt, angry eyes. "That thong isn't going to do you any good. Drop it."

"I'm not taking off my panties," she said firmly, covering her lower body with her hands.

Ryan leaned up on the sofa and shoved his hand into his pocket. When he pulled his hand out holding his cell phone, she growled and hooked her thumbs into the thin black elastic at her hips and pushed them down. Ryan couldn't stop his eyes from locking on the soft blonde fluff at the apex of her thighs. He also couldn't help his body going rock hard as the need to see her soft, wet center slammed into him. She stood there staring at him with accusation and hatred in her icy blue eyes. If they were laser beams he'd be frozen solid where he sat.

Swallowing hard, he tried to regulate his uneven breathing, slow his galloping heart. "Take your top off," he instructed, cringing at the rusty quality to his voice.

"I don't have on a bra," she informed gruffly.

"I know that. You're wearing it as a damned top. Take it off. I think you know what naked means, Twyla. You were halfway there before you started undressing."

Her hands shook harder as she grabbed the band of the sports bra. She stopped and the shaking encompassed her whole body, even her lower lip trembled. "Don't make me do this, Ryan," she begged, her voice barely above a whisper.

"This is what I paid you for, Twyla. What you

were willing to do for Boss Hog's money too. There's no difference. Now, take your damned top off!" Her eyes filled, and Ryan fought the sickness in his gut. She spun around giving him a nice view of her round ass, while she fought to get the top over her head. She finally got it and tossed it to the side.

"I can't dance without music," she said, and he heard the wobble in her voice.

Twyla Taylor was one of the strongest women he knew. He had never seen her cry before, and didn't want to see it now. It would kill him to be the cause of it. Ryan didn't want to break her, he just wanted to teach her a lesson.

"Suck it up buttercup. This is what you choose to do for money. I paid you, now act like a professional and shake your ass for me," he said coldly as he got up from the sofa. He picked up the remote for the television. He turned it on and scrolled down until he found the country music channel, then tossed it back on the table and sat back down.

And wasn't it just appropriate that Luke Bryan's Country Girl was playing?

Ryan pushed the button on the remote to turn up the volume, so he didn't have to hear her sniffling. He had to get through this, and he wouldn't be able to if he heard her crying.

"Nice ass. Now turn around and show me your tits," Ryan ordered, flinching at using that term with a woman he used to have the ultimate respect for. Never in his life had he ever said that to a woman, especially in that way. But Twyla needed to know this is what she could expect from paying customers if she didn't get the hell away from here. Ryan was determined to get her out of here. If this was the only way he could make that happen, then he would do it. "Do it, Twyla," he growled then held up the cell phone. "Or if you want to back out I have Grandma Sibley on speed dial."

She spun around to face him, but her hands covered her breasts. Her eyes shot icy blue daggers at him, as her hips found stilted time with the music. She wasn't dancing, she was swaying, and that just wasn't enough. The need to see her pert little breasts, the beautiful mounds he'd fantasized about seeing for ten years, hit him in the center of the chest. This would probably be his only chance. "Move your goddamn hands, Twyla. I said I want to see your tits!" he shouted angrily, one hand squeezing his cell phone tighter, while the other stroked his cock.

Twyla whimpered, her hands fluttered down to her sides, and she closed her eyes. His eyes locked on her pink areolas in the center of perfect, handful-sized mounds. Perfect mouthful-sized mounds he corrected, as his mouth watered for a taste of her. His tongue tingled to feel the raspy roughness of the rigid berry-colored buttons at the center. She finally danced now, popping her hips, and her breasts bounced as she danced. Ryan's heart was pounding in his chest and he fought for breath. His fucking palms burned to test the weight of those peaks, to tease her nipples until she screamed. God, he wanted to hear her scream his name. To make her come for him, so he could see her face.

That would be the ultimate turn-on, his ultimate satisfaction, but Ryan knew it wasn't happening. This was a lesson, not a prelude to sex, he reminded himself. He had no plans to satisfy the desire clawing at his insides. But damn if that wasn't just what he wanted to do, Zack and the Taylor family be damned. The orgasm building inside his body was like a lava flow from a dormant volcano that was long overdue due to erupt. The ultimate satisfaction would be burying himself in her tight body and finally knowing how damned sweet she was as he found his release.

Save a Horse Ride a Cowboy followed the previous song, Ryan's balls tightened and he bit back a groan. He wondered if there was some cosmic DJ picking the music for that station, because that's exactly what he wanted this long, tall cowgirl to do to him right then. He'd have to settle for the next best thing. "Come over here and give me a lap dance, and it better be good."

Twyla's movements stuttered then stopped. "I can't do that," she said in a raw voice. Ryan refused to look at her eyes, because he knew he'd find tears there again.

"Oh, yeah you can. I know you probably do that at the bar for tips too. You'd have done it at that party." He finally dragged his eyes to hers. "I paid you a thousand bucks, and you're going to give me a fucking lap dance. And it better be a good one, Twyla. The best one I've ever had, or I'm calling Granny."

Ryan stood and shoved his jeans and underwear down, he toed off his boots, then stepped out of the jeans. When he stood back up, Twyla was staring at his engorged dick, gnawing her lower lip. Her chest heaved with her breaths, and her fists were curled at her sides. Ryan fisted himself then sat back on the couch. He didn't want to see her face while she did this, and he didn't want her to see him come. It would be too weird. And he knew he was going to come when he imagined himself sliding up into her tight, wet heat, as her hips moved over him while she danced.

He was almost there already.

"Turn around and show me your ass. Bend over when you dance like you did at the bar. I want to see your wet pussy."

Her eyes flew to his. "Stop being vulgar! I am not doing that!" she said, her tone rising an octave with each word.

Ryan shrugged with a helluva lot more nonchalance than he was feeling. "Won't be anything I haven't seen, Twyla, and you're a pro at this remember? I could almost see the goodies at that bar in those shorts anyway."

"I am a dancer, not a stripper or whore!" she shouted, then held out her hand. "I'm not letting you treat me this way! Give me your damned phone and I'll call Zack and tell him!"

"Dancer, stripper, whore. Half a dozen of one or six of the other," he replied calmly meeting her angry gaze. "I don't think your family would like to hear that you're doing any of them," he challenged, and sat his phone on the sofa beside him. "What do you think?"

Her face fell, and she looked down at her hands, which were now twisting in front of her.

"You think they'd be proud of what you're doing here, Twy?" he repeated, wanting her to admit what she was doing was wrong. "Are you proud of yourself?"

A big fat teardrop landed on her hands followed by another, then it was raining on her hands, and her body shook violently. He thought her knees might give out she was shaking so hard, so he pulled her to him and onto his lap. His arms closed around her and she buried her face in his shoulder. It wasn't long before her tears soaked his shirt. He held her tight and rocked her, until the tremors became intermittent, then he kissed her hair. Guilt swamped him, when she whimpered. "I'm sorry, baby. I didn't mean to talk to you like that…but you needed to see."

She sat up and dragged in a shuddering breath, then scrubbed her eyes with the back of her hands and came away with black streaks. "You are a bastard," she ground out, then pushed off of his lap. She started to walk off toward the bathroom, but he grabbed her wrist.

"I won't argue with you there. I have been a bastard for years, and that's not likely to change.

You, however, are not a whore, honey."

"I'm not going to dance forever. Just until I get enough money to buy my guns and tack."

Ryan stood, then gently took her shoulders to turn her to face him. Her face was a mess, black streaks tracked to the corners of her mouth, which was swollen from her gnawing. "What the hell do you need guns for? And what were you doing out there with that cowboy today?"

Her eyes dropped to his throat. "Learning to do cowboy mounted shooting. Randy is a world champion shooter, he's teaching me. That is what I want to be doing."

"Well, Randy wants to be doing you," Ryan growled his fingers digging into her soft skin. "And that's not happening." She sniffled, and blew out a breath, then pushed against his chest, but Ryan held her. "I'm not going to let it happen, Twyla."

Twyla slammed her fist into his shoulder. "You're worse than Zack! Why the hell not? Randy is a good man!"

"He's not good enough for you," Ryan said evenly. She looked up at him with so much misery in her eyes, he wanted to hold her until it went away. To do whatever it took to make sure she never looked that way again.

"According to you and my brother, no man is good enough." Her lower lip wobbled again, and his eyes fixed there as she fought to still it. "I should just join a damned nunnery and you two will be happy. I like Randy and I want him too."

Ryan heard the words, saw her lips move to form them, but his brain refused to accept them. Those beautiful lips tightened, and her breath whispered against his throat, as she said, "I'm a grown woman, Ryan, but y'all refuse to accept that. A woman with needs. Y'all are hound dogs, have whoever you damn well please, but every time I find a man I might be interested in, who might be interested in me, you get in the middle. Where's the fairness in that?"

The only part of her statement Ryan could focus on was the fact that Twyla wanted a man other than him, was contemplating being with another man. Jealousy punched him in the gut and stole his breath. He couldn't even find enough to speak.

"It's not fair, and I'm old enough to make my own choices. I'm done letting you, or Zack make them for me." She pushed against his chest again, and Ryan was so stunned he let her go. "Just leave me alone, Ryan. If it upsets you that much, and you think it would upset the family, I'll get a job at the burger joint, and work part time at the barn to pay my board. It'll take me twice as long to get where I need to be, while paying half the expenses here, but I'll do it. If you and Zack will just leave me alone, I'll do that."

Leave her alone. To be with Randy.

A sense of loss more profound than he'd ever felt in his life engulfed him as he watched her walk toward her bedroom. Emotion shot up to his head and it pounded in time with his heart. Ryan staggered back to sit on the sofa. For ten years, he'd pushed Twyla away, dodged her advances and fought his attraction to her. It looked like he didn't have to push anymore, and the fight was over. She was walking away on her own accord.

Now that she said she'd quit the bar, he really had no reason to stay here. She would be safe living here with Heather, as long as she wasn't at that bar, he admitted grudgingly. It wasn't optimal in his opinion, but his opinion didn't matter. Twyla was grown and could make her own decisions. One of those decisions was she had evidently outgrown him. He knew now she had a roof over her head, and food in her refrigerator, he'd looked. Twyla didn't need him, and she didn't need her brother.

She would have Randy, the man she wanted. And a new career eventually. A life that didn't include either Ryan or Zack.

He did need to find out more about that cowboy mounted shooting to make sure she could support herself, after investing so much into it. But that really wasn't his business either, now was it? From what he'd seen, the sport wasn't any more dangerous than barrel racing, and Twyla seemed to like it. She was a grown woman and didn't need him telling her what to do.

With a feeling of numbness inside, Ryan got up and put on his underwear and jeans. He staggered to the front door and unlocked the three locks, then walked out, closing it quietly behind him. He definitely wasn't feeling the peace he thought he'd feel when Twyla was no longer chasing him, when he didn't have to dodge her.

He felt strange, empty…lost.

***

Twyla scrubbed her face until every trace of the thick makeup was gone, every ounce of the heartache was purged from her system. Well, every ounce of this new wave. That feeling was going to be with her for a long time. Half of her heart would always be on the road, tucked into Ryan Easter's back pocket. She just had to accept that. Seeing him again told her that no matter how hard she tried to separate herself from those feelings, they would always be with her. He would always be a part of her.

But Randy also gave her hope today that she might eventually be able to move on. She needed to move on. Ryan Easter was finished business, and she just needed to accept that. Why then was her heart bleeding so badly in her chest?

Because what he'd done to her a few minutes ago had been a reality check. Ryan had been trying to teach her a lesson, and had succeeded tenfold. Two points had been driven home during his instruction. One was that Ryan Easter did not want her that way, and never would. Never had. When she was sitting naked and raw in his lap, he would have at least kissed her, if there was even a spark there. The second lesson was she was not cut out to be an exotic dancer. Heather had the moves and attitude for it, but Twyla didn't.

Ryan was right that her family would be

mortified if they knew.

Telling Ryan she would give it up hadn't been difficult. Twyla hated it. His shock therapy tactics convinced her of that. It also convinced her that he would never want her the way she had always wanted him, waited for him to want her. After he'd extracted a promise from her that she'd give up the dancing, he'd lit out of here like his tail was on fire. That proved his sole purpose for coming to Dallas was to check up on her for Zack. To make sure she wasn't doing anything they didn't approve of. He hadn't come here to tell her he missed her and wanted more.

Because he didn't.

For ten years, Twyla had been kidding herself that there was something there. Ten wasted fucking years on a man who thought she was his kid sister. Ryan hadn't been staying away from her because of Zack's threats, and posturing like she thought. He just plain didn't want more from her. She was his sister, and he had his buckle bunnies. Why the hell would he look twice at an irritating, gangly tomboy who mooned after him like a lost puppy?

He wouldn't.

Twyla threw the washrag into the sink with disgust at herself. She dropped her chin to her chest and took deep calming breaths, exhaling slowly. When she finally thought she had herself together, she grabbed her worn terry bath robe from the hook on the back of the bathroom door and put it on. She yanked the ends of the tie tight, and pulled the front together tighter across her chest. Damn, she wished she had a box of Twinkies. If ever she needed them, it was now. Maybe she'd get dressed again and run to the store, she thought, as she left the bathroom to go to her room. She would Twinkie Ryan Easter right out of her system.

But that wouldn't do a damned thing except make her sicker than she already felt. It was still early, maybe she'd call Randy and tell him her plans had changed. At least that would be a distraction from her misery. She reversed direction and headed for the phone in the kitchen, but a loud knock sounded at the front door.

With a groan, she padded toward the door wondering who the hell it could be. Heather wouldn't be knocking, and Ryan was gone. Maybe it was Bud the maintenance man who liked to pay them surprise visits, she thought, as she went to unlock the door and saw all three latches were undone. Ryan hadn't even locked the bottom lock, which surprised her.

She twisted the knob and opened it a crack to stick her face out through the opening. Her heart squeezed then shot up to her throat, when she saw Ryan standing there with a wilted bunch of wildflowers in one hand, and a brand new box of Twinkies in the other.

CHAPTER NINE

Stunned, Twyla stepped back to open the door. Ryan walked inside and she shut the door, then flipped the locks. She turned, and their eyes met. There was something different in his deep blue eyes now. Remorse, and maybe an apology. The prickly attitude from earlier, his arrogance from an hour ago, was gone.

"I bought these earlier on the way here to apologize for what happened at the barn." He held out the gifts to her. "I forgot them in the truck when I saw you leaving with Boss Hog."

Twyla just stared at the gifts until he shoved them into her chest. Her hands shook a little as she took them from him. Who was this man and what the hell did this mean? More of the push and pull she'd been dealing with for years? In all the years she'd watched him chase women, Twyla had never seen Ryan buy any of them flowers. He'd bought her Twinkies before, because he knew they made her feel better when she was upset.

His shoulders tensed, his mouth opened and closed a couple of times, before he huffed a breath and put his hands on his hips. "I just wanted to give them to you." He dropped his chin to his chest and started at the toes of his boots. "I, ah…also wanted to say goodbye, and to tell you to take care of yourself." He sighed deeply. "If you ever need anything, just call and I'll be here, Twy."

Anger surged through her. Her brother had come back up here with a peace offering. These weren't gifts from a man to a woman he was interested in. They were to appease his guilty conscience evidently. Grease her up, so when they met up at family things in the future, there wouldn't be any hard feelings. Well, there certainly were hard feelings, and she didn't want the gifts, or his apology. The only thing she needed from him was him to leave.

Enough was enough.

Twyla shoved the box and flowers into his chest. "I don't want 'em. Maybe they'll keep until you get back to the rodeo. You can pawn them off on a bunny to get you a little. Leave, Ryan. Don't come back." How many times had she told him that now? Too many. Why wouldn't he just leave her the hell alone?

His eyes flew up to lock with hers, and what she saw there shocked her. Heat, passion, and something that looked like desperation to her. His chest rose and fell rapidly, as his eyes burned her. He continued to stare at her until Twyla's fingers went numb from gripping the box and stems so tightly.

Suddenly, his hands shot out to grab her shoulders. The flowers and box fell to the floor between them. "I didn't buy them for a fucking bunny, Twyla. I bought them for you," Ryan growled, and before Twyla could catch a breath, he jerked her into his body. His mouth slammed down over hers, and a tremor shook her as his incredible taste shocked her system, his heat and delicious outdoorsy scent surrounded her. Her heart stopped, then took a giant leap in her chest that left her dizzy when the kiss turned even hotter. Twyla moaned as every bone in her body melted under his fierce assault on her mouth. She leaned into him to keep from falling as her knees turned to water. The kiss was all that she'd ever imagined it would be and more.

But this whole thing bordered on the surreal. Was she dreaming this? Had she gone off the deep end? Or was Ryan Easter really standing in her living room kissing the stuffing out of her?

He slid his mouth from hers, dragging in heavy breaths. His hands shook as his fingers found the sash on her robe and he jerked it open. Cold air rushed over her still damp skin and her nipples pebbled to tight points. Ryan's hot blue eyes fixed there, and it felt like they branded her skin. "And I don't fucking want a buckle bunny. I want you." He met her eyes and repeated the words she'd waited ten years to hear, as if they cost him dearly. "I want *you*, Twyla."

An electrical field of tense emotion buzzed between them, and Twyla was too shocked to move. Twenty-thousand volts and ten years of pure awareness heated Twyla's blood, but she held back, because she didn't trust him. This could be another of his games to get her to go back to the rodeo with him.

"I finally write you off and try to move on, and now you tell me this?" she asked incredulously then took a step back. "You're definitely a slow mover, cowboy. Too slow."

Ryan grabbed her shoulders. "I've missed the hell out of you, Twy..."

"You missed me?" Twyla's heart melted in her chest, but then she stiffened her shoulders, as another thought hit her. He'd been without his buckle bunnies for a few days. "Or are you just horny, and any willing woman will do?"

"*No!*" he shouted, jerking her back to him. Ryan's arm was a tight band around her waist. Twyla put her hand on his chest to keep some space between them, and his heart pounded against her palm. Her eyes met his burning gaze and her own heart tripped in her chest. "This has been going on too long. I've *let* it go on too long. We need to see what's going on between us, regardless of your brother, or if I lose your family because I can't keep my hands off of you."

A knot settled in Twyla's throat, and she couldn't find her voice, so she just nodded. Her body relaxed against him, and Ryan's arm loosened around her. A smile that she'd only seen him give other women eased up the corners of his lips, and Twyla put her palm on his beard-roughened cheek. His eyes spoke to her, as his head lowered. His mouth hovered over hers for a moment, his sweet, uneven breaths brushing her lips.

His lips finally met hers gently, and Twyla sighed. After several fleeting passes of his mouth over hers, the tip of his tongue rasped over her lower lip lighting up every nerve ending in her body. The nerves at the top of her thighs beat in time with her heart, as her body anticipated him deepening the kiss, wanted him to deepen it. Needed it more than her next breath. But Ryan took his time making several more slow passes over her mouth, before he stopped a moment to hover there with their lips millimeters apart.

"Remember you wanted this tomorrow," he growled, then shock rocked her when his teeth clamped down on her lower lip, and he tugged it as he roughly shoved her robe from her shoulders. Cool air swept over her upper body and she shivered. Without the padding of her new bras, Twyla knew he would find her lacking there. Heat flooded her face, as she tried to free her arms to cover herself, but his fists closed in the material trapping her arms at her sides.

His hot eyes drank their fill for several moments, before he muttered, "Fucking perfect." His dark head lowered toward her left breast, Twyla held her breath. Ryan's lips only whispered over her nipple though. Instead he made slow irritating strokes over her nipple with his beard roughened chin, nuzzled it with his equally rough cheek.

It felt like sandpaper on the sensitive bud, and was painful. Her nails curled into her palms, and she bore the pain until she couldn't take anymore. Just as she opened her mouth to protest though, something shifted inside of her and the damndest thing happened. The pain suddenly transformed to the ultimate pleasure. Sharp pangs of desire hit her in the center of her being, and instead of complaining, Twyla threw her head back to moan long and low in her throat. Ryan's tongue made soothing circles around her nipple and she mewled.

The wet heat of his mouth finally covered her, but he wasn't gentle with that either. He sucked her nipple into his mouth hard, and Twyla felt the tug at her core. She screamed his name, her inner muscles clamped down, and her knees went weak. Ryan held her upright by the lapels of her robe, and turned her toward the door. He slammed her limp body against it, lifting her before pinning her there with his hips. He looked up into her eyes, as he reached between them to shove his hand under her robe, between her legs. He ran a finger along her folds and dipped it inside of her. Twyla whimpered when he carried her moisture to where she throbbed and slathered it there. His voice low and tortured, he said, "You have been every woman I've fucked for the last ten years. I want the real thing."

His mouth drifted down to cover her right breast, but his words floated through her lust-clouded brain to settle there, and a shock wave rippled through her. For ten years, while he'd been fucking those other women, she'd been waiting for him. Wanting him to be her first. Now that it was finally happening, how the hell did a cowgirl tell a man she was a twenty-six-year-old virgin? She'd had opportunities, but between her brother and him, those opportunities were lost. She should be pissed and not want anything to do with this man for reminding her of that, but she couldn't get there. She was too turned on, needed him too badly. Had waited too long.

Her body tensed. "Ryan, I, ah...well."

He lifted his eyes to hers, and his eyebrows slammed down over his eyes. He tempered the fierce look with a sexy smile she felt in her gut. "No changing your mind now, Daisy. The cow is out of the barn, and the branding iron is hot, hard and ready."

She knew the women Ryan was used to were experienced, as far from virgins as women could get. They were like the women she danced with at that bar. This was finally happening, and Twyla was not about to disappoint him by being inexperienced.

Daisy. The stage name that Leon had pinned on her. She needed to channel her inner Daisy to get through this. *Fake it til you make it.*

That had been Heather's advice, and so far it had served her well. So had her new test of asking herself what Heather would do, given the same situation. Twyla forced what she hoped was a cocky grin. "You really are slow moving, aren't you?" She swallowed the bitterness on her tongue before it could seep into her tone. "I've watched you fuck those women for ten years and wanted to feel you inside of me. Now, get a move on, cowboy. I don't want another ten to go by, while you work up the courage to fuck me."

Ryan's cheeks turned red, and his smile faded.

With a growl he eased her down to her feet, and yanked her robe downward. It whispered down her body to pool at her feet, then he grabbed her wrist to tow her behind him toward the breakfast nook. Jerking out one of the plain wooden chairs he spun it to face her, then pinned her with an angry glare. "You got whiskey and a shot glass?"

"Um, yeah?" She crossed her arms over her breasts, suddenly self-conscious now just standing there naked in front of him.

"Get it," he ordered flatly, as he unfastened his jeans. "I need a damned drink."

Twyla felt his eyes burning her back as she stumbled into the kitchen. She opened the cabinet over the sink, and pulled down the bottle of rotgut bourbon that Heather kept there for emergencies, as she called it. Twyla felt sure this situation qualified. She found the shot glasses on the bottom shelf, and grabbed two.

The way things were going, the only way Twyla would be able to maintain her Daisy confidence and persona was with a little false courage herself. She sat the bottle down and opened it, poured herself a shot then downed it. The bitter taste numbed her taste buds, as the fiery liquid scorched all the way down to her toes. Thankfully, she felt the edge on her nervousness blur, as she recapped the bottle and picked up the spare glass. When she rounded the corner, she stumbled as her eyes fell on Ryan, who was completely naked now, leaning on the table with his arms crossed over his muscular chest.

A sly, sexy grin creased his face. "Good girl," he praised, as he took the bottle and glass from her numb fingers to slam them down on the table. Uncapping the bottle, he filled the shot glass, before turning back to her. He motioned to the table and the amber liquid swirled in the shot glass. "Now, hop your pretty little ass up on that table."

Disbelief shot through her. "*What?*"

"I want my gut shot with a *Daisy* chaser," he informed, toasting her with the glass.

A shiver worked itself down her spine to settle between her legs. Heather taking a shot off of her stomach didn't do a damned thing for her, it was an act. Somehow, she didn't think Ryan was acting. And she had a feeling she wouldn't have to fake the result either.

When she didn't move his eyes narrowed. "Who's a slow mover now, Daisy?" he taunted smugly. "I thought you were in a hurry to get to the fireworks?"

"I, ah..." *haven't ever had sex, much less on a table.*

Ryan tossed back the shot, and flinched, before refilling the glass. "Better hurry up, or I might be too drunk to perform," he said without looking up. He slapped his hand to his forehead, as he stood. "Oh yeah, what am I thinking? You're used to drunk men pawing you. Probably fucked plenty of them too, right?" He gave her a nasty wink, and a leering grin.

It was obvious he was trying to hurt her, by making her feel like a piece of meat. He was doing a good job of it. "Fuck you," tumbled out of her mouth, before she could stop it.

Twyla wondered if he treated all the women he slept with like this. If that was the case, no wonder there weren't many who came back for a repeat performance. Why he went through so many of them, but none had stuck.

Anger flashed in his eyes, but he grinned. "That's the idea, baby. Now, if you want that to happen sometime tonight, you'll get your ass up on that table."

Hurt punched her in the gut to mix with the nasty whiskey. Twyla felt it rise up to her throat and swallowed it back down. "You know, I don't think I do want it to happen tonight, or ever for that matter. You're not the man I thought you were." She turned to stomp across the living room and bent to pick up her robe. "Maybe you treat your bunnies like this, but you sure as hell aren't going to treat me like this." She turned with the robe clutched to her chest and ran smack into Ryan's muscular chest.

His arms clamped around her, and he pinned her with intense eyes. "Drop your Daisy act, Twy—I know you better than that too and it pisses me off. You're not that woman." His arms loosened, and he moved one hand under her chin to tip her face up to look at him. "Daisy is hot as a two-dollar pistol, but she isn't the woman I want." His head drifted down, and his lips closed over hers in a sweet kiss she felt all the way to her toes. "I want Twyla, the beautiful, crazy cowgirl who has chased me since she was sixteen," he whispered over her mouth.

Twyla sighed, as his words, the sincerity in his voice, melted the ice covering her heart. The robe slipped from her fingers, and her palms burned as she slid them up his chest to his shoulders to circle his neck. She tiptoed to press her lips to his, and Ryan lifted her against him. His mouth claimed hers again, and she leaned into him. Her heart met his, and she felt the strong, steady beat of his against her sternum, as the soft fur on his chest abraded her tender nipples.

She sucked his lower lip into her mouth, and Ryan moaned. His fingers dug into her ass, and his tongue traced the seam of her lips. Twyla opened her mouth, his tongue found hers and they danced. Her hips moved in time with their tongues, and his hardness dug into her hip. His heart skipped a few beats, and hers did too.

Needing him much closer, Twyla wrapped her calf around his thigh. She made small pleading circles with her hips. Ryan shifted his hips, and groaned when his thick erection slid between her legs. Twyla made long strokes with her body along his cock, craving to know what that thickness would feel like inside of her. Ryan groaned loudly, then breathing hard, he bent to grab the back of her thighs. He lifted her, then growled, "Put your legs around my waist."

Twyla held onto his neck and wrapped her legs around him. Ryan looked down at her and smiled as he carried her swiftly to the breakfast nook. He sat down on the chair with her on his lap. "You have no idea how many times I've fantasized about having those long legs of yours wrapped around me, having you ride me like this."

Ryan leaned over to grab his jeans. He shoved his hand into the pocket, and pulled out his wallet. Flipping it open, he rifled through it with trembling hands to pull out a foil wrapped packet. With his teeth he opened it, then a condom appeared between his fingers. His voice bristled with excitement and need, as he held it up to her and said, "Put it on me, and ride me to the barn, cowgirl."

Twyla stared at the flesh-colored circle like it had fangs. Her eyes darted to his, then back to the condom pinched between his fingers. She tried to channel her inner Daisy, but the bitch had evidently run for the barn. And Ryan didn't want her anyway. She gnawed her lower lip, and thought about lying, but she knew if she did it wrong there could be dire consequences for both of them. "Ryan, you need to know something."

"Yeah?" he asked his hand dropping to his thigh, as his eyebrows slammed down over his concerned blue eyes.

"I haven't ever done this before, don't know how to put it on you." Twyla notched her chin up an inch, waiting for his laughter or to see the disgust he had to be feeling to show itself. When his passion-glazed eyes just looked a little confused, she slid off of his lap and held out her hand. "I can do it, just tell me how."

"You've never put a condom on a man?" he

asked, then his eyes lit up, and his eyebrows raised. "Are you on birth control then?"

Twyla didn't miss the hopefulness in his voice, or the message. He didn't get that she'd never done *this* before. Had sex. It was going to take her bluntly telling him she was a virgin. All the blood in her body rushed to her face, as she stammered, "Between you and Zack, how the hell could I have ever had a chance to have sex? I didn't need birth control."

All the starch went out of his body, and Ryan slid down in the chair to rest his head on the back. "Twyla tell me that I'm not about to deflower you, as well as have sex with you. Your brother is going to kill me."

"What Zack doesn't know won't kill you," she said shortly. "But I will if you don't put that damned condom on and have sex with me."

Ryan opened his eyes, and studied her for a minute, then laughed. He sat up in the chair to position the latex ring at the thick head of his cock, before expertly rolling it down to the base.

"That's what I lo—like about you Twy— you're blunt. And come hell or high water, you're gonna get what you want." He looked up at her. "Even if it takes ten years."

"And you are definitely a slow mover, Ryan Easter. Get the molasses out of your ass, and let's go to the bedroom. You've got some catching up to do."

CHAPTER TEN

"No ma'am—I've decided your first time is not going to be in the bedroom. I want you to remember it a hundred years from now. It's going to be right here on this table, just like I planned. If Zack kills me, I'm going to make damned sure it's worth it."

Ryan stood, and shoved the chair aside then walked over to her. "But I definitely need another drink for this," he said with a grin as he took her hand and tugged her back to the table. Grabbing her hips, he sat her there, then shoved her shoulder toward the table. "Lay back and relax, baby." With a sigh, Twyla complied, folding her hands at her waist.

Twyla watched Ryan open the whiskey bottle and pour himself another drink. He sat the bottle on the floor, then nudged her knees apart to step between them. "Shove back a little," he urged, and she scooted back until her feet were on the table top. He gripped her ankles to bend her legs, then spread her knees wide. Heat flooded her face when he stepped back and just studied her like she was a patient he was examining or something, while he sipped his drink with a contemplative look on his handsome face. "Scoot your ass closer to your heels," he grumbled.

Twyla leaned up and did as he asked, but he still didn't move on with things. He did smile, however, when she eased her back onto the table again with her hands at her sides. He stepped to the edge of the table and spread her heels even farther apart. Like a comet, his eyes zipped down her body, leaving a fiery trail behind, then he smiled that smile that twisted her insides, as his eyes fixed on her breasts.

"Mmm...that's perfect. You're perfect, Twy." The heat zipped back up her body to her face, and she fought the urge to cover her breasts with her hands.

"I'm not perfect, Ryan," she argued, trying to wake him up from his obvious trance. It had to be the alcohol, but he hadn't drank much. The man must be seeing things, if he thought that. He was the only man on earth who did. But then he was the only one on earth who she cared what he thought about her.

Ignoring her comment, and what had to be her obvious discomfort, Ryan stepped forward, leaned over her to balance his shot glass about two inches under her navel. Heather always put it at the base of her ribcage, so a little would spill into her navel, but Ryan had put his lower. Her muscles contracted there, as the cold glass touched her skin. She thought about him licking her up to the glass, the amber liquid sloshed in the glass, and he frowned.

"No spilling, Twy, or there will be consequences." His eyes met hers and his pupils were dilated almost as large as the blue irises. His breathing came in short spurts, and she could see his pulse pounding at the side of his throat. The look on his handsome face said he would relish delivering those unknown consequences. "By the time I'm done, I'll really need that drink."

A shiver worked itself up her body from her toes, and the glass wobbled again. She gasped and contracted her muscles to steady it. Agitation bristled through her. "Why don't you just have the damned shot then, and get on with this?" That's what *she* really wanted.

His hand clamped on her ankle, and he grinned. "Patience is a virtue, darlin'. Slow is not always a bad thing, and I'm about to teach you that, and a lot more." His voice was heavy with anticipation, and his sensual threat was punctuated by his tongue making a slow trip around his hot lips. Her eyes followed it around and heat sizzled along her nerves to singe her at the apex of her thighs. Maybe this is why all those bunnies she saw leaving his trailer were smiling. They must have had the patience Ryan was talking about, and liked that Ryan was slow as a turtle in his lovemaking. Twyla wasn't sold on it yet, but decided to try to find the patience he asked her to have. She huffed a breath then relaxed and uncurled her fists.

What the hell did she know about all this, anyway? She was green as grass at this, he knew what he was doing. Had done it many times. Too many.

"Get on with it, then," she grumbled, settling her focus on keeping that shot glass steady on her lower abdomen. Ryan's dark head appeared in her line of vision, and Twyla gasped.

His eyes met hers over the plane of her tummy, and were filled with mischief and purpose. His hot breath tickled her thighs when he warned, "Keep it still, Twyla. Remember, no spilling."

He slid his hands behind her calves, and under her thighs to hold her hands at her sides. Turning his face, he planted a wet kiss on her inner thigh, before his mouth latched there and he sucked, while his tongue swirled on her skin. Fire zipped up to her core, and Twyla whimpered. The glass wobbled again and she knew then that she was in big trouble.

Twyla held her breath until the liquid settled, then breathed again when his mouth unglued from her skin. Her relief was short-lived though. His mouth landed again, this time closer to the crease where her thighs met her torso. Her most intimate part quivered, her fists clenched and she moaned. She sucked in a gulping breath to croak, "Gah, how am I supposed to stay still?"

Ryan's chuckle vibrated along her folds, as he stopped there for a second, his hot breath just teasing her. "Goddamn you smell like heaven, sweetheart. I bet you taste like it too," he said breathlessly, before she felt his hot tongue take a swipe over her.

Twyla's body jerked and she tried to scoot upward, but his hands tightened over hers holding her prisoner. Cold liquid splashed onto her skin, reminding her of the shot glass. Her body tensed, and she whimpered, afraid to look to see how much she'd spilled. Twin trails leaked to the edge of her hipbones and pooled there. The feeling was a lot less than comfortable. Nothing about this was comfortable.

Ryan tsked a couple of times. "You're wasting my whiskey, baby."

His hand crept up to her hipbone, and he dipped a finger into the liquid. His hand slid under her thigh, and Twyla put her chin on her chest, planting her heels on the table to see what he was doing. His finger disappeared between her legs and she clenched her teeth to fight the tremor in her body, as she felt that finger trail over the nub at the top of her thighs, along her folds and downward to finally stop at her anus. His finger lingered there, and his eyes slid up to meet hers. He smiled that smile and a sharp shot of electricity zipped through her body, as he brushed her anus with his finger.

"No," she pleaded weakly, bearing down, bracing, in case he was going to do what she thought he would do.

Her breathing became practically non-existent, as she waited to see what he'd do. If he did that, there was no way she would be able to keep that shot from spilling all over her. He grinned as he slid his finger upward again. Twyla breathed a sigh of relief, but that was short-lived. Ryan watched her face, as he slowly dipped his finger deep inside her body and swirled it.

Twyla moaned as her nails curled into her palms, and she sucked in a sharp breath, trying to focus on keeping still. Not spilling the whiskey that swirled in that shot glass. Ryan hit a spot inside her body that made her inner muscles spasm.

She fought her reaction with everything she had, but then Ryan added another finger to the mix, and the incredible stretching burn incited her muscles to clamp down. She gritted her teeth, fighting the tremor that started in her legs. Ryan stretched her even more by adding a third finger, and Twyla couldn't stop her throaty moan, or the tremor that rocked her. After a moment Ryan set a slow and steady rhythm in and out of her body with his fingers, and of their own accord, her hips made small circles in time with his hand, her pleasure inching up with each thrust.

Her breathing became even shallower, as something delicious built inside of her. Twyla closed her eyes to reach for it, wanting it, needing it. She heard Ryan's ragged breathing, and was glad she wasn't the only one affected. Liquid splashed on her skin, trailing up her stomach to settle in her navel. Twyla's body went rigid, as her eyes flew open. She saw the spilled liquid and groaned, her heart beating out of control in her chest. The shot glass was now three-quarters empty. "I'm sorry," she said hoarsely, dragging her eyes to Ryan's to gauge his reaction.

Ryan's fingers stilled but he didn't remove them from her body. He shook his head solemnly. "I told you there would be consequences, Twyla," his deep voice rumbled along her nerves, which were already at the point of snapping.

He reached for the shot glass, and downed

what was left of the whiskey, before setting the glass beside her on the table. When he eased his fingers from her body, her muscles protested. Their game was evidently over, and Twyla was happy, because maybe that meant he'd get on with things now. But she was surprised to be a little disappointed too.

This was pretty damned exciting. Ryan Easter was exciting, unpredictable. He always had been, and Twyla thought that's why she hadn't been able to work this man out from under her skin for so long. But then he turned his back to her, she saw his beautiful rear end, one she'd studied fully clothed many times, and knew that wasn't why. It was only part of the reason. The other was that this man was so damned delicious she hadn't been able to even think about being with another man before him. After this, the bar would probably be set so high, no man would ever compare. With Ryan Easter as her first lover, she'd wait a long time to find someone who came within miles of him. Probably as long as she'd waited for this moment.

If that wasn't a show of patience, she didn't know what was.

Ryan bent, and when he raised back up he held the bottle of whiskey. Instead of refilling the glass, he unscrewed the cap and set it on the table by her hip. "Put your hands over your head and grab the top of the table, Twy," he said gruffly. "Since you refuse to let me have my whiskey in a glass, I guess I'm going to have to figure out some other way to enjoy it."

A thrill zipped along her spine, as she slowly raised her hands above her head to grip the edge of the table. His eyes narrowed and he waggled his brows, as he warned, "Don't let go, no matter what. If you do, I'll tie 'em there." His voice was soft and a little slurry, probably from the shots he'd already consumed. It was damned cute, as if he needed something to up his cute factor. This man was already lethally cute.

He just stood there staring at her breasts and her nipples hardened painfully. Twyla decided she could use another shot herself. It felt like her entire body was laying on a live wire, as his eyes scorched every inch of her, while she waited to see what he was going to do to her next. The anticipation was killing her, and he probably knew that. Ryan upped her aggravation when he dragged a chair out from under the table and turned it around to straddle it, the bottle just dangled between his fingers. A puzzled look crossed his face, and his eyes slid down between her legs.

"I'm trying to figure something out, baby,"

"What's that?" she asked, all the blood in her veins all converging between her legs, as if drawn there by his hot gaze, pinpointing at the top of her thighs to beat there in time with her heart.

"How in the hell are you still a virgin? And how the hell have I kept my damned hands off of you so long?"

"You were afraid of my brother," she reminded him. "And Zack watched me like I was the crown jewels or something, when I went off to rodeo with y'all."

The corner of Ryan's mouth kicked up. "Then I'm a chickenshit moron."

Twyla laughed, and rolled her eyes. "That's what I've been trying to tell you for years. Glad you finally get it."

"Oh, I get it now." His eyes darkened, and he frowned. "And I'm going to get more. All night long. If you can walk tomorrow, you'll be damned lucky."

If Ryan didn't hurry up, it would be tomorrow before he got to the good part. "And you better take it easy on the liquor, cowboy, or you'll be lucky if your head doesn't feel like I took a sledgehammer to it, which I might do if you don't get a move on with *getting* it. I think you're taking slow to a new level just to torture me, turtle boy."

Ryan shoved up to his feet, and laughed. "Turtle boy?" he repeated indignantly. He stepped to the table to push her knees wider, and his eyes pinned her. "You think I'm torturing you? You ain't seen nothing yet, sweetheart. You better hold on tight, because I wasn't kidding about making sure you do, one way or another."

He held the bottle above her thighs, and Twyla gasped when he tilted the bottle and the liquid slid along her folds to pool beneath her butt on the table. A glazed, determined look took over his face, as he moved to the side of the table to trickle a stream of amber liquid up her belly to the valley between her breasts. He stopped a moment to dribble some over her left breast, before doing the same to her right. The cold air mixed with the liquid and cooled. She shivered, and her nipples tightened. "I'm cold, Ryan."

"You won't be saying that long," he promised, as he bent to set the bottle on the floor. He leaned over and put his lips to hers. His tongue forced itself inside her mouth, and he plunged in and out, mimicking what he'd done to her a few minutes ago. She tasted the sweetness of the whiskey he'd drank, mixed with something strange, earthy and musky. She realized that was herself she was tasting on his swollen lips, and moaned. Ryan had tasted her there, drank his fill of her, and now he was sharing it with her in the most intimate kiss a man could give a woman.

Twyla lapped up his kisses, tried to lift her head for more, but his hand trapped her hair, held her still, while he plundered her mouth. With a final hard nip to her lower lip, he released her and stood. Her tongue darted out for a final taste, and his eyes fixed on her mouth. Twyla's chest heaved with her breaths, as his eyes slid down her body to her toes, before moving back up to her eyes. His hand dropped on her thigh, and Twyla shivered.

"I've got some pigging strings out in my truck. Do I need to tie your feet, so you keep your legs open for me?" Twyla realized then that her knees had drifted down to the table while he kissed her, and he evidently wasn't happy about it. She dragged her heels up and bent her legs again. "Wider," he coaxed, moving to the end of the table. Twyla inched her heels farther apart and let her knees fall open. "That's better," he said, seeming satisfied with himself as he dragged a chair up to the table and sat down.

Ryan grabbed her hips and pulled her closer to him. Her body was stretched to the max, as she tried to maintain her grip on the table, or she thought it was, until he picked up her calves and laid them on his shoulders. He scooted the chair closer, then slid his hands under her ass to lift her up, propping her weight on his elbows.

"Now for the consequences," he muttered as he leaned his face into her. "I'm about to drive you as crazy as you've driven me for ten years, sugar." Ryan's tongue took a long slow lick up her body, stopping at the top.

Twyla gasped, enjoying the pleasant feathery sensations that tickled her insides. But then his tongue flicked the nub at the top of her folds in rapid fire hits. Those feathery sensations ignited into something so intense, she lost her breath. Her heels dug into his shoulders, as she wiggled against his hold, but Ryan held her firm, while he continued his sensual assault. With every strike of his tongue on the sensitive bud, the tension inside of her built, her agitation increased. When her insides felt like they were coming apart, Twyla whimpered, twisted her hips trying to get away from his mouth, but Ryan's fingers dug into her skin to hold her still.

A scream built in her throat, she bit her lower lip and her fingers dug into the wooden table. The incredible feeling rushed up her body to her head, and she felt dizzy as black dots danced behind her closed lids. Between gasping breaths, she realized something wonderful floated just out of her reach, and lifted her hips toward his hot mouth to grab for it. Suddenly his mouth left her body, and Twyla was left floating in limbo, adrift on an angry sea of sensations with no particular destination. Frustration quickly replaced whatever had been happening to her, what she assumed had been a near orgasm. Exactly what Heather told her she needed to fake when she did the shot off of her belly at the bar. Heather had laughed herself silly when Twyla told her she had no idea what that was, or how to fake it, since she'd never had one before. Thanks to the man breathing heavily between her legs, Twyla still didn't know.

Her body wilted, as Ryan lowered her hips to the table. She pinned him with an angry glare. "What the hell was that?" she growled, her fingers releasing the table. She flexed the feeling back into them, wanting to feel them squeezing around Ryan Easter's neck.

"The consequences of you wasting my whiskey are you don't come until I decide to *let* you come," he said smugly, as he leaned back in the chair and folded his arms over his chest. "I'm not ready to let that happen just yet, until you beg me to make you come."

"Now let's try this one more time shall we?"

he drawled, as he stood and walked to pick up the bottle. He poured the last of the whiskey into the shot glass, then Twyla watched as he sat it in the exact same spot as before, right below her navel, right on top of the place that quivered uncontrollably when he almost brought her there a minute ago.

With a groan Twyla laid her head on the table and shut her eyes. Somehow she was going to make Ryan Easter pay for this torture later. But right now, she focused on keeping perfectly still, so he would finally give her what she needed more than her next breath. She wanted that feeling again, wanted to see where it ended. But she'd be damned if she'd beg the cocky bastard for it. He had a long row to hoe if he thought she was going to do that. That might work on his bunnies, maybe he got some kind of thrill from the begging, but he was about to find out how long a tough cowgirl could hold out against his sexual blackmail.

She heard him sigh, then his hair tickled her breast right before his hot mouth covered her right breast. He tugged on it gently, suckling her, as his raspy tongue swirled slow even circles around her nipple. A slow burn started in her midsection, and moisture gathered between her thighs with each of his gentle tugs on her breast. Those feathery feelings returned, and Twyla mewled wanting to stretch her body like a cat. Pinching the top of her thighs together with the tugs, helped her keep from doing that. Yes, Ryan definitely had his work cut out if he planned on breaking her, she thought, and the corners of her mouth crept up into a smile.

That went on for long minutes, the suckling, and the swirl of his tongue around her nipple. The same rhythm and pattern over and over. And over. After a while, it became frustrating, monotonous. Ryan didn't touch her in any other way. The rest of her body was cool from the air conditioning vent blowing directly on her body above the table. The only warm part on her entire body was her right breast.

It wasn't just warm, her breast was hot, burning up, and the friction of his tongue on her nipple was irritating to the point of pain. That was all she could focus on. Even the shot glass was forgotten. Twyla didn't realize her legs were shaking until she felt a splash of liquid on her stomach. Her body tensed and her eyes flew to Ryan, but he didn't seem to notice thank, God.

Twyla huffed a breath and closed her eyes again. Immediately the trembling returned, and she realized what was causing it too. With every circuit of his rough tongue around her nipple now, one of those feathers inside her went up in flames. As each one incinerated, inching her closer to that lovely place she'd been before, her inner muscles clenched and released.

Twyla whimpered, as she felt another splash hit her stomach. Cold air wisped over her nipple shocking her, right before pain shot through her as Ryan bit down on her nipple. Her brain seized, and a gurgling scream came from her throat, and a violent tremor rocked her body. Liquid splashed onto her skin, filled her navel, then tickled a cold trail over the sides of her waist. Twyla whimpered, tensing her body enough to keep the shot glass from toppling over. Ryan held the pressure with his teeth, as she fought the waves of mixed messages washing through her body. Pleasure, pain, anger and joy fought for control of her, as she dug her fingers into the table, while her eyes fixed on the shot glass wobbling on her belly, trying to keep it from toppling.

Ryan finally released her and Twyla's breath gushed out, as her heart pounded in her ears and between her legs. Frustration filled her. "Gaaah, I want to come. Let me come," she begged as she laid back on the table, done with this game.

"Please let me come, Ryan," he corrected with a laugh, as he leaned down to lick up the whiskey she had spilled. Her muscles contracted under his tongue, and her insides quivered, spilling more from the glass. His tongue darted into her navel, her body shook, and Twyla watched in horror as the glass toppled, sending a stream of liquid toward her mound. The whiskey trickled through her folds to pool on the table.

Ryan shook his head, as he walked to the end of the table and shoved her legs apart. He stepped between them, and Twyla groaned knowing more of what he was doing to her was about to come. What wasn't coming was an orgasm.

But Ryan surprised her when his dark head lowered over her, and he licked a heated trail up from her mound to the glass. He looked up at her over the plane of her tummy, and a small smile kicked up the corner of his mouth, before his lips closed around the shot glass. He lifted it, throwing his head back as he stood to take the last few drops in the glass.

He wiped his mouth with his forearm, then set the glass on the table beside her. "Say it, Twyla." He lifted a dark brow. "Or if you prefer, I can keep this up all night."

The words rolled off her tongue before she could stop them, "Make me come, please, Ryan." She sounded weak, like one of his bunnies. But Twyla couldn't help herself. She needed him to make her come. And she needed it now, not next week.

He held out his hand to her. Her fingers were sore from gripping the table, almost bloodless, as she took his hand. She scooted to the edge of the table and he helped her down, then grabbed a chair and sat down. He pulled her to him to straddle him, with his massive erection between them. With his hands on her hips, he looked up into her eyes. "I'm putting you in charge of this part, baby. I don't want to hurt you."

He was putting her in charge? That was pretty stupid on his part, considering what he'd just done to her. Twyla wasn't about to let the opportunity to get a little payback pass. She grabbed his hands on her hips and bent to put them on the sides of the chair, and squeezed his fingers around the edge. "Keep your hands right there, and put on your seatbelt then."

"But I can't touch you then," Ryan complained, and his smile faded.

"Exactly," she purred as she turned and sashayed into the living room.

She flipped on the television, and put it on CMT, then found her straw hat and patted it down on her head, then stuffed her feet in her fringed boots. Buck naked save her boots and hat, Twyla waltzed back into the nook, making the fringe on her boots whisper in time with her hips.

Her effort wasn't lost on Ryan. He sucked in a sharp breath and his eyes heated, as they locked onto her breasts. He reached for his cock, but she waved her finger at him. "No touching me or yourself. That's my rule. Grab the sides of that chair, cowboy and don't turn loose, or there will be consequences."

"Twyla what the hell are you doing?" he griped, and his lower lip jutted out.

"You asked me to dance for you before," she said with a wide smile. "I'm dancing for you right now." She bit back a laugh when Get Me Some of That echoed through the apartment. Ryan Easter was gonna want some really bad when she was finished with him. The jury was still out whether he would get any.

Ryan's eyes darkened, but he grabbed the sides of the chair and his cock stood proudly between his muscular thighs, still sheathed in the condom he'd put on earlier. The sight thrilled her, but scared her too. She was a little glad she had time to work up to this next step. Twyla walked over to him and ran her fingernail from the base of his cock to the head, and he shivered.

"I thought you said no touching," he hissed through his teeth.

Her eyes swung up to his and she smiled. "I said *you* can't touch. I can do whatever the hell I please." She straightened, then gripped the back of the chair and straddled his legs. Holding his eyes, Twyla mocked sitting on him, and felt his heat scorch her inner thighs as she hovered over him popping her hips with the music. She sank closer to his thighs, mouthing the words to the song, making sure her mound brushed his cock with each slow upward pass, enjoying the odd little gurgling sounds he made in his throat. As tight as his jaw was clenched, his teeth would probably be dust by the time she finished with him.

Twyla leaned in closer, arched her back toward him, and slowly rose, bringing her breasts within millimeters of his mouth. His chin followed her upward, but he didn't try to touch her with his mouth. A faster song came on, and Twyla decided to up the ante, speed things along. She squeezed her thighs together, clamping his cock between them as she slowly lifted off of him.

"Arrgh...you're killing me," Ryan groaned hoarsely, throwing his head back as every muscle in his body went rigid. His breaths were short and shallow, and his heart pounded at the side of his throat.

He only thought he was dying, Twyla thought, as she grinned evilly and reached between them to position his cock at her opening. His eyes popped open, and desperation filled them. He couldn't be any more desperate than she was feeling right now. This little *dance* that she was doing, they were doing with each other, was taking a toll on her too. But the score was even now, and she was determined to win.

Mr. Easter needed a lesson about messing with cowgirls. Bunnies might put up with his bullcrap, but cowgirls would make you pay, and pay big, for messing with them. Twyla might be a virgin, but she was and always had been a cowgirl. She was not a prissy, girly girl like the women he was used to dating. No, not dating, fucking. Ryan didn't date.

He wanted her to remember her first time a hundred years from now?

Well, Twyla was going to make sure he didn't forget her lesson in that time too. A lesson about teasing a woman that might do the women he fucked in the future a favor. That thought caused her heart to sink a little in her chest. Ryan might be here with her tonight, but as much as she wanted it to be, she knew this wasn't going to be a lasting thing with them. Ryan Easter was about as ready to settle down as the bucking broncs he rode for a living. He ran from clingy women. Hell, she'd helped him avoid them often enough herself to know.

Twyla was determined not to become a clinger just because they'd had sex. She never wanted to be on his run from list. Ryan had been a part of her life for a long time now, and she didn't want to lose him. But the thought that she might have to watch him be with other women again after this made her stomach curl. That was just something she knew she would have to deal with though. Just like she always had.

"You okay?" he asked and she realized she'd stopped moving.

"Yeah, just doing my best to make you sweat, big boy," she said with a forced laugh as she reached between them to position his cock at her opening.

His voice was raw and hoarse, his breathing uneven, when he said, "Don't worry, I'm sweating, baby." Twyla eased down on his shaft, taking his head inside, and Ryan groaned, laying his head against the back of the chair. She leaned back and took a little more of him, and the muscles in his forearms became rock hard against her legs. The burning stretch was incredible, and her inner muscles clenched and released around him, urging her to take more of him. Her fingers bit into the slats of the chair as she gritted her teeth to keep from doing that, taking slow even breaths until her body adjusted.

Beneath her thighs, she felt his hands release the chair, his fingers flexed and she pinned him with her eyes. "Do it and I get up," she warned.

His fingers immediately curled again, and she smiled, as she lifted to make the first circle with her hips, feeling his thickness swell inside of her even more. Ryan growled, stretching his neck as far back as it would go, and a muscle ticked at his jaw. A slow, sexy song came on the station and Twyla found the rhythm with her movements, holding the chair in a death grip to make sure she didn't sink down on him. Between her thighs, his knees pinched together tightly, and he made that gurgling sound again, followed by a couple of weak whimpers.

"What's wrong, Ryan? Can't take your own medicine?" she asked smugly.

Ryan's body went rigid, his jaw worked, and he ground his teeth. A fierce roar erupted from his throat, and his hands appeared out of nowhere to grip her hips. He pushed her hips downward as he pistoned his own up into her, burying his cock halfway inside of her body. Twyla lost her breath from the intense stretching burn, and her body throbbed against the invasion. Ryan's nostrils flared, as he dragged in short, uneven breaths through his nose and exhaled through his mouth. Twyla couldn't breathe at all, she was too overwhelmed by the shocking pain. Every muscle in her body was clenched.

Ryan's thumb rubbed soothing, but irritating circles at her hip. "Relax baby, and just ease on down. I'll help you," he begged, his voice raw and ragged.

Relax? How the hell could she relax? She was impaled on his massive cock, and was afraid to move. Ease on down? There was nothing easy about this. What she had of him hurt like hell. Taking the rest of him would probably rip her in two. No, she'd just stay where she was until she caught her breath and then she'd get up.

She was done with this. Maybe forever.

"It won't hurt anymore, baby. Sit on me, Twyla, I'll make you feel good, I promise."

She gasped when his hand eased between her legs. His long fingers gently massaged the nub there, and her breath hitched as her inner muscles miraculously relaxed a little. Her thigh muscles followed, and it was a good thing, because her legs were shaking so badly she thought for sure she'd collapse.

"Kiss me, Twy," he encouraged leaning his mouth a little closer to hers, his eyes pleading. Her death grip on the back slats of the chair loosened a little. When she didn't move closer, he closed the distance between them to meld his lips to hers, making a couple of exploratory passes over her mouth. With each slow rotation he made, each delicious fleeting kiss, she relaxed a little more, and he sank a little deeper inside her body. When she was fully seated on him, had taken all of him, she released a shuddering sigh.

Pulling his mouth away, Ryan rested his forehead to hers. "So tight, so damned tight," he groaned. "You okay, sweetheart?"

"Yeah," she muttered weakly. Now that he was inside of her, it didn't feel so bad. It actually felt pretty damned good. And now, she was no longer a virgin, and Ryan was her first.

"I'm sorry it happened this way. So damned sorry. I went about all this the wrong way. We should've gone to the bedroom, and I should have gone slower with you."

"If you went any slower, we'd have been going backwards," Twyla replied with a laugh, sitting up straighter to rest her hands on his shoulders. 'Okay now what? Is this it?"

If it was, in the morning Twyla would be sorely disappointed along with being sore.

Ryan's face relaxed, and he grinned. "Not by a long shot, darlin'," he replied.

He leaned her back over his arm, and his head descended to take her left breast into his mouth. He sucked her gently, and Twyla's inner muscles clenched around him. The tension didn't inch up inside of her this time, it shot straight to her head to make her dizzy.

Her breath came in short uneven pants, as he sucked her with a little more pressure, while his other hand moved between them to find her clit. He rolled it between his fingers, teasing that tension even higher. It became rubber band tight inside of her, as lights flashed behind her eyes, her ears rang, and her inner muscles clamped around him.

Ryan groaned against her skin, but he didn't let up. He played her body, until those lights converged, the elastic band snapped and then she felt like she was floating above them, looking down on her body shaking in his arms as she made nonsensical noises. The tremors lessened, and Ryan eased her back up, hugging her to his chest, until they ceased. He kissed the side of her hair, then pushed her away.

"How do you feel?"

Twyla gave him a wobbly smile, and grabbed the back of the chair, then put her feet on the floor. Her body itched inside now to feel him moving inside of her. She pushed up, and slowly lowered herself back down. No pain now, just extreme pleasure at the drag and fullness of his cock inside her body. "Like I need to ride," she said, easing her body up again.

"Oh, God, Twy—" he moaned, dropping his chin to his chest to make that gurgling sound in his throat that she loved. As she moved her body faster over him, Ryan's hands dug into her ass, spreading her wider, so she sank lower, took him deeper.

"That's it, baby. So fucking good," he mumbled hoarsely, his fingers digging in even deeper. Twyla clenched her inner muscles as she rose, figuring that would give him extra pleasure. The surprising part was it added to her pleasure too. With each movement, she felt herself getting nearer another climax. The tension built and built, her breathing shallowed right along with his. She knew the signs now, so when she saw the lights, she reached for them, focused. A tremor started in her thighs, then moved up to take over her body. Ryan roared, and Twyla moaned his name reverently as her body vibrated with his.

Her body melted into his arms, Ryan held her tightly to his chest, kissing her hair and whispering things she couldn't hear over the pounding of her heart in her ears. His fingers dug into the underside of her thighs and he lifted her. Twyla wrapped her legs around his back, then rested her tired head in the crook of Ryan's neck, as he carried her to the bedroom.

CHAPTER ELEVEN

Muffled banging and cursing woke Twyla from a dead sleep. She tried to roll over, but couldn't. She was trapped by a very muscular, lightly furred leg, which was draped over both of hers. It felt like she was cozied up next to a blast furnace. She tried to move Ryan's leg, without waking him, so she could get up. Twyla felt sure she knew why her roommate was cussing.

Heather was a neat freak, and they had left the evidence of their hours-long lovemaking session all over the breakfast nook and the kitchen. Their two a.m. midnight snack had turned into a snack of a different kind. They had been so exhausted afterward Twyla just didn't have the energy to clean up the chocolate syrup and ice cream from the counter. That had made a shower mandatory, and the round in the shower had been so hot, she ended up on her knees, unable to even stand to walk to bed. Ryan had carried her.

Twyla's heart melted and flowed right down to her lady parts. She sighed and glanced over at the man snoring softly beside her. He looked so young and carefree, relaxed. The bruise under his eye was fading now, thank goodness. His nose wasn't swollen any more either. She brought her finger up to the bridge of his nose and skimmed it to the tip. Ryan wiggled his nose and swatted at her hand. Twyla laughed, then traced the fading bruise under his eye.

When she reached the corner, that eye popped open and she was skewered by a heated blue-eyed stare.

Twyla smiled shyly, then traced the seam of his lips with her finger. "Morning." Ryan, nipped the end of her finger, and she yelped.

"Don't you know better than to poke the bear, darlin'?" He shoved his hips forward to press his rock solid erection to the side of her thigh. "He might poke back," he drawled in a sexy, sleepy voice that did things to her insides. A little thrill zipped down her spine when the fact that she was actually laying here with Ryan sank into her brain.

"I might like being poked by the bear," she said and felt her cheeks heat.

His hand came up and he fingered a strand of her hair. "And the bear might like being woken up, as long as it's Goldilocks doing the waking." A loud bang followed by a crash and a salty curse made Ryan flinch. He dropped her hair to massage his temples. "Someone shoeing a mule with ten penny nails out there?"

Twyla laughed. "Nah, just in your head, baby. I told you not to drink that rotgut."

Ryan cut his eyes at her, and groaned. "Told you so, ain't helping me, baby. I'd do it again in a heartbeat the way you served it." He tried to smile, but grimaced instead. "But I need some fricking aspirin."

With a heavy sigh, Twyla threw her leg over him and rolled to get out of bed, but Ryan's hands landed on her ass to stop her. He ground his hips against her, and smiled. "On second thought, the aspirin can wait. My head is splitting but if I die, I'll die happy."

Twyla liked this playful side of Ryan. A lot. It's not one she'd seen often in the fourteen or so years she'd known him. If they weren't arguing, he was usually cut and dry with her, brotherly, when he wasn't running somewhere. Probably hiding from her. But there wasn't a damned thing brotherly about what he was grinding against her right now. Molten lava replaced the blood in her veins. "That thing loaded, son?" she asked, circling her hips with him.

His eyes dilated and his nostrils flared, as the corners of his mouth eased up into a sexy smile. "Loaded for bear, baby," Ryan growled, as he rolled her under him, pinning her to the mattress with his body, as his mouth covered hers in a scorching kiss. His hand smoothed over her hip and crept between her legs. Twyla's hips shot up and she moaned into his mouth, dug her nails into his back and rotated her hips in time with his hand. Ryan's hips ground into her, as he continued driving her mindless with his kiss and his fingers.

Things heated up very fast, their bodies ground together faster, then suddenly a loud splintering crack broke the sensual spell. Twyla yelped as the bottom came out from under her butt and she was momentarily suspended in thin air, before her body slammed down on the mattress, a foot below where it had been a moment ago. She grunted when Ryan's body slammed on top of hers, and they bounced together. Their eyes met, and he looked as stunned as she felt.

"Good Lord, buddy, we broke the bed," she said in awe, covering her mouth with her hand to suppress a giggle. His look was so comical laughter bubbled in her chest. Twyla couldn't stop it, so she threw back her head and let it free. After a minute she was beating her fist on the mattress trying to catch her breath. Laughter rumbled in Ryan's chest too then exploded from him. He rolled onto his back, holding his stomach as it overcame him.

Loud banging rattled the wooden bedroom door on its hinges. They stopped laughing and their eyes met. "Ut oh, I think we're in trouble," Twyla whispered dramatically, then slapped her hand over her mouth to stop another round of giggles.

"Twyla get your narrow ass out here and help me clean up this mess!" Heather screeched.

"Be there in a minute," Twyla yelled back holding her finger over Ryan's mouth. He nipped the end of her finger, and then sucked it into his mouth and Twyla gasped as heat flooded her body. She yanked it out and hid her hand under her hip.

"*Now*, Twyla. This place is a wreck! And was that my grandma's bed I heard breaking in there?" Twyla pictured her friend standing outside that door with her hand on her curvy hip, tapping her toe like a grandmother would, like her mother used to do. Her tone was very similar and agitation bristled inside of her. Yeah, they'd left the front rooms a wreck, but she had planned to get up and take care of it this morning. She didn't think Heather would be home so early.

"I'll fix it!" Twyla yelled back. "It's just the bed boards!" *And I'll start looking for a place of my own this afternoon.* Heather was awesome for letting her stay here, a great friend and amazing woman, but two women who were so different living together for very long wasn't going to work.

"You need your own place," Ryan said with a sigh, as if reading her mind.

She looked over at him. "Can't afford it." Unless she kept dancing at the Cowgirl.

"I'll help you. I have a couple of days before I have to go back."

Twyla rolled over and put her hand on his chest. "Ryan, I can't afford it if I quit the bar. I do need my own place, but to get that I need that job at the bar. Leon and Teddy don't let the men touch us." She ran her thumb over his fading bruise. "You know that."

His body tensed. "I don't want you working there. They might not touch, but they sure as hell look, and I don't like it. I don't think your family would either." His eyes narrowed, as he reminded, "You promised you'd quit, so I don't have to tell them."

"*Twy*la!" Heather yelled again, and Twyla huffed a breath, scooted to the end of the bed and got to her feet.

With a final glance at Ryan, she grabbed her clothes off of the floor, and hopped into them as she walked to the door. She opened it and the scent of Pine Sol immediately smacked her in the face. Her stomach rolled. God, she hated that stuff, had told Heather it made her nauseous, but Heather seemed to love it in an obsessive kind of way. She absolutely did need her own place, Twyla thought, as she walked into the living room to see Heather in the breakfast nook on her hands and knees scrubbing the floor with a sponge. How the hell she wasn't passed out from the fumes, Twyla didn't know.

"I bought some Mr. Clean, Heather," Twyla said, as she walked into the nook.

"Mr. Clean can't even get these whiskey stains out of my floor. They're gonna take that out of my deposit, Twyla." Heather sat back on her heels, breathing hard. She swiped her forearm across her brow, then said, "You said a couple of weeks. It's been a couple of weeks. You need to find your own place. Teddy told me about a garage apartment over by the bar."

"I'm sorry, Heather. Thanks for taking me in for as long as you did. I'll talk to Teddy tonight."

"Tonight?" Ryan said gruffly behind her. Twyla spun around and her mouth flapped when she saw the heat in his face, the anger in his eyes.

Twyla tried to keep her voice even, but her voice didn't cooperate. Her frustration was more than obvious when she said, "I have to support myself, Ryan. Now, I have to pay for a place to live. It's unreasonable for you to ask me to quit my job right now. I have a competition coming up too, so I need to save money for that, buy equipment."

"You don't owe him explanations for how you live your life, Twyla, or any man for that matter," Heather said stepping to her side. "The man fucked you on my table, and one of the legs is weak now. And on my breakfast bar from the looks of it. Really? It was her first time and that's the best you could do?" she asked in dismay giving Ryan a once over.

"Who the hell are you to judge me?" Ryan said, his fists tightening at his sides. "You're a damned stripper, and you've gotten that same innocent woman into it too."

Heather's left eyebrow raised sky high, she tilted her head to the side to put her hand with the sponge in it on her hip. Twyla knew it was on when Heather didn't even notice the soapy water dripping down her leg into her boot.

Ryan was in deep shit, if she didn't step in.

Heather might be small, but her tongue could rip a man to shreds at fifty paces, not to mention where she was fond of planting the toe of her cowboy boot when cowboys got fresh with her. She was sweet as pie, until you ruffled her feathers, then there was no telling what would come out of her mouth.

Twyla stepped in front of Heather to put her hands on her shoulders. "I'm going to talk to Teddy about the apartment right now. I have a thousand bucks," she said glancing over her shoulder at Ryan, giving him a look that told him to keep his mouth shut. "I'll buy you another table, and I'll find someone to come and fix the bed today."

"I'll fix it," Ryan ground out, pinning Heather with a glare, before swinging his gaze to Twyla. "And I'll take you to go see about the apartment, and help you find another job."

Her overbearing brother was back. The patient and exciting lover from last night who'd taught her the joys of sex, and the playful lover from this morning had both left the building.

"I don't need you to fix things for me, Ryan," Twyla said angrily. "I've found out I'm more than capable of taking care of myself, and deciding the best way to do that."

"If this is an example of you taking care of yourself," he said waving his hand expansively around the apartment, finishing with a little dip toward Heather. "I beg to differ with you, and I'm sure your brother would too."

Anger pushed Twyla's heart up to her throat. It lodged there, making it almost too hard to speak. After last night, she thought things might be different between them, but she was wrong. Dead wrong. Twyla walked over to Ryan and tilted her chin up to meet his eyes. "Well, it's a good thing Zack isn't here, isn't it?" She poked him in his bare chest with her finger. "And it's a good thing you won't be here either. Neither of you will have to see anything." She poked him again, and he stepped back. "As far as you telling my family? Go ahead, I dare you. I have a few things they'd probably be interested in hearing too." Twyla winked at him and shoved his shoulder. "Get back to your own business, Ryan. I have things to do today."

Ryan's jaw dropped, and he went to grab her shoulders, but Twyla dodged him. He rounded on her. "Twyla we have things to discuss. What happened last night—"

"Is over, Ryan. Thanks for a good time," she said with another wink and a tight smile. "I'm sure those lessons will come in handy in the future for both of us."

"God*dammit*, Twyla!" he growled in frustration. "You are one hardheaded woman."

"Why yes, I am," Twyla replied in a sing-song tone. She stabbed a finger in his direction. "And you are one hard-*hearted* cowboy. I guess that makes us even." With a shake of her head, she turned to walk back to the bedroom and get ready. She had a lot of things to do today, and arguing with Ryan Easter all day long wasn't getting them done.

Ryan banged on the bathroom door, until his knuckles were blue. It's a wonder the damned thing wasn't in splinters by now he'd knocked so long. He heard the shower running, and Twyla moving around inside, but she wouldn't answer the damned door. He slammed his palm against the door beside where his head rested.

"Twyla, please open the door," he repeated, his voice hoarse from calling her name.

This was the last time he'd try. Ryan knew he'd be better off beating his head on the door than continuing to try to get her to listen to him. He'd been at this almost an hour now. Since Heather left to go to her dance studio, after they had final heated words that almost ended with a cowboy boot in his crotch. That woman was a pistol, and any man who tried to tame that one had his work cut out for him. Almost as much work as Ryan had for himself with Twyla.

Some battles were better left for another day though. This was one of them. He had to get back to the circuit tomorrow, and she was going to do what she damned well pleased anyway. Hanging around wasn't going to get him anywhere. From past experience he knew letting her cool off was probably his best option at the moment. His next break was in two weeks. Ryan would come back then and try again to convince her to quit that damned bar. That was probably the most he could hope for, because he didn't think he was ever going to convince her to come back with him.

He thought he'd made a little progress there, but that two-minute argument with Twyla and Heather had undone any headway he'd made with Twyla. He'd shot off his mouth before he thought about what he was saying, then stuffed his foot in his mouth to boot. Insulting both women at the same time had been taking his life into his hands, he realized now.

"I'm sorry, Twy—I'm leaving now, but I'll call to check on you," he mumbled as he pushed away from the door. Heaving a sigh, Ryan gathered up his stuff, and finished dressing. He grabbed his wallet from the dresser, and his heart skidded to a stop at seeing the condom wrapper sitting on the dresser beside it. Good God, that last time they made love in the kitchen on the counter, he hadn't worn a condom. Hadn't even thought about it. His head rocked back on his shoulders and he sucked in a sharp breath through his nose. It came out in a rush, as he massaged his pounding temples. "I'm a fucking moron," he grated as he shoved the wallet into his back pocket. "A total complete idiot."

Ryan had never forgotten before.

It was something he remembered religiously. Hell, he kept almost a gross of them behind his seat in the truck. He didn't want a kid, and he didn't want something that wouldn't be cured in nine months either. That was something his old man had taught him before he left them, the only thing really. Ryan found out later there was a reason for his expertise on the subject that he passed on to a fourteen-year-old boy. He was a serial cheater, a man who had slept with everything that had two legs and a split. That accidental knowledge about his father's activities had come to him through his stepfather, who said at least he didn't cheat, when Ryan confronted him about hitting his mother.

Like that made the black eye she sported that day, a lot of days, okay.

The old anger dredged up from deep inside him to wash through his body. His fingers flexed wanting to feel that bastard's throat under his hands again like he had the day he almost killed him. The day his mother told him not to come back around. That day she had chosen between them. She chose to have a relationship with a man who beat the living hell out of her on a daily basis rather than her eighteen-year-old son who had only been trying to protect her. At the time it hadn't made any sense to him, and it still didn't. Relationships were the luck of the draw, and his mother had drawn two deuces, but she decided to play them.

That is why Ryan chose not to get involved in the mess that came with relationships. He stuck to temporary women who could give him temporary relief. Last night though, he knew beyond a shadow of a doubt, he had stepped off into uncharted territory with Twyla. He did have feelings for her, he just didn't know what they were. The possibility of him having some kind of non-familial relationship with her now had tickled his brain, but Ryan planned on taking one day at a time to see where things went, while he sorted out those feelings, and she untangled the mess she'd made of her life. Both would take time.

If Twyla turned up pregnant though, that plan would change quickly. The sand would rush to the bottom of the hourglass. Ryan would marry her, and do the right thing. That's what the only family he'd ever, her family, had taught him to do, would expect of him. What he expected of himself, because he cared about her and the family.

At the moment though, the right thing was to give her some space to get over her temper, and get his ass back in the saddle. Once he thought she'd cooled down, he'd try to call her. If she didn't take his call, on his next break he'd be back down here to try again, and find out if anything had taken root from his stupid mistake.

That was all he could do.

CHAPTER TWELVE

During a break between rounds in Amarillo, their second stop on the circuit since he'd left Twyla a week ago, Ryan found an empty corner in the locker room, to make his third call to Heather's apartment. Twyla didn't have a damned cell phone, so he had to call Heather's apartment. It was the only number he had for her. Ryan was going to rectify that situation when he went back to Dallas. He needed to be able to get ahold of her, and she needed to be able to make a call in case she needed help. Lord, just the thought that she might need help and not be able to call for it sent cold chills zipping down his spine.

Maybe he should tell Zack. Or her family.

It was bad enough when she was living there with Heather, but now she was really alone, in an apartment by herself, and she was still dancing at that bar. At least Heather had half a lick of sense about protecting herself. Ryan could attest to that firsthand. But Twyla was naïve and unsophisticated, not used to taking care of herself, because she'd always had him and Zack watching out for her. When it came to men, and what they were capable of, Twyla didn't have a clue. Ryan had a clue, and so did his mother. Zack knew too, because his best friend was the only person on the planet he'd talked to about it. Which could be part of the reason he'd always sheltered Twyla like he had. They both had.

Dancing in that bar, there was no telling what

kind of man could attach himself to her. Just thinking about the many things that could happen gave him cold sweats at night. Or it could be the damned dreams giving him cold sweats. Every time he shut his eyes, which hadn't been often since he left her, because those hot moments in Heather's apartment kept replaying in his mind like a broken record, he saw her face as she came, heard her delicious moans. In his dreams though, that slick shooting instructor's face was the one he saw on the man making love to Twyla, not his own.

His heart jerked in his chest as he punched out Heather's number on his cell phone. He slammed the phone to his ear and heard it ringing. Heather telling him, "She's doing fine, and I'll tell her you called," wasn't going to cut it this time. Heather was going to get Twyla to call him back, or he was going to Dallas. Ryan felt someone walk up behind him, and turned to see Zack lean a hip against the row of lockers and cross his arms over his chest. Wouldn't you know he would show up at just that moment, Heather's impatient voice came over the line? His luck had definitely gone south, and not only with his riding since Twyla left.

After a huffed breath, Heather started in with, "Look Ryan, your apology might've worked with me, because I really don't give a shit what you think of me, but I can't make her call you. I've told her you called. That's all I can do. Now, I'm going to hang up, because I'm busy trying to get ready for a gig."

Ryan dragged his eyes from Zack's interested

blue gaze, and turned to face the wall. "*Wait*! Can you at least go by there and check on her?" he said, then covered his mouth to whisper into the phone. "I'm worried about her. I really need to talk to her." What Ryan was worried about, he definitely couldn't be saying out loud with Zack standing behind him. "Um, how's her apartment? How's the job and her shooting lessons?" *Has she started her period?*

"She's fine. The job's fine. I haven't seen the apartment yet. She and Randy are not seeing each other as far as I know. I know that's what your real question is," Heather said with a dry laugh. "And if it will get you to stop calling, yes, I'll stop by on my way out."

The tension in Ryan's shoulders eased a little. Heather definitely wasn't the one he'd choose to go by and do a welfare check on Twyla, that was sort of like sending a fox to check the hen house, but she was his only choice. "Can you call me back and let me know she's okay? I'll probably be riding, but you can leave a message."

Heather sighed, and he could imagine her rolling her green eyes. "I'll leave a message, but don't call me again. I have a lot on my plate, without playing go between. If you're that damned worried, get your butt down here and find out for yourself how she's doing."

The line disconnected, before he could even mutter thank you.

Go to Dallas is exactly what he was going to do in six days and ten hours. He turned back toward

Zack, and his friend was still there, but his look had changed from interested to concerned. "Why the hell are you so worried about Twyla? That's the second time I've caught you sneaking off to call to check on her. You said she had a job at a burger joint, and was taking shooting lessons. How much trouble could she get into?"

More than you could ever imagine. Blood shot up to Ryan's face and it felt like it was on fire, as he stammered, "I'm just worried because she's so damned green about men." *A lot less green than before I paid her a visit.* His heart took a sick dive to his toes. "You know how guys are." *Guys like him. Or worse, guys like his stepfather.* Ryan fought off a shiver, and shoved his phone into his pocket.

Zack's brows slammed down over his eyes, and his arms fell to his sides. "Was she seeing someone while you were there?"

Seeing someone? No, but she was having sex with me. Ryan's blood rushed to follow his heart to his toes, making him a little dizzy.

Zack's eyes narrowed. "Is there something you're not telling me, bro?"

Only that I slept with your sister, and would do it again, if given the opportunity. Oh, and the little fact that she's dancing at a bar. Other than that no. Good God, Ryan had lied to the man he thought of as a brother. Something he'd never done before. That man's sister was into all kinds of things she shouldn't be, and Ryan couldn't tell him, or do a damned thing to stop her from doing those things. And now he was going to have to lie again.

"Um, no," his voice cracked and he cleared his throat. "Twy was fine." He used Heather's tactic, and it evidently worked, because Zack's face relaxed.

"Well, that's good then, because you only have five minutes to get ready for your ride, dude." Zack put his arm around Ryan's shoulder and slapped his back. "You're up first next round. That's why I was surprised when you ran off. We need to check-in at the pens, or they'll scratch you."

The last thing Ryan wanted to do was ride right now, unless he was riding a wild ass cowgirl he couldn't get off his mind, he thought as he walked back to the arena with Zack.

***

Twyla reached beside her to fumble blindly for the half-empty Twinkie box on the floor. It was one of those Twinkie kind of days today. Had been for the last couple of days. When she needed it most, her tips at the bar Saturday night hadn't been good, and Leon wasn't happy. Twyla just couldn't seem to find any sexy to put into her routines these days. Because she wasn't feeling very sexy, not that she ever had. She was feeling dirty. Because Ryan had made her feel that way. Tried to make Heather feel that way too, but her friend just didn't care what he or anyone else thought. Twyla wished she could manage that.

Even though it was all an act that Heather had helped her perfect, like she had perfected her own, to make ridiculously easy money to help her follow her dreams, Twyla felt dirty and cheap now when she danced. She wasn't anymore a stripper than Heather was, or that kind of dancer, but Randy thought she was. Because of Ryan.

At their shooting lessons now, Randy was treating her like she had the clap. It had become obvious there wasn't a snowball's chance in hell now he'd ask her out again after what Ryan told him. Randy didn't even look at her the same now. He left after they finished the lessons like his ass was on fire.

Stuffy, judgmental asshole.

Even if she was a stripper, that wasn't any way to treat someone you'd asked out not a week ago. But something else was bothering her more. Although it pissed her off to admit it, she was missing the hell out of Ryan. Since he left a week ago, she had intentionally refused to talk to him, trying to get on her way to forgetting him, but she was paying the price. Twyla wondered if the heartsick feeling in her gut would ever go away.

Heather said he'd called her apartment a couple of times looking for her, but Twyla hadn't found the gumption to call him back. If he gave her more of the same that he'd given her while he was there, she'd get more pissed off at him. Might never want to talk to him again. Twyla didn't want to end up hating him, because she became so frustrated. Hell, after ten years of it, she was surprised she wasn't already at that point. But dammit she wasn't.

She missed him more every day, wondered if he was making time with the bunnies again after he'd made love to her like he had. If she knew that was the case, it would be over for sure. But they weren't committed. She was as free to date anyone she wanted as he was. The problem was she didn't want to date anyone else. Hadn't ever wanted to be with anyone else. Unless she changed her attitude on that, she probably never would be over Ryan Easter. She'd spend her life alone pining for him.

Her lips wobbled as she shucked the crinkly wrapper from the yellow cake in her hands. She crammed it in her mouth and tossed the wrapper over the side of the sofa. Another dead soldier. She quit counting how many she'd had in the last two days. It didn't matter really if she ended up weighing two hundred pounds or not. No man wanted her anyway. Would ever want her. At least she wasn't a virgin anymore. But that made things worse, because now that she'd had sex, she wanted more. With Ryan. Twyla's nose burned, and she rubbed it. She was not going to cry dammit.

Of course her feelings could be exaggerated, magnified, because on top of all that she started her fucking period this morning. Twyla definitely wasn't feeling up to dancing tomorrow. Leon would probably fire her.

Hell, today was her day off and she didn't feel like doing anything other than laying here on this ratty pullout loveseat, the only piece of furniture in her new *furnished* apartment, which consisted of one room with a hotplate on a vanity, and stare at the dingy walls, while stuffing her face full of Twinkies. A

Twinkie pity party is what she was having, and this time it wasn't making her feel better. She actually felt a little sick. Twyla reached for another Twinkie, but someone knocked at her front door.

She groaned wondering if it was her pinched-face little bald landlord coming to perform one of his 'surprise' inspections' he informed her he performed occasionally. She hadn't even been here two weeks, but she wouldn't put it past him. The only person who needed to be inspecting this rat hole apartment was the fire marshal. Or the health inspector maybe. Her eyes fell to the nasty carpet, which she thought used to be olive green. Now, it was a puce color. In places anyway. Lord knew what was growing in the long shag strands.

The knock came again and she glanced at the deadbolt, saw it was locked, and breathed a sigh of relief. He couldn't get in with the spare key. Maybe if she just kept quiet he'd go away. Twyla slid down on the sofa so her head was below the back, but that just meant her legs hung further over the arm at the end. If he looked in the window beside the door, she knew he would see her. This loveseat was definitely not meant for a person over five foot four, and she was six inches taller.

"Twyla I know you're in there, I see your damned truck parked out here!" Heather shouted at the top of her lungs. "Open the door!"

With a groan, Twyla sat up and shoved her feet into her boots, because there was no way she was walking across that carpet barefoot until she could have it cleaned. The knocking became banging by the time she got to the door and flipped the locks. Heather stood there dressed like she was ready for a concert at the Grand Ole Opry in a rhinestone studded black shirt with red rose embroidery and fringe on the V across her bosom, with a snazzy black fringed skirt, and high heeled studded black boots. On her head she wore a black felt hat with a rhinestone band. This was as close to formalwear as a country girl could get. She must have a gig tonight.

Twyla couldn't help but laugh, even though it came out a little rusty. "Damn girl, you look like you hit a garage sale at Loretta Lynn's place."

"Very funny. I have a gig," Heather said as she brushed past her into the apartment. "Ugh…" she said walking further inside. "What the hell is that smell?"

"The landlord said the tenant before me had a ferret. I'll get the carpet cleaned when I get my check. I need the money to get my pistols for the competition this weekend."

"You need that pistol to shoot the damned landlord you mean?" Heather turned around. "That bastard should've cleaned the carpet, before you moved in. I'll talk to him for you. And you need to get your priorities straight. Food other than Twinkies, a decent place to live, and then pistols." Heather looked at the floor in front of the sofa, then put her hands on her hips. "What's up with the Twinkie fest?'

Twyla huffed a breath and shut the door, then

walked back around the sofa. Bending she pulled the last Twinkie from the box, then stood to hold it up to Heather. Her Twinkie party or the reason for it was none of Heather's business. Twyla was getting damned tired of people telling her what to do, butting in her damned business.

"You should try it sometimes. If a girl has enough Twinkies, she can solve most any problem." Twyla jerked open the end and shoved the wrapper down then bit off half of the cake. She shoved it into her cheek. Tilting her head, she asked sharply, "You dress up to come over here to talk about my eating habits? Or did you need something?"

"Damn girl, who pissed in your corn flakes this morning?" Heather asked with a laugh. "Can't I come over just to see how you're doing?"

"I'm doing fine." Twyla said around the knot in her throat that was her Twinkie. She walked to the mini-fridge and opened the door to take out the pint of milk she'd bought last night with her Twinkies. Unscrewing the cap she took a big swig, shock rocked her and she blew it right back out. Wiping her arm over her mouth, she spit a few more times while she tried to keep her Twinkies from reappearing. She took a deep gasping breath once she was sure that wasn't going to happen.

"Are you okay?" Heather asked walking over there.

"Damn milk I bought last night is clabbered," Twyla said gagging again. She took another deep breath and waited as her stomach rolled yet again.

Heather walked to the tiny refrigerator and opened the door to stick her hand inside. "This thing probably hasn't worked in ten years or so."

Twyla sighed heavily, then got a glass and filled it with water at the tiny sink beside the vanity. After a long swallow, she said, "Guess that's what I get for two-hundred dollars a month furnished. I probably should've looked around more."

"Ya think?" Heather asked with a laugh, then her eyes took a tour over Twyla's holey gray sweatpants, her now stained white t-shirt. Paired with her cowboy boots and haphazard braid, Twyla knew she had to look absurd. But she really didn't give a shit.

How she looked was exactly how she felt.

Heather shook her head, and grinned. "Girlfriend you are a hot damn mess. You been in this place since yesterday?" Heather's eyes took another tour around the room, and her face looked a little disgusted.

"Where the hell else do you think I've been?" Twyla replied gruffly.

"Didn't you have a shooting lesson yesterday?"

"Canceled it. Didn't feel like going. I'm sure Randy didn't mind, he thinks I'm a stripper." Twyla walked back to the loveseat and sat down to rest her head in her hands.

"Why would he think you're a stripper?" Heather asked in amazement.

"Because Ryan told him I was a stripper."

"Why the hell would he do that? He knows you're not a stripper. He saw you dance!" Heather said angrily. "What was he doing out at the barn anyway?"

"He followed me evidently, saw me at my lesson with Randy and decided there was something going on that needed his interference."

Twyla heard her gasp. "That sonofabitch was jealous."

"Not jealous. He was standing in for my obsessively over-protective older brother, which he thinks is his role when Zack isn't around. He ran off Randy just like Zack has done with any other man I was interested in since I hit puberty."

"Honey, I don't know where you grew up, but where I'm from brothers don't look at their sister the way Ryan Easter looks at you. And they surely don't—"

"Leave it, Heather!" Twyla shouted, shooting up to her feet. "I really don't want to talk about it." She pushed Heather toward the door. "And you need to leave. You don't want to be late for your gig." And Twyla didn't know how much more of her friend's mothering she could take before she broke down. The last thing she wanted to do was that. If she broke, it would be when she was alone. And the odds were as soon as she flipped that deadbolt, that is exactly what was going to happen.

Heather pushed back, before Twyla could get her over the threshold and spun to face her. "You need to get out and do something. Drowning yourself in junk food isn't going to help a damned thing. I've got a gig at a very nice bar in town. Get your ass dressed and you're going with me."

"I started and I don't feel like it," Twyla replied with a frustrated breath.

Heather's chin cocked up and she crossed her arms over her chest. "Well, if you don't want me to call big brother and give him a report on your situation, you'll get dressed so we can go. Now hop to it. I'm going to be late."

"Ryan called again?" Twyla asked and dammit if her heart didn't do a little dance in her chest. Mentally, she slapped it and it stilled.

"Yeah he called, and wants a report. It's the last time I'll be giving him one though. I told him if he's that damned concerned, he needs to come and check on you himself."

A little satisfaction flowed through her. "He was worried about me?"

"Sounded pretty damned worried to me, and not in a brotherly kind of way either."

"What do you mean?"

"I think he's worried that his little trick with Randy didn't stick, and that you might be dating him."

Twyla snorted. "Fat chance of that. I don't think he's the type of man to date strippers."

"You're not a stripper," Heather reminded.

Twyla sighed. "He thinks I am. That's all that matters."

"No, what matters is you found out what kind

of man he is before you got involved with him. Anyone who judges you like that without cause, based on someone else's off-the-cuff words doesn't deserve you. And a man who sleeps with you then takes off when you get a little pissy with him, instead of sticking around to duke it out doesn't deserve you either."

Heather made sense, but Twyla's heart still wasn't convinced. "Where's your gig?"

"The Red Rooster Saloon," Heather replied. "My agent got me the gig. It's downtown in the hob knob section. That's why I'm dressed like this. Spent five hundred bucks on this outfit," she said with a shrug.

"Oh my God, Heather," Twyla said breathless. "Five hundred bucks?"

"I figured once they see how great I am, they'll call me again, so I can use it again later."

Heather grinned widely, but Twyla saw the doubt in her eyes. Her friend had been trying to break into the music business, since she left the rodeo. Road block after road block had prevented that. But Heather was determined. And she was damned good. She deserved a break. She also deserved Twyla's support. "I'll be ready in twenty minutes."

CHAPTER THIRTEEN

Twyla smoothed her blue jean skirt then yanked the hem down a little more, as she walked back to the table with her beer in her hand. Heather was up on stage talking to the backup guitarist and the drummer, who were up there with her. She looked like a star up there with the lights reflecting off of the rhinestones on her shirt and hat. Twyla hoped something broke loose soon for her on the career her friend had been working so hard to achieve for so long. Even when she rode rodeo, Heather was singing at every open mic night she could find at every stop. When they finished riding, she was running for her truck to go sing somewhere.

From her lackluster performance in rodeo, it was obvious her passions laid elsewhere. Dancing was a little better for her, but it too was just a device to get her where she wanted to be. Up on that stage singing. Twyla had gone to watch her several times after races. That's how they'd become friends. The rest of the barrel racers had other things to do, or were jealous of her, but Twyla was in awe of her talent.

It was still early and a Monday, so the crowd was thin. Twyla had her choice of tables up by the stage. She took one at the center, so she had a good view and sat down. She crossed her legs then took a long sip of what would probably not be her only beer. She was glad Heather had made her come now. With a shower and getting fixed up to come, she felt about fifty-percent better than she had in that dreary apartment. She imagined with another couple of beers that would be up to seventy-five percent. Or she hoped anyway.

She raised her bottle to take another sip of her beer, but stopped when someone sat down in the chair across the table from her. A tall, handsome cowboy in a black hat and black shirt with a very sexy grin. He looked quite a bit older than her, but he was extremely good looking. Maybe she needed an older man who wasn't so immature he couldn't accept she could make her own choices, and let her make them. Someone who wouldn't play childish games with her for ten years while they kept her on the hook chasing them. Someone who had no desire to be her brother, or anything like him.

"Hi, pretty lady," the cowboy said sticking his hand out to her. "I just wanted to say hello to you before the band starts up and it's too loud to do that. I'd have kicked myself in the butt all the way home if I didn't. I'm Jared."

Twyla's eyes fell to his other hand, which rested on the table. No wedding ring, or ridge from one. He looked harmless, and was well dressed. One thing was for sure, unless she opened up to another man, she'd never find that someone. Her eyes swung back up to his and she smiled, as she sat her bottle down, wiped her hand on her skirt, then took his hand. "I'm Twyla. Nice to meet you, Jared."

His eyes fell on her beer. "I'd ask if I could

buy you a beer, but it looks like you're set for now. Can I sit here and wait until you're ready for one?" he asked hopefully.

Damn this man was smooth, she thought, as she pulled her hand from his. "Tables aren't reserved," she replied with a laugh and eased back in her chair. "What brings you here?"

He pointed at the stage. "I want to hear that little lady sing. I've heard good things about her, and wanted to hear for myself."

Twyla gasped. "Really?"

He glanced at her and smiled. "Yeah, I'm an agent. I can do big things for her, if she's ready to ditch the schmuck she's with."

"She's been with him a long time."

"You know Heather?" he asked curiously, turning to lean in closer.

"She's a friend."

"Well, if you're her friend, you'll tell her what's holding her back is her agent. If she's been with Lester that long, and this place is the best he can do for her, then she needs to go agent shopping, and I'm her man."

Twyla got this tickling sensation at the back of her neck, but had no idea what that was about. "How'd you hear about Heather?"

"I went to the Crazy Cowgirl awhile back and saw her dance. Leon told me she's a singer too, so I decided to check her out." He shrugged. "Heard she had a gig here tonight."

"You know Leon?" Twyla asked picking up

her beer, because that tickling sensation turned into a full blown buzz that zipped down her spine. She'd never seen this guy at the Cowgirl, but then again she hadn't been there long. And she tried her best not to notice men there anyway. If she didn't make eye contact, she found she didn't get so grossed out with them staring at her. Jared said it was a while back, so maybe it was before she started there. And he knew Leon. Maybe he wasn't some crazy stalker who had latched onto Heather at the bar. He didn't appear to be that type.

His eyes swung back to Twyla, and he smiled as his eyes took a quick tour of her breasts, before he volleyed, "Question is, how do you know him?"

Twyla wasn't about to tell him she was a dancer there. Look how that knowledge had turned out with Randy. And this man knew what the Cowgirl was. "Um, through Heather."

"Well, Leon and I go way back. We used to own a bar together before I got into talent management." When his eyes met Heather's up on stage and she waved, Twyla felt a little better. She relaxed and picked up her beer, chastising herself for being so paranoid. She was going to sit here and drink her beer, let this man buy her another, and enjoy her night.

Maybe that would help her forget that payphone she'd seen in the hall near the bathroom, the one that had called to her on the way in to pick it up and call Ryan Easter. The one at the Crazy Cowgirl was out of service, so she hadn't been tempted at work. But damn she was tempted here, and she doubted it was broken. This place was too upscale for that to happen.

It was Monday, so he was probably on his way to the next venue anyway. Out in the boonies where cell service was sketchy. At least that's what she was telling herself so she didn't run over there to call. She was not going to call him, she thought with determination as she lifted her beer and downed it. When she sat the bottle on the table, Jared was watching her. "You ready for another one?"

Twyla nodded and he smiled then pushed up to stand. "Be right back."

She watched Jared walk toward the bar, then her gaze swung back to the stage as Heather introduced herself. Her voice shook a little, and Twyla recognized it was nerves causing the shake in her usually confident friend's tone. She also noticed Heather's eyes were following Jared across the bar too as she spoke, and she wasn't smiling now. But with a nod to the others on stage, she strummed her acoustic guitar then sang the first note of her first song.

Twyla got caught up in the magical, pitch perfect sound of the sad country ballad and sighed, resting her chin on the heel of her palm. Jared came back and slid a beer across the table to her as he sat down. He relaxed back with his own and before long he seemed as wrapped up in the music as Twyla was. That was a good thing, she thought. Maybe he would help Heather. Two songs later, Twyla was convinced he was sold. Jared was leaning forward with his elbows on his knees, seeming to be totally into Heather.

That's why it surprised her when he sat up and turned toward her. "I've seen all I need to see. She's definitely a star. I have another act to go see tonight. You want to ride with me? I can drop you back here later? I need to talk to Heather anyway," he asked with that sexy grin.

Twyla gnawed her lower lip and her hand tightened on her half full beer bottle. For some reason the beer was going straight to her head tonight, and she felt loose as a goose. But she had enough sense left to know if she turned this man down, knowing he held Heather's future in his palm, he would probably get pissed and not help her. She could probably help grease him up to offer to help Heather anyway. She owed her friend a lot for helping her. Maybe she could return the favor now.

"Sure, why not?" fell out of her strangely numb lips. Twyla got to her feet and wobbled a little, but Jared flew around the table to put his hand on her arm to steady her.

"Whoa there, cowgirl. No more beer for you," he said with a laugh.

Cowgirl. That's what Ryan called her. Her heart jerked in her chest, but she mentally slapped it, and stiffened her shoulders to walk with Jared to the front door of the bar.

***

Ryan watched the miles pass as he drove toward Cheyenne, the farthest stop on the tour this year. Not even a hundred miles into the drive from Mesa, he had a long road trip ahead of him. He settled in and wandered off into his thoughts, which hadn't left Twyla at all. Not even when the bronc he drew in that last round kicked his ass.

Mostly because Heather hadn't called and left a message like she said she would.

He blamed her for him getting his ass kicked. And Twyla who still refused to call him. He just wasn't paying attention, wasn't able to focus on anything else. Shifting in his seat to get more comfortable, Ryan held his arm against his side to cushion his bruised ribs. They were taped, and he knew in a few days they'd feel better. But right now? He felt just like he'd been mule-kicked in the ribs, which isn't far off from what actually happened.

Tonight, he ended up fourth, completely out of the money. Ryan couldn't expect to keep that up and be in the finals. This year would be a bust if he wasn't careful, in more ways than one.

Things just weren't right in his world anymore. Twyla had always been with them. Always around. His head cheerleader wasn't there at the rail waving her arms and egging him on to the buzzer. Twyla was irritating at times, but she had been a fixture in his life for a long time. Ryan had taken it for granted that she would always be around to irritate him, to push him. Laugh at him, and tease him to the point of madness with her damned antics to get his attention.

She definitely had his attention now, the kind

she'd been looking for all along, and she didn't want it. What he knew all along would eventually happen between them, had happened, and the morning after she'd kicked him out. Now, she wasn't taking his call. Was avoiding him.

Like he'd done to plenty of bunnies himself.

Ryan couldn't say he liked the role reversal. Not one bit.

He was beginning to think he was Twyla's sacrificial bunny to get the worrisome problem of her virginity behind her. Now, the path was clear for her to date other men, be with other men, without having to explain herself. There was only one problem in her thinking.

They had had unprotected sex, and she could very well be pregnant with his child right now, while she was dating those other men. That wasn't going to work at all.

He was going to tell her that, if he ever got ahold of her. And a helluva lot more.

Ryan banged his fist against the steering wheel again. As soon as this Cheyenne gig was over, he was heading straight to Dallas. But that was another fricking six days, almost five now. As bad as he was riding these days, he should just bow out and go now. The writing was on the wall as to where he would finish this year. He could probably use this latest injury as an excuse. The doctor had offered him one, but he had refused. All it would take is a phone call probably.

He needed Twyla back with him now. With

them, he corrected. With him and Zack. So they could watch out for her. Yeah that was it. It wasn't because missing her was driving him fucking insane. Or because his good luck had left with her. Or that she was probably fucking that damned slick cowboy.

Who the hell was he kidding? It was all those reasons, and plenty more.

Ryan's hand tightened on the steering wheel. But he didn't need to go off half-cocked. He needed to think things through, before he turned his truck around. What he would say to her to make her change her mind? If he tossed in the towel for the year, what would he tell Zack that wouldn't give away everything? He knew his friend was going to grill him about it. Zack was already asking about his bad attitude and poor riding. His friend who knew him better than anyone, knew something was up, but Ryan had managed to dance around telling him for now. He didn't want to open that can of worms if he didn't have to.

He flicked on the radio, hoping it would distract him, but wouldn't you know that damned song *You're Gonna Miss Me When I'm Gone* would be playing? There was that cosmic DJ again, probably sitting on the other end of those radio waves laughing his ass off at Ryan. The next song snapped his patience in two, *She Won't Be Lonely Long*. With a growl, Ryan flicked off the radio, but the tune still echoed through his head, like the thought echoed through his soul.

Ryan jerked the steering wheel when he

realized he'd drifted to the shoulder. He shook his head and righted the truck on the road. He was so damned tired, he was going to have to stop soon at a rest stop or hotel if he could find one out here in the boonies. Then in the morning he'd decide if he was heading back the way he came, or going on to Cheyenne.

Maybe he'd try to call Heather again too. Or maybe he'd just bite the bullet and call Zack and fess up. Tell him that he and Twyla...nah, not yet, that would be suicide. But if it came down to it, that's exactly what he would do, because he'd welcome death if it meant Twyla was safe and back on the right track with her life.

The phone in his pocket rang, and Ryan fished it out at the expense of another shot of pain between his ribs. His breath was short as he pushed the button, and cradled the phone between his shoulder and ear. "Yeah?"

"This is Zack. I'm not going to Cheyenne, I'm heading to Dallas. Twyla's in the hospital. Mom and Dad are on their way there too."

Ryan's heart skidded to a stop, then headlights hit him in the eyes, as he swerved just in time to avoid a head on collision with an SUV. His brain was so stunned, he hadn't even realized he'd drifted over the center line. "What happened?" he asked breathlessly.

"Hospital didn't say. They just said they needed someone there as soon as possible. They called me, because she told them I was her next of kin," Zack explained, his voice sounding as sick as

Ryan was feeling. Zack told him which hospital Twyla was in, and Ryan spun the truck in road and fishtailed on loose gravel, before regaining control and slamming his foot down on the accelerator.

"I'm on my way," Ryan finally managed to say past the lump in his throat. "I'm about four hours out though." Four fucking hours. He should have headed straight to Dallas when he left the arena and he'd be there by now. And Twyla wouldn't be in the hospital, probably hurt bad or dead. His heart plummeted to his feet, and emotion built like a powderkeg inside his head.

Please, Lord, don't let her be dead.

"I'm six out. I'll meet you there," Zack said, then Ryan heard him blow his horn impatiently. "If you get there first, call me and let me know what's going on. I'll call the folks. They may get there first, since they're closer."

Blood pounding in his ears in time with his heart, Ryan disconnected the call, tossed his phone up onto the dash, and shoved the accelerator to the floor. He had to get to Dallas and find out what was going on. *Please, Lord, don't let her be dead. I'll deal with the rest.*

Forty-five minutes later, Ryan's phone rattled on the dash, and as it rang it danced toward the passenger side of the truck. He almost ran off the road trying to grab it, but finally managed to close his hand over it. By then it had stopped ringing, and his fricking ribs hurt like a bitch, but not worse than his heart. He flipped on the overhead light, saw it was

Heather and hit redial. Maybe she knew what was going on, or he hoped she did. On the third ring, she answered.

"Ryan you've got to come to Dallas and help me find Twyla."

"I'm on my way to Dallas. Her brother called and she's in the hospital." Ryan mentioned which one, but told her he had no idea what happened.

"I know what happened. Jared Wilkins happened. She left with him from the bar where I had my gig, and I couldn't stop her."

Ryan sat up in the seat as worry shot through him, followed very closely by anger. "Who the fuck is Jared Wilkins?"

"Leon's old business partner, and a customer at the Cowgirl."

Hearing the disgusted tone in Heather's voice, Ryan's stomach rolled. "What kind of business, and who the hell is he?"

"He and Leon owned a strip club together several years ago. Leon cut ties with him because rumor has it he liked to audition the girls personally, before they were hired in his trailer, behind the bar."

"At the Cowgirl?!?" Ryan shouted, his heart doing weird lunges in his chest now.

"No, no. It was another club. Leon puts up with him coming around the Cowgirl, because he tips well, and drinks a lot. I guess his money is as green as the next guy. Leon told us to be friendly with him, not to piss him off. He said to let Teddy know if he got out of line." She sighed deeply, and there was a long pause before she continued. "Jared hadn't been around in a while, so I didn't think to warn Twyla about him when she started working there. He showed up at my gig tonight, and she left with him, before I could stop her. There's no telling what the man told her to get her to go with him. He's a liar and a sleazeball. Ryan, I'm really worried."

Now that he knew the story. Ryan was more than worried. That sat like a lead weight in the pit of his gut, and unimaginable fear sat on top of it. And then there was anger. His whole body burned with it. The road blurred before Ryan's eyes he was so mad. Everything seemed to be covered in a red haze. His face felt like it was on fire, and his eyes burned.

"Find out where that bastard is by the time I get there, Heather. I'm three hours out, that should give you plenty of time. And gather up bail money, because I'll probably need it."

Ryan disconnected the phone and tried to breathe. Between his anger and his ribs that was nearly impossible. Flashes of that mystery man with his hands on Twyla like his stepfather had put his hands on Ryan's mother pierced his brain, and that old helpless rage returned.

First he was going to that hospital to check on Twyla, then he was going to find the man who put her there and that sonofabitch was going to be the one in the hospital by morning.

CHAPTER FOURTEEN

Twyla felt like she had lead weights on her eyes, and it took every ounce of her strength to breathe. Just lifting her chest to inhale was a chore. And the voices, the strange voices she'd been hearing for what seemed like hours now, were getting louder now. Angry voices. Wailing voices. They sounded familiar, but she couldn't wrap her mind around who those voices belonged to.

She wondered what the heck was happening to her. Her body felt like there was a rubberband stretched tight from her skull to her toes. If it snapped, her insides might shatter into a million pieces. And her damned head hurt. That damned beeping she had been hearing felt like nails being driven into her brain with each ping. She wished someone would cut whatever was causing it off.

"It was a roofie, a date rape drug. She was in and out when she was brought into the ER, so the police haven't had a chance to talk to her yet. I know you want the person responsible arrested, but we can't find out who that is until she wakes up. We've given her medication to counteract the effects of the drug, but it could take a while for her to come around. Her vitals are stable now with the added help breathing we've given her, sir. We're doing everything we can for your daughter, so please just relax."

"Was my daughter *raped*?!?" her daddy's voice

boomed. Twyla had finally placed his voice. Her daddy was there. She had missed him so much. Twyla was so glad he was there, because she really didn't feel good right now. He would hold her, and take care of her. Help her feel better. If she could just open her eyes, she would ask him to do that.

"No, sir! I told you that," the man replied, sounding frustrated. "She got away from her attacker and staggered into the bar before she passed out. Someone there brought her here, and it's a good thing they did. Is there someone coming to be with you, Mr. Taylor? I think you need someone here with you."

"My sons are on the way, and someone is driving my wife here. She was at a horse show, and too upset to drive herself."

"Good. I've got some things to do right now, but I will be closely monitoring Twyla's condition. If anything changes, I will let you know right away. The best thing you can do right now, Mr. Taylor, is relax. Take a deep breath, and keep it together so you can help your daughter when she does wake up."

"Easier said than done, doc. She took off from her brothers, set out on her own, against our wishes, and now look what's happened. We were already worried, and for good reason."

As it continued, Twyla could hear the conversation, but it was like it was coming to her from down a long, dark hallway, echoing in her head. Why the hell did she feel so weird? And sick? She felt like she wanted to throw up, but her throat was too numb to even gag.

Between the voices being muffled and that incessant beeping, Twyla gave up on trying to hear the conversation. She faded off into the darkness of the hallway, but as she drifted off she heard a new voice, Heather's voice, join the two men's. Heather didn't know her daddy though, so that couldn't be right. Peace settled through her, as Twyla heard her daddy's voice again. He would take care of her. She let herself float off into nothingness when it became too hard to think anymore.

When Ryan finally got to the hospital dawn was breaking. He didn't park when he reached the Emergency Room entrance parking lot, he pulled right up under the unloading canopy, and barely put his truck in park. He didn't have time for formality. Twyla was unconscious according to her father, who had called Zack, who had called him to tell him she wasn't doing well at all about an hour ago. Ryan was damned scared, as he flung open the truck door and sprinted through the double sliding doors.

A nurse looked up and smiled when he stopped at the counter in the ER, breathing hard. It took him a minute to force the words past the lump of fear in his throat. "Please tell me where Twyla Taylor is."

The nurse typed on her keyboard, stared at the screen a second, then typed again. Her eyes finally shot back to his. "She's been moved to ICU, sir, but…" She lifted her wrist to look at her watch. "But visiting hours aren't for another couple of hours.

Maybe you could have some coffee in the cafeteria."

Coffee hell, visiting hours be damned. Ryan was seeing Twyla. Now. Not in a couple of hours. Right this minute. "Thank you," Ryan said shortly, as he staggered down the corridor, following the signs until he stopped in front of a map of the hospital.

His finger traced the board, until he found the intensive care unit. Fifth floor, and the elevator just happened to be behind him on the other wall. He stabbed the button to call the elevator, then folded his arms over his chest. He was going up to that floor, and they would let him see her, or he would raise the roof on this place. There was no way he was leaving this hospital without seeing Twyla. Because after he did, there was no telling when he'd see her again. He'd probably be in jail, because he was finding the bastard who hurt her, and that man was going to learn to keep his hands off of women.

The elevator opened on the fifth floor and Ryan strode with purpose to the nurse's station. He slapped his hand down on the counter. "Where's Twyla Taylor?"

"Visiting isn't until eight," the nurse informed without looking up at him.

"I'm her goddamn fiance' and I want to see her *now*," he ground out. Ryan had thought of that tactic in the elevator. He knew they'd let family in. Well, he was family. As much as her brother was, as her daddy was and her mama. He loved her just as much.

"Don't curse at me, please," she said primly,

giving him the stink eye like his third grade teacher had done many times. She pointed her ink pen down the hall. "She's in room five ten, but someone is in with her now. We only allow one—" she started, but Ryan walked down the hall, his eyes fixed on the small placard outside of room five ten.

Ryan pushed through the door, and his eyes immediately landed on Twyla's pale face. The only color in her face was a purple bruise on her cheek in the shape of four fingers. One of her lifeless arms resting on top of the blanket was in a splint. Anger almost blew off the top of his head as he dragged his eyes to fix on her beautiful mouth, because her lower lip looked to be split. A damned tube separated her lips, and a machine whooshed beside the bed, evidently pumping oxygen into her lungs. Good God, she was on life support. His knees went weak, and a wail worked up from his toes to his throat to cut off his breath.

"What the hell are you doing here?" Carrick Taylor demanded, and Ryan's eyes swung up to meet those of Twyla's dad.

"Zack called me and told me Twyla was here. I had to come help."

His jaw tightened, and Ryan noticed Mr. Taylor's fists were clenched at his sides. "Well the kind of help you've been giving her, we don't need, son."

The hatred and anger in Mr. Taylor's voice stunned him. Ryan staggered back, and steadied himself with a hand on the door. "I love Twyla, sir. I came to find who did this to her and take care of it. He won't be hurting a woman again, and he definitely won't be hurting Twyla. Why are you angry at me?"

Mr. Taylor's lips curled, and he sauntered around the bed to stop in front of Ryan and put his finger in Ryan's chest. "You love her huh? Is that why you didn't tell Zack she was dancing at a titty bar, son? That she had gone hog ass wild and was going to clubs to meet strange men?"

He emphasized his words with a hard poke to Ryan's shoulder, and Ryan's heart lurched up to his throat. The cat was out of the bag. Evidently Heather had been here and gone. That was the only way he could've known. Ryan was going to kill her.

"*That* is why she's in this fix. Because you didn't think enough of us to tell us so we could stop it. If that's your definition of love, of caring for a family member, you definitely don't belong in this family." With a disgusted push against Ryan's chest, he spun and walked back to Twyla's bedside.

"I'm sorry, Mr. Taylor," Ryan croaked, holding back the bile that sautéed his heart in his throat. "I do l-l-ove her. Love y'all. The Crazy Cowgirl is not a strip club, sir, but I was still wrong not telling you."

Mr. Taylor spun and there were tears in his blue eyes. "Damn straight you were. You made a big mistake, boy. I trusted you, helped you when you were in trouble, and this is how you repay our family?"

"I'm sorry, sir." Ryan was so damned sorry.

He'd not only hurt Twyla, allowed her to be hurt, he'd hurt the man he considered a father. God only knew what Zack would want to do to him when he saw him. Ryan would deserve every damned blow, would probably stand there and let his friend beat the shit out of him, if it would fix this situation. Ryan was damned scared nothing would though. These people he loved like his own hated him now. Nothing short of him ceasing to breathe was going to fix the situation.

And he might just do that when Zack got ahold of him.

Ryan should have told them what Twyla was doing. Mr. Taylor was right, this was all his fault. But he had to try to talk to Twyla, before he left. His eyes fixed on her pale, still face again, and he swallowed down the despair trying to overwhelm him.

"Sir, could I please have a minute with Twy to...to..." His voice cracked, and Ryan sucked in a sharp breath through his burning nose. "To say goodbye to her?"

"I'll tell her you came by and said goodbye," he replied gruffly. "If she ever wakes up."

Ryan couldn't help the whimper that came from his throat, any more than he could stop the tears that overflowed his lower lids to burn twin trails down his face. "Did they say she might not wake up?" *Please God, let her wake up.*

"That's none of your damned business now. Just get your ass back on the circuit and forget we ever existed. Leave us in peace."

Ryan's phone rang in his pocket, and his eyes flew to the sign on the wall saying they weren't allowed to be used inside the room. He fumbled behind him for the handle to the door and pushed it down. "I'll be back to check on her once things settle down," he said jerking the door open to stagger into the hallway.

His eyes fell on another no cell phone sign, and he all but ran for the elevator. Pulling the phone from his pocket, he saw it was Zack. He didn't have the guts to talk to him. There wasn't anything Zack could say to him that would make him feel worse than he did right now. And honestly, he wasn't in any shape for the confrontation right now.

One thing he could do for his surrogate family though was get retribution from the man who hurt Twyla. Because he needed to. It wouldn't even begin to repair the damage he'd caused though, nothing would. Ryan had fucked up the best thing that ever happened to him for good, but at least that would give him an outlet for the rage burning inside him. And maybe it would give the family some kind of relief from their own rage at him.

Ryan walked out of the sliding doors at the front of the emergency room, and his truck was not there. Could things get any worse for him today? His damned truck had evidently been towed with his wallet inside. He only realized his cell phone was in his hand when it rang. It was probably Zack again, he thought, and went to push the ignore button. Instead, it was Heather, so he pushed talk. "You have totally fucked me," he growled before she could speak, as he walked over to a bench beside the door to sit down.

"No, that's Twyla's job. Be thankful I didn't tell them that though. They're pissed, but maybe you can talk your way out of it. If I'd have added that other little tidbit about you sleeping with her, you'd probably be in the hospital with Twyla."

"She's in a coma!" Ryan shouted into the phone.

"She's not in a coma. They have her sedated for the ventilator until the drugs Jared gave her wear off and she can breathe on her own again."

"Drugs?" Ryan repeated, shooting to his feet.

"He slipped her a roofie."

"I'm going to kill that bastard," Ryan growled, taking deep breaths as his heart tried to beat out of his chest. "Where the fuck is he?"

"The police are trying to find him. I talked to them at the hospital and gave them as much information as I could. I haven't been able to find Leon yet to see if he can tell me more. He's not usually up until after noon."

"You know where Leon lives? I'll wake him up, and he will tell us where to find that slimy friend of his, or I'll peel his fucking skin off."

"Calm down, tiger," Heather said with a laugh that inched Ryan's anger up a notch. This woman didn't seem to know exactly how bad this situation was. "Don't bite the hand that can help us. Leon can't stand Jared either. Just puts up with him, because…well, I don't know why exactly, but he does."

"I need a ride. My truck's been towed and my damned wallet is in it."

"Where are you?" Heather asked.

"Outside the front of the hospital. I need to get out of here before Zack gets here, or there won't be anything left of me to take care of Jared Wilkins. I'll meet you on the west side of the hospital." If he stayed outside the emergency room, he knew he'd run into Zack.

"Twyla's brother?" Heather asked with a laugh. "You scared of him? He's not all that big and bad. He's just an uptight asshole."

"No, I'm not scared of him, I just don't want to fight with him. That man is as close to a brother as I'll ever get. And he is not an uptight asshole, Zack is just…" Well, Ryan had to admit Zack could be an uptight asshole at times.

Heather laughed. "I'm on my way. Ten minutes."

The line disconnected, and Ryan shoved his phone in his pocket. His eyes snagged on a familiar truck waiting in line to turn into the parking lot, and quickened his steps. He flew around the corner, and stood with his back against the wall between a row of tall hedges. He didn't let down his guard until nine minutes later Heather's truck rounded the corner and stopped. He saw her looking around the lot, and stepped out of the bushes. He glanced around himself for Zack as he walked to the truck and got inside.

"Whew, that was close," he said resting his head on the back of the seat.

"You really are a chicken, aren't you?" Heather needled, as she put the truck in gear. "I'm glad I could come and save your sorry ass. It's worth it to see you like this, Mr. Bad Ass Cowboy." Heather leaned forward over the wheel to look left and right, before merging into traffic, then looked over at him with a smug grin. "I'll loan you my mace if it'll make you feel better."

"I'm not a fucking chicken. My ribs are busted! I got stomped on by a damned bronc last night. I don't need to be stomped on by Zack too," Ryan growled, pinning her with a lethal stare.

This woman was just irritating, and aggravating and seemed to enjoy it. She had no filter between her brain and damned mouth. Either that or she really didn't give a shit what people thought of her. A lot like Twyla, but at least Twyla had more couth and somewhat of a filter. Not much more, but some. Twyla teased him as well, where Heather didn't, she was just brash and abrasive. Heather wasn't flirty at all, thank God. That was one woman he wouldn't touch with a ten foot pole. But Twyla he would touch, ten times today and twice on Sunday.

Ryan's feelings for the beautiful woman he'd tried to think of as a sister for so long had definitely transitioned into more. It was more than brotherly, more than hot sex. Since Twyla had been gone he realized something. When she wasn't around, he just didn't feel right. When she left him, it seemed like she had pulled the spark plug out of his life. He was still living it, he just had no pep or energy. Like the broncs he spurred to get reactions and more points from during his ride, Twyla spurred him. That's exactly what it was like. She spurred him to do better, be better and face and feel things he'd otherwise hide from.

Like the fact that he'd been in love with the girl for ten years.

Ryan was going to do something about that, just as soon as he fixed this and the slight problem that her family now hated him. They were a very close family unit. Having any kind of relationship with Twyla would be impossible unless he convinced the Taylors he wasn't the scum of the earth.

They drove a few minutes, then Heather picked up her cell phone from the console and cursed. "I was going to try to call Leon again, but my phone is dead. I forgot to pick up my charger on the way out the door."

Ryan lifted up and pulled his out of his pocket. He shoved it at her. "Use mine."

That would give him Leon's number too, so if he had to track the man down later himself he could. Another avenue to get in touch with Twyla too, just in case. He hoped he never had to call that man though. Ryan was going to do his best to make sure Twyla never stepped foot in the Crazy Cowgirl again. Maybe she would listen now, because of what happened to her. If he couldn't convince her, maybe her family could. Since they knew now, maybe she would feel differently about working there.

He sure as hell hoped that was the case.

Heather dialed, cradled the phone to her ear, and whistled. Ryan's eyes shot over to her, as she said, "Thank, God, Leon. I thought I was going to have to get a bloodhound to find you. I need to know where I can find Jared Wilkins."

She pursed her mouth and listened for a minute, and Ryan held his breath.

"I know I don't need to be around him, but he tried to rape Twyla last night. I need to find him."

More silence followed that inched up Ryan's agitation to know what was going on.

"Leon, I'm not going to do anything stupid. The cops need to know where he is so they can arrest his scummy ass." She rolled her eyes, and then said, "I can't help it if he has photos. You'll just have to deal with Layla if it happens. But I promise I won't tell him you told."

Huffing out a breath, Heather pushed the button to disconnect the call, and threw the phone into the console of the dash. "Damn, Leon and the shit he gets himself into," she grumbled. "He's a good man mostly, he's just stupid like most men are."

Heather sure had a low opinion of the male gender. Ryan wondered what in the hell had happened to her to cause it, but he had other things to worry about. Like what information she'd gotten from Leon. "What the hell was that about?" Ryan sat up straighter in his seat, and turned to face her. "Did you find out where Wilkins is?"

"Yeah, I found out. Bastard must shit where he sleeps. He has a trailer parked behind his strip club."

It didn't matter to Ryan, but he was too curious not to ask. "What was that he said about photos?"

Heather glanced at him and frowned. "None of your business," she said shortly. "Doesn't have anything to do with this situation. Besides, we have more important things to discuss." She glanced over at him with a mischievous grin stretching her full lips. "I think I know how we can keep you out of jail, but still pay that asshole back."

Because of what happened with his stepfather previously, serving time was a very real possibility if he got caught this time. He wasn't keen on spending time in jail or adding to his record, but he wasn't letting that stop him. One way or another he was going to stomp Jared Wilkins ass into the ground. But if Heather had other ideas, he was definitely going listen.

"Spill it. I'm listening."

CHAPTER FIFTEEN

Something was wrong. Twyla's throat hurt, and she felt like her head was stuffed with cotton. Every inch of her body hurt. Did she have the flu? She didn't remember being sick. But her brain was so foggy, she didn't remember much anyway. Dragging her eyes open, it felt to her like sandpaper lined the inside of her eyelids. They scraped as she pried them open.

The first thing she saw was a man in a white coat leaning over her. Next her eyes slid to the man standing beside him with tears in his eyes. Her daddy. She'd never seen him cry before, but slow tears rolled down his face.

Fear shot through her. Had somebody died? She tried to talk, but nothing would come out. Her hand flew up to her throat to massage her vocal chords.

"Water," she managed to croak. Her throat felt raw, and slick it was so dry.

A glass immediately appeared on her left side, held by her mother. Twyla reached for it, but couldn't lift her arm. She looked down and saw her left arm was in a splint. Her eyebrows pinched as she reached her right hand across her body to take the glass. She put the cup to her lips and drank greedily. The water flowed down her throat reviving it like the brown grass of winter by the first spring rain. She drank the last drop, then tried to smile, but her lips felt cracked, so she flattened them back out.

What the hell happened to her?

"Where am I?" she asked, looking past her mother at the supply station against the wall. She was evidently in the hospital for some reason.

"You don't remember what happened?" her daddy asked, seeming a little relieved.

Twyla searched her blank memory and nodded. Whatever it was must've been bad gauging from the look on her daddy's face.

"That's typical, Mr. Taylor," the doctor interjected, then cleared his throat. "The drug she was given causes that. But the good news, it's out of her system now. Her memory will improve, and she'll regain her strength very fast—"

"*Drug*?!?" Twyla screeched, trying to sit up, but then falling back against the pillow.

"Yeah, darlin'. Some bastard gave you a roofie."

Twyla had heard that term at the bar before. Had been warned never to take drinks from anyone other than the bartender, and to never leave it unattended on a table or the bar. Her mind ticked back to the last thing she could remember. She'd gone out to watch Heather's gig, and had had a beer, but she had bought it, drank it at the table. Then that agent had bought her a beer.

Good God had that man drugged her?

"Jared slipped something in my beer?" she asked incredulously.

"He did more than that, sweetie," her mother

said, her hand dropping on Twyla's shoulder. "But you're alive. That's what's important. The police will get him."

"How did I get banged up?" Twyla focused on her lower regions and didn't feel sore there, so she figured she at least wasn't raped.

Her daddy's lips wobbled, and he cleared his throat. "He assaulted you in the parking lot of his strip bar, and you fought back." He ran his hand over his beard-roughened face, and a tremor shook him. "I'm so proud of you, baby girl. You got yourself out of what could've been a very bad situation. If Ryan had told us what you were doing before now, none of this would've happened."

A shot of adrenaline when through her, and Twyla wasn't foggy anymore. "What I was doing?" she asked, playing dumb, because she prayed it wasn't what she thought. Oh, God. Her daddy knew she'd been dancing at the Crazy Cowgirl, and Lord only knew what else, if Ryan was the one doing the telling, and it looked like he was.

Twyla glanced at her mother, and those blue eyes that usually held patience and love, narrowed and heated. "Don't play dumb, Twy—we know what you've been doing." Her gaze darted to her husband across the bed, then she looked back at Twyla. "You should be ashamed of yourself. I know we raised you better than that. Your grandmother is going to be very disappointed when she hears too."

If Ryan had told us before now what you were doing...

Twyla was sure he hadn't sold himself out though by telling them he was her first lover, had used his knowledge of her dancing to try and blackmail her into having sex with him.

Blinding anger hitched a ride with the adrenaline coursing through her. Telling them was right on the tip of her tongue. But she stopped herself, because that would most likely mean none of them would ever speak to him again. And having *any* kind of relationship with the man would be impossible. She just couldn't make herself do that.

One thing was for sure though. Ryan Easter needed to choose a side, either brother or lover. Riding the fence had just gotten splinters in his ass. Twyla was choosing the side for him now. Brother. She was done with that man as anything other than that. And the brother role was even questionable now. If she got her hands on him, she was most likely going to kill him, or at least make him wish he were dead.

Another thought hit Twyla.

If her parents knew, the odds were Zack knew too. He was probably twice as mad as her parents. The odds were he was hunting down Ryan right now. Another layer of fear plopped down on the mountain in her chest. Her brother could be a bear sometimes, especially when it came to her. If Zack knew too, Ryan could very well be getting his ass kicked somewhere.

Both of them would likely end up in jail, or right here in this hospital bed with her. They had rodeo careers to think of, but she knew from past experience that wasn't their first concern when they were pissed at each other.

"Where are Zack and Ryan?"

"Ryan Easter is dead to this family. He is no longer welcome in our home," her father replied angrily. "Your brother is out helping the police try to find the man who assaulted you."

Twyla's heart jerked in her chest, and emotion surged up to her eyes. Her daddy was serious about cutting Ryan from the family. She was pissed at him, but she couldn't let that happen. He'd been through too much in his life.

"Daddy, I asked him not to tell," she said taking the bullet for him.

"That doesn't make a hill of beans, daughter. He had a responsibility to this family, and he knew better. He made a choice, and needs to face the consequences of that choice. He's a grown man and your safety and our sanity should've been his first concern, if he was concerned at all about our family, which he was not."

Frustration took the lead in the emotions fighting for control inside of Twyla. "Daddy, I wasn't doing a damned thing illegal or immoral at that bar. I was dancing, and making good money. I had to find something to do when I quit racing."

"Well, if you don't see that it was wrong, that's a problem. There were plenty of other choices you could have made too, Twyla Renee," he said with disappointment in his tone.

God, she hated that tone. Twyla had heard it enough in her life to know it when she heard it. And the two-name thing magnified it tenfold. This fight would be better left for another day, when her family wasn't so upset. She'd let them cool off, and try again.

"Mr. Taylor," the doctor said putting his hand on her father's shoulder. "I'm going to sign Twyla's release papers. She's going to feel better tomorrow, but she needs to take it easy for at least a couple of weeks. Her arm should be ready to take the splint off then. The nurse will give you more instructions when she comes in."

Why was this man talking to her daddy, when she was a grown woman, over the age of majority, who was responsible for taking care of herself now?

The doctor stuck his hand out and her daddy took it. "Thank you for everything, doc. I'm sorry if I got a little agitated with you before."

The doctor laughed. "You're not the first. When our kids are in trouble, it's understandable. Call me if you need anything." With a sympathetic smile and a final shake of hands, the doctor turned and walked to the door.

Kid? Twyla was a kid?

That was the problem here. Had been the problem for years. Her family thought she was a kid, her brother thought she was a kid, and Ryan Easter, even though he knew firsthand she wasn't, thought she was a child. Someone weak who needed protecting and directing. Yeah, she'd gotten herself into a bad situation, because she'd been stupid. It could have turned out bad. But she wasn't a child. The decision to walk out of that bar with Jared Wilkins had been hers to make. Shock rocked her when she realized she'd remembered she'd done that.

Twyla huffed out a breath, and closed her eyes trying to remember more, but nothing would come. Maybe she'd eventually remember. And maybe Ryan wouldn't end up in a coffin, and Zack in prison. While she had her eyes closed, she said a silent prayer that was the case.

"We're taking you back to the ranch with us so you can recover," her father said shortly, and Twyla's eyes flew open.

Twyla stiffened her chin, and shored up her confidence. This was the first time in her life she'd ever stood up to her parents. "I have a shooting competition this weekend, but I won't be able to go because of my arm. I'm still going to watch, and can practice for the one in two weeks. Besides, Tango is here. I can't leave him. I'm not leaving."

"You are leaving little girl. Your mother will help you get dressed, and I'm going to pull the truck around to the front of the hospital. We'll stop to pick up Tango on the way out and haul him home."

"I'm not going anywhere, daddy," Twyla replied firmly. "I'm going to my apartment until I get back on my feet, and I'm going to stay here and train for the mounted shooting competition. That's what I want to do with my life now, and I'm going to do it."

Her father's head rocked back on his

shoulders and he looked both angry and surprised. "You're getting very big for your britches there, little girl."

"My britches fit just fine, daddy. I'm not a little girl anymore. I'm glad y'all care about me, and came to take care of me, but I've got it now. I'm not ashamed of what I was doing at the Cowgirl, and I'm not going to apologize. I was being an adult, figuring things out for myself. I learned a lesson with Jared that I won't forget. But I need you to let me grow up and learn those lessons myself." Her eyes darted to her mother who was quietly weeping. Twyla's heart squeezed, but she knew she had to do this while she had a head of steam worked up. "I just need all of you to let me grow up." She smiled at her father. "But I would appreciate a ride to my apartment on your way out. I don't have my truck here."

A weight lifted off of Twyla's chest and she felt like she could breathe a little better. Finally, she could breathe. And live her life the way she wanted to live it. An overwhelming sense of freedom made her feel a little giddy, as she tossed back the covers and sat on the edge of the bed. Things happened for a reason. Twyla didn't want what happened with Jared Wilkins to happen, but she was almost glad it did. This was the first day of the rest of her life.

The first day she didn't answer to a soul but herself and God.

***

Ryan watched as Heather bent to grab her bag from beside his leg and rifle through it. When she raised back up, she smiled and held her hand up to him. "You remember what this looks like, don't you, big boy?"

"Oh, yeah, I remember," Ryan replied, rolling down the passenger side window of the truck so he could hear if she screamed. "Just don't let him take it from you like I did. Stay back." He wasn't sold on this harebrained plan of Heather's, but it looked like she wasn't giving him much choice. He'd tried to tell her he could handle it just fine alone, but his words had fallen on deaf ears. Her response was it was either her way, or she was calling the police to let them know exactly where Jared Wilkins was staying.

If she did that, Ryan wouldn't have the chance to get his hands on the man before they hauled him off to jail. There was no way Ryan was going to let that happen. Ryan heard the quiet hum of the air conditioner inside the small Airstream trailer. "And make sure you're not downwind of the air conditioner, or you'll wind up with a noseful of it too."

"Yes, daddy," Heather replied with a snort, as she opened the door of the truck. She looked back at him one last time. "If you hear him screaming, just stay where you are. I have a few things to teach Mr. Wilkins, before I give you what's left."

"Just do what you're gonna do, and call me."

She laughed as she hopped to the ground, then shut the door. Ryan watched Heather stop to jerk her short top down further, and push her breasts up into more cleavage, and just shook his head. She stuffed the can of mace into her pocket and wiped hands on her very short shorts, before walking up to the trailer door to knock. Ryan ducked down below the dash, so Wilkins wouldn't see him when he opened the door. He just hoped Heather could convince him to leave the door open so he could hear.

Ryan waited until he thought she was inside then took a peek over the dash. Sitting upright, he tuned his ears into the faint words of the conversation going on inside the trailer.

"Hey, honey. I saw you at the Rooster last night. Why didn't you stick around to talk to me? I saw you leave with Twyla and was a little jealous," Heather purred, and Ryan could imagine her raking her fingernail down his chest. Don't get too close darlin', he thought, his fists clenching. "Did you come to hear me sing?"

"Yeah, I have someone interested in signing you. But I think I need a little more convincing, before I recommend you."

"Well, I have another gig set up for next weekend. You could come see me," Heather said, ignoring the slimy undertone in Jared Wilkin's words that Ryan heard clearly. The convincing Wilkins wanted involved her with her knees beside her ears. Anger made him almost light headed, as Ryan's hand shot to the door handle.

"I had a little something else in mind, beautiful," Wilkins drawled, and there was silence for a second.

"Get your damned hands off of me!" Heather yelled loudly. Ryan opened the truck door, ready to run in there and beat the ever living shit out of that slimy bastard, but then he heard a grunt, a loud squeal, followed by loud moans and another grunt or two.

From the sound of it, if Ryan didn't get in there, there wouldn't be anything left for him. It sounded like Heather was killing the bastard. The trailer actually rocked a few times, before she appeared at the door grinning widely to wave him inside.

Ryan held back a laugh as he jogged to the door. "Help! He assaulted me, and I think he's getting up again," Heather said in a distressed voice, followed by a chuckle.

She moved aside so Ryan could enter the nasty trailer. It smelled like sex and stale beer. A perfect combination to inflame Ryan to the point of murdering the bastard.

He walked over to the built-in table and jerked Wilkins to his feet. The man moved his hands from his eyes to push on Ryan's chest, giving him the perfect opening to plant his fist in the man's face. Ryan jerked him up again, then spun him around to hold him against the wall, while he landed blow after blow. With every punch he landed, every pained grunt he made, Ryan's anger inched down a notch.

Before he knocked him unconscious though, which seemed to be very close, Ryan wanted to let the man know exactly what the beating was for. Holding

Wilkins up by the throat, Ryan kept him on his feet against the wall. "If you ever get the urge to do to another woman what you did to the one I love, you remember this," Ryan growled, before he landed a quick, but deadly punch to Jared Wilkin's nose. He heard a sickening crunch, and the man's body went limp.

Ryan eased his grip on the bastard's throat and let his body slide down the wall to the ground. His head lolled over to rest on his chest, and his nose bled profusely. Ryan's adrenaline finally cleared a little, and a dull pain shot through his ribs. He grabbed them, and looked at Heather, who was leaning in the doorway with her nose stuck out into the fresh air. He needed some fresh air too.

"Although, I'd like to leave the bastard here to bleed to death, call the police and an ambulance." Ryan stopped to grab a towel off the counter. He wiped his bloody knuckles, and then threw it in the tiny sink.

"Okay," Heather said pushing off to walk down the two steps. Ryan followed behind her, and stood by the front of the truck, while she made the call. Once it was done, she walked around to lean beside him on the truck. "So you love Twyla, huh?"

"Doesn't matter if I do or don't. Her family hates me now, and she probably does too," he said pushing away from the truck. He took one step back toward the trailer when he heard his ring tone. He spun back toward Heather, who was staring at the screen of his phone, which was in her hand. "Says, mom," she said with a curious smile, as she held it out to him.

CHAPTER SIXTEEN

Ryan ran over and snatched the phone from Heather's hand. His hand shook as he fumbled for the talk button, and his heart pounded in his chest. Something had to have happened, and whatever it was it probably wasn't good.

"Mom?" he said around the knot in his throat.

"No, this is Montgomery County Hospital. Is this Ryan Easter?"

After a dull thud in his chest, Ryan's heart sank to his toes and settled there. "Yes, ma'am, this is he," Ryan replied breathlessly.

"Sir, I need you to come here as soon as possible. We have your mother here and need to talk to her next of kin. We found your number in her cell phone."

The rage he'd just moved beyond by pummeling Jared Wilkins came right back, bigger and brighter than it had been before. This had to have something to do with the bastard who was his stepfather. If it didn't, Clarence James would be there with her and they wouldn't be calling him.

"Is my stepfather there?"

"Um, uh, no sir," the nurse replied hesitantly. "How long will it be before you get here?"

"I'm up by Dallas, so probably several hours, but I'm on my way."

"The sooner the better, please."

"Yes, ma'am," Ryan said, hanging up the

phone with the sick feeling in his gut telling him whatever he found at that hospital wasn't going to be good. The bastard had finally done it. He'd killed Ryan's mother. A tremor rocked through him, and Ryan grabbed the truck as his knees went weak.

"Hey, what's wrong?" Heather asked, putting a hand on his arm.

"My mom is bad off and I have to get to Houston. Can you take me to get my truck?"

"Where is it?" Heather asked, sliding her hand to his back when his knees tried to buckle again.

"I don't' know." Right now Ryan didn't know much of anything, other than round two of his shitty day was about to begin. And his stepfather was likely to end up worse off than Jared Wilkins before this day ended.

"What do you mean you don't know?"

"The hospital had it towed, and I don't know where it is." Ryan swung his gaze to hers, as desperation gathered inside him. "I've got to get to Houston."

"I can take you, but we really should wait for the police," Heather said.

Just that quick, Ryan had forgotten about the police that were on their way. His priority, his whole life had shifted with one phone call.

"I've got to get to Houston," he repeated, scrolling through his phone looking for a number to a cab company. "I'll call a cab or—" Ryan looked up when he heard tires squealing on asphalt. As if things couldn't get worse, Zack's pickup slid to a stop beside

Heather's and before it even stopped, he flew out of the door and ran full out toward Ryan.

The look on his face said that Ryan was about to join his mother in Heaven very shortly. Right now, that might be the best place for him. It was a lot better than the hell of this reality. With a deep sigh, Ryan handed his phone to Heather, waiting for it.

Sirens blared in the distance, just as Zack took a flying leap at him. The impact jarred his teeth, then Zack landed on top of him on the ground. Ryan lost his breath, as his bruised ribs crushed inward. Zack landed a blow to his chin that stunned him. Ryan sucked in a breath finally, and gathered his strength to push upward and roll Zack under him. He wasn't going to hit him, but he did try to hold him down. That didn't work long, Ryan saw the world spin as Zack rolled him again, and delivered another blow to his jaw.

Ryan lifted his arms to shield his face, just as another punch landed. At least it landed on his forearm instead of his just now healing eye. Or worse his barely healed nose. "Stop it, Zack!" he growled.

"Stop hell, I'm just getting started, asshole!" Zack shouted and tried to pry Ryan's arms from his face.

"Zack, get your ass off of him!" Heather shouted. Over the blood pounding in his ears, Ryan heard loud sirens, tires on gravel, then running feet.

"Step back ma'am," a firm authoritative voice, that could only belong to a cop, said.

"You two turn over on your bellies and put

your hands over your heads. *Now.*"

Breathing hard, Zack shot him a glare then slid off of him. Ryan rolled, and groaned as a shot of pain sliced through his ribcage. He spread his hands over his head and waited for the cold steel bracelets he knew were coming.

Fuck this was not what he needed right now. His mother was in a hospital and he was going to jail. He could feel the tension in the arm that jerked his up behind his back, before the cold metal touched his skin. It looked like he and Heather's plan had worked perfectly, but they hadn't figured on one thing. Zack showing up at exactly the wrong time to throw a wrench into things.

"Which one of these two assaulted you ma'am?" the policeman asked as he jerked Ryan up to his feet.

"Neither of them. The guy in the trailer assaulted me."

"Another one?" The cop asked with a groan. "Looks like y'all are all going to jail until we figure this out." He pushed Ryan toward his squad car, and he stumbled. He glanced back and saw Zack being pushed toward another car, as the ambulance pulled up and skidded to a stop in front of the trailer.

The cop turned him sideways and Ryan stepped in, as the cop pushed the top of his head down to shove him inside. Ryan got settled and the door shut. Through the tempered glass, he saw Heather talking to one of the cops with her hands waving and her neck rocking. He wouldn't be surprised if the mouthy brunette wound up in a cell beside his. The cop she was talking to didn't look too happy.

Ryan groaned and laid his head against the seat to close his eyes. This was a nightmare. It had to be. Nobody could have a day like this. He needed to find out how Twyla was doing, if they were going to release her from the hospital. But that wasn't his business now. Her daddy wasn't going to let him see her again. He needed to focus on getting his ass out of jail and getting to Houston for his mother. But he didn't even have his wallet to bail himself out. It was in the truck they towed. He was screwed and would probably be spending the night in jail at least.

Frustration built inside of him, and Ryan fought the burning behind his eyelids. All he could do is go along for the ride on this runaway train. He wasn't in control. He could only roll with the punches, and deal with what he could control. Right now that was keeping himself from bawling like a baby, and feeling sorry for himself. That wasn't going to get him anywhere.

The cop who'd stuffed him in the car finally got into the front seat. With a glance at him in the mirror he cranked the car, mumbled something into the radio, then Ryan was on his way to the pokey. As they pulled out he saw the medics carrying Jared Wilkins out of the trailer on a stretcher. The man still didn't seem to be moving, and Ryan prayed he was just hurt, and that in his rage he hadn't killed the slimy bastard. If he was dead, Ryan had no hope of getting out of jail anytime soon. He'd probably be spending the rest of his life in prison.

Please don't let him be dead.

***

Twyla had just settled on the loveseat with a sandwich and a soda, when loud knocking came at her door. If it was the landlord she had a few things to say to that man. She was not going to pay him two-hundred dollars a week for a place that smelled like a ferret. He was going to clean her damned carpet. After her fallout with her parents, when they saw how and where she was living, she was primed for it. Because of it, her daddy tried to force her back to the ranch, had actually started pulling her clothes out of her closet, when her mother finally stopped him.

Thank God, her mother had a little sense and at least she realized Twyla was a grown woman. It had taken both of them to get her father back in his truck, so they could leave. Twyla hadn't been in any shape to deal with that, and she still wasn't. There wasn't a damn soul she wanted to see right now. Not Ryan, certainly not Zack or her parents.

Twyla just wanted to be left alone.

That damned interrogation the police had put her through before she left the hospital had taken every ounce of energy she had left. She couldn't handle anything else right now. All she wanted was this sandwich, a nap and a little peace. Whoever was at the door could just go away. She was not answering that door.

The knocking continued, so Twyla reached for the remote for the new television her daddy had brought back as a peace offering. She turned the volume up as far as it would go, then tossed the remote on the table. She imagined her mother was behind that gift, but she was thankful to whomever decided to get it for her. At least now she'd have something to do other than watch the wallpaper at the corner of the kitchenette slowly peel away from the wall.

Twyla didn't hear the knocking any more now, but she imagined the people in the house next door would complain to the landlord about the Jerry Springer free-for-all blaring from her apartment. Jerry Springer had nothing on her life lately though. The show that usually made her feel better about her own life, was making her want to cry today.

Her life was such a damned mess. Twyla had no idea how she was going to fix things either. She was out of the dancing business, out of the shooting business too for at least two weeks. Two weeks of no income would mean she'd probably be kicked out of this nasty little apartment. Then her life would really be at rock bottom.

Who got kicked out of an apartment like this?

Someone who should be on the Jerry Springer show, instead of sitting here watching it on the television. Maybe she could pawn the new TV to get through this week at least. Her rent was due on Friday. She'd just have a Jerry Springer-fest until then.

God she was bored already. And to make matters worse, she discovered after she got home she was freaking out of Twinkies. Hell, the next two weeks were going to be sheer hell.

The window beside the door rattled from the knocking now. With a sigh, Twyla sat her sandwich plate on the end table and walked to the door. Twyla glanced out the window and saw it was Heather on her doorstep. She flipped the locks and swung the door inward.

"I'm getting damned tired of standing on your doorstep while you ignore me," Heather grated as she pushed her way inside. "I went to the hospital and you were discharged already. I figured you'd be here."

Twyla snorted, and walked back to the sofa. She picked up her sandwich and sat down. "I wouldn't be here if my parents had their way. They tried to drag me back home," she said then took a big bite of her sandwich.

"Well it's a good thing you're here. I need help untangling the damned mess your brother and Ryan have gotten themselves into."

Twyla stopped with the sandwich halfway to her mouth. "What do they have to do with me? What they do or who they do it with is not my problem. They can untangle their own messes from here on out. I'm looking out for me from now on," Twyla informed, lifting her chin. She dragged her eyes back to her sandwich, and took another bite then chewed it angrily.

"Turn down that damned TV!" Heather shouted, grabbing the remote, before Twyla could. She pressed the off button, then threw it back down "You have enough of your own drama going on. You don't need to watch that crap. And now I'm right in the middle of it, thank you so much."

"What do you mean?" Twyla asked angrily. "It was pretty damned peaceful until you got here." Finally peaceful. Boring as shit, but peaceful. Twyla took another nibble off the corner of her sandwich. She was not going to let herself get upset again.

"Your brother and Ryan are in jail. Are you sitting here telling me you don't give a shit?"

The bite of sandwich turned to sawdust in Twyla's mouth. She grabbed her soda and took a long drink. "In jail?" she asked incredulously.

"Yeah, I just thought you'd want to know. But if you don't care, I sure as heck don't. I'll just be going," Heather replied shortly, as she turned to walk back toward the door.

"*Wait!*" Twyla yelled and left her sandwich on the sofa to follow Heather.

Heather stopped at the door, and turned back toward her with her arms folded over her chest. "What? I have things to do."

"What happened?" Twyla's voice shook, because she just couldn't maintain her front any longer. Especially when both Ryan and her brother were in jail. Probably because they'd been fighting over her. But that wasn't her fault. They were grown men, stupid, but grown. Way past the age they should be fighting over anything. But secretly she hoped Zack got a few good blows in, because Ryan deserved everything he got for telling her parents what he had.

Heather huffed out a breath. "You better sit down, because this isn't a short story."

Fifteen minutes later, Twyla took a drink of soda, because her heart was in her throat. "Ryan's mother is in the hospital?" she asked, swallowing again. Ryan had a rough childhood. Zack didn't tell her all of it, but he told her enough. His stepfather liked to use his mother as a punching bag. "What's wrong with her?"

"I don't know but he was pretty shook up after he got that call."

"And now he's stuck in jail?"

Heather nodded, her face grave, and Twyla's heart bounced back up to her throat. Ryan was in jail, because of her damned brother, and because he had been beating up the man who had assaulted her. As far as Twyla was concerned, that wasn't a crime.

In the police's eyes though, she was sure it was. But he and Heather would have gotten away with it, if her brother hadn't shown up there and attacked Ryan. Zack needed to stay out of her business too, and she needed to tell him the same thing she'd told her parents.

If she needed them, she would call them. Butt out otherwise.

Twyla glanced at her new television, then back at Heather. "How much is the bail?"

Heather shrugged. "I didn't stop by the jail, but if that cop was right, Ryan was getting charged with two counts of assault. I tried to tell the bastard cop that Jared had assaulted me, and Ryan had only defended me. I also told him that Zack had attacked Ryan first, he had only been defending himself. His response was that the judge would sort it out."

Twyla stood and brushed the crumbs off of her shirt. "Let's go find out what his bail is and figure out how we can scrape it up," she said calmly. "We need to get his truck out of impound too, because he might have some money in there. I'm not letting him go to Houston by himself either, if he's upset. That situation isn't good, and he could wind up in hot water down there too if he goes by himself. Zack said Ryan's stepdaddy has a restraining order against him."

"Really? Girl, you just got out of the hospital. You don't need to be going anywhere. I just came by here to tell you what was going on, since you don't have a damned phone. I can handle getting them, or at least Ryan, out of jail. I found some pictures that Leon wants."

"I'm fine. I've had worse from falling off my horse during a ride..." Twyla started, but her eyes flew up. "What kind of pictures?"

"Pictures of him and some woman who isn't his wife doing the nasty. Pictures that Jared has been using to blackmail him for years. It took me a while to find them, but that freezer had lots of other photos in it too. Awful, degrading stuff. Most of the women looked to be drugged or unconscious. They may have even been strippers at his club. I took the ones I wanted and called the police to come and get the rest."

Anger and fear shot through Twyla, making her knees weak. Those photos could have been of her, if she hadn't fought him, and succeeded in getting away. That is the bastard who should be locked up in jail. Not Ryan. "Where's Jared now?"

Heather laughed. "Probably in the hospital wishing he'd never met me or Ryan. He was in bad shape when they hauled his sorry ass off."

"Good, I hope they arrest him as soon as he opens his eyes. They sure grilled me for information long enough after I was released."

"Could you tell them anything?"

"No, I can't remember. The doctor said it was from the drugs he gave me. He said I might remember later, but as of right now, I just remember leaving the bar."

Heather's eyes clouded, and she hugged Twyla, then stepped back. "You're damned lucky you're a fighter. It could've been bad."

"I know, and I'll be smarter next time. He told me he was an agent and had a big contract he was thinking of recommending you for. I was trying to help."

"He's an agent alright. An agent of evil. I would rather sing in dives for the rest of my life than ever have him on my team." Heather put her hand on Twyla's shoulder. "Thanks for the thought, but I'll make it when I make it. You just stand back and watch."

"You work so damned hard. You deserve it, and I can't wait til it happens for you."

"We both work hard and deserve our successes. Just remember don't put your dreams on hold for a man. I made that mistake once. If I hadn't I might already be there."

"Got it." Twyla read between the lines of what her friend was saying. Don't give up her dreams to chase Ryan, or put her life on hold for him. It was a good message, because that's exactly what Twyla had been doing for ten years. But she was past that stage now. Her dream of doing cowboy mounted shooting was delayed a couple of weeks, but it was going to happen.

Twyla had a couple of weeks now though to help Ryan with whatever problem he had with his mother to pay him back for defending her. After that they'd be even, and Twyla was coming back here to resume her new life without Ryan Easter.

"Ryan came to my defense, now it's my turn to help him. I can't dance or shoot right now anyway," she said with a laugh. "If I stay here and stare at the walls, I'll go nuts."

Maybe those two weeks would give her time to say goodbye too. Something she hadn't done when she left the rodeo, and him. That was the adult thing to do. Bury the hatchet, and leave without regrets. Twyla thought she could do that now that her initial anger was gone.

Yeah, she was mad at him again, because he

told her parents, but in reality Ryan had done her a favor. Ryan had given her the opportunity to publicly claim her new life. If anyone didn't like what she was doing with that life, then it was too damned bad. From here on out, Twyla would do what she pleased and hold her chin up while she did it.

Helping Ryan would also give her the chance to prove to him she was a grown woman capable of helping him for a change. Maybe he'd finally realize she didn't need him watching over her shoulder, or bailing her out when she fell into a mess. She was up to her knees in one now, and she was doing fine. She was just fine. Without any of them.

She was the one bailing him out for a change, and it felt damned good.

CHAPTER SEVENTEEN

"Holy hell, girl. You were amazing in there," Twyla said, almost bouncing on the seat with excitement as she recounted the thirty-five-hundred bucks Heather had gotten from Leon. He had waffled, hedged and even tried to threaten to fire her if she didn't give him the photos. But she'd sat there in his office cool-as-a-cucumber calm, and waited him out. It had paid off.

Heather shrugged, but even in the dim interior of the truck, Twyla saw the satisfied little smile that curved her friends lips. "I know what buttons to push, and how Leon works."

"Well you pushed those buttons like a pro! We have enough money to get Ryan's truck out and post his bail."

"Yeah, if Leon's wife got a hold of those photos, she'd have cleaned that safe out for him. What we asked for was a pittance compared to what Layla would've done. But we didn't get enough to bail both of them out. I didn't want to push my luck."

"Zack can rot in there, or my parents can bail him out. I don't really care. Maybe it'll teach him a lesson." Twyla did care, she cared a lot. But Zack did need a lesson about getting in her business. Maybe from here on out, he'd mind his own.

Heather pulled into the driveway of the impound lot and stopped in front of the brick building. They'd pushed the envelope on getting here. The place was closing in five minutes. If she didn't hurry she'd miss the window to get Ryan out of jail tonight too. Twyla leaned across the seat and kissed Heather's cheek. "Thanks for everything, Heather."

"Good luck," Heather said, then gave her a penetrating stare. "Remember what I said, girl."

"I will," Twyla said with a sigh. Twyla just hoped that seeing Ryan again, especially if he was beat up and hurting over the situation with his mother, didn't make her get weak and female. Fall in love with him again. She could not afford to do that.

Ryan didn't love her, and she'd be setting herself up for more of the hurt he'd dished out to her for ten years. They'd made love, but there hadn't been anything warm and fuzzy about it. There was just heat. Incredible heat. Twyla would remember it always, but she had come to the conclusion that isn't what she wanted from a man.

She was a tough tomboy cowgirl, but she wanted those soft feelings that came with being in love too. The same feelings she'd nurtured for Ryan for so many years. Giddy, girly and completely feminine, because she knew her man thought she was the best thing since sliced bread. Adult feelings that came from mutual respect, and didn't get lost in her man trying to protect her from living her life the way she wanted to live it.

Twyla had come to the conclusion that Ryan was incapable of that kind of love. He would never be that man, and she wasn't accepting less than adult love. It was a crying damned shame, but the truth about him nonetheless.

Stiffening her shoulders and her resolve, Twyla stuffed the money into the paper sack Heather had gotten at the Cowgirl. With a confident smile, she opened the door. "I'll call and let you know what happens."

"I'll be waiting with baited breath," Heather said sarcastically, with a roll of her eyes. Twyla hopped down, and was just closing the door when Heather spoke again. "Tell Ryan I said to get his head out of his ass and do something about it."

"What?" she asked.

"Give Ryan a message for me...tell him I said to get his head out of his ass and do something about it. That's all." Heather repeated with a secretive smile. "Oh, and here's his cell phone." She leaned over to toss it across the seat.

Twyla was confused, but smiled back as she reached for the phone. "Thanks, and I will," she said with a laugh. "Anyone ever told you you're a weird chick?"

"I've heard it plenty," Heather replied with another laugh. "Now get your ass out of my truck. I have things to do tonight."

Twyla shook her head and shut the door. She shoved the phone into the pocket of her jean shorts, as she walked to the front door. Her eyes fell on the neon sign on the door that said Open and breathed a sigh of relief, as she twisted the knob. She walked up to the counter, and turned her face when a musty old wall unit blew smoke-tinged air into her face. She fumbled for the bell on the counter and hit it several times.

A dirty-looking older man walked through the doorway. "Yeah?" he said his eyes immediately fixing on her breasts. They slid down to her waist, which was the only other part of her body visible above the counter, and she felt like his eyes left a mud trail on her body.

"Eyes up here mister," she said with a wave of her hand in his line of vision. "I need to get a truck out. It's big and black. You picked it up from in front of the hospital earlier today."

"Is it your truck?" he asked and his words whistled through the gap left by his missing front teeth.

"No, it's, um, my boyfriend's truck. He's, ah, in the hospital and can't come get to it. He sent me to pick it up."

"Sorry, lady. Owner has to pick it up and pay the fines, and my bill."

"I have the money to pay the fines," Twyla replied, her fist clenching on the brown paper sack in her hand, making it crinkle.

"Can't do that. Has to be the owner," he said gruffly, turning his back to walk through the doorway to leave her standing there.

"Wait!" she shouted and he turned back. Channeling the negotiation skills she'd seen Heather use earlier, Twyla pasted on what she hoped was a sexy smile. "How bout I give you double your fee, if you just let me have the truck?"

"Can't do that," he said, but Twyla saw the interest in his eyes.

"Triple?" she offered, counting up in her mind what that was likely to be. He hadn't given her a price yet, so she dared not go any higher until she found out. She still needed enough to bail Ryan out of jail.

"Pay me a thousand dollars, and I'll forget it was ever here."

"Not doing that," Twyla replied, turning toward the door.

"Five hundred," he countered, when she grabbed the door knob.

"Four hundred," she volleyed, without turning around.

"Four-fifty."

That's the amount she had in mind for triple his fee. It must be more though, if he was settling for that to let her walk out of here with the truck. Forget it was here meant he'd just wipe out any record of it to cover his ass. Unless Ryan reported it stolen, which he wouldn't, this man was off the hook, and she had transportation to get to the jail.

It sounded like a bargain to her, and it would save time. Her other option was getting a cab to the jail, then bringing Ryan back here to get his truck. That would be cheaper, and evidently legal, but definitely not more efficient, since the jail was forty-five minutes away.

Twyla released the door knob and sifted through the money in the bag to count out the right amount, then twisted it closed and walked back to the counter. She slapped it down on the counter. "Keys first, please."

The way they were doing business was illegal, and Twyla wasn't taking the chance of this man trying to scam her. He could take the money, and then just walk to the back. She wouldn't be able to call the police, because the only crime committed was her trying to buy Ryan's truck.

He studied her a minute, then turned toward the doorway. "Only truck I picked up today, so I guess I know which one you mean," he grumbled as he disappeared through the doorway. He reappeared with the keys in his hand and slammed them down on the counter.

"Let's go back to your lot, and make sure they fit," Twyla suggested. The man rolled his eyes, but swept the keys up in his beefy fist, and walked around the counter. He opened the door for her and Twyla walked through with the greenbacks clutched in her hand.

Since she'd been around Heather more, Twyla felt like she was getting a grip on being smarter about the way she did things, handled people. Even though her friends approach was don't trust anyone, so far it was serving her as well as it did Heather.

The lot was dark, and the cars packed in tight, but she saw Ryan's truck at the back, parked crossways taking up two spots. At least it was backed in so she'd be able to get the monstrosity out easier. Why that man needed such a big truck she didn't know. He was a bronc rider, so he didn't have a trailer to haul. The only thing he hauled was his ass and gear from venue to venue. Twyla knew firsthand that Ryan wasn't compensating for shortcomings in another area, like all the cowgirls on the circuit joked about men who drove big trucks.

That thought brought heat to her cheeks, and a throb to other areas of her body. It was starting already, and she hadn't even gotten to the jail to see him again. Between here and the jail, Twyla needed to get a grip on herself and the excitement at seeing him that tickled her insides. If she didn't, she was in for a long haul for the next two weeks.

They stopped beside the truck, and he inserted the keys, leaving them hanging there while he pulled open the door. He stepped back and held out his hand, palm up, with a long-suffering look on his lined face. Twyla slapped the bills into his hand and smiled. "Nice doing business with you," she said jerking the keys out of the door.

With a shake of his head, the man turned and walked back toward the office. Twyla hopped up into the truck, and inserted the keys feeling a sense of victory she hadn't felt in a long time. But then she went to crank the truck, looked down and saw the stick shift. She had forgotten Ryan's truck was a stick. How the hell could she have forgotten? Twyla hadn't ever driven it for that reason. She'd only ever driven her beat up old *automatic* truck.

"Dammit!" she cursed and slammed her back against the seat to huff out a breath. What the hell was she going to do now? The truck was too damned big to wing it and try. She knew she'd end up in a ditch, or stalled in the middle of the road with someone plowing into the rear end. If that happened, she'd never get to the jail in time.

Her eyes darted back to the office. She'd bet that old geezer would know how to drive a stick. If she could get to Ryan, he could drop the man back off here, or they could pay for a cab ride for him back here. But Twyla knew he wasn't going to do it for free, or for the fifty bucks she had in spare change in the bag. Getting Ryan out would take twenty-five-hundred dollars even. The person they'd talk to on the phone said so.

What did she have that she could bargain with to get him to agree to help her? The vision of his eyes tracking down her body flitted into her head. Her arm was busted, her lip was busted, and her cheek was bruised, but he sure hadn't seemed to mind when he was eating her up with his eyes earlier. She couldn't dance at the Cowgirl in the shape she was in, but she could sure dance for him. She just hoped he'd go for it. Twyla grabbed the handle, and then hopped down. She stopped to stuff the sack of money behind the seat then locked the door.

With purposeful strides, Twyla walked to the backdoor, and knocked loudly. She reached down to unbutton the top two buttons of her shirt to show more of her miracle cleavage, hoping it would perform a miracle and this man would agree to her proposition. He didn't open the door, so she knocked again, pounded her fist on the door.

The door opened, and he stuck his head outside. "What do you want now?"

"You ever heard of the Crazy Cowgirl?"

"No, but I do know when I'm looking at one," he said with a shake of his head. She saw his eyes track down her body to her toes again, before he dragged them back up to her breasts. That bra had been worth every penny she spent on it, Twyla thought, arching her back a little to give him a better look.

"Yeah, I am crazy. Because I forgot that damned truck is standard, and I don't know how to drive it. I have a proposition for you, mister. I'm a dancer at the Crazy Cowgirl, and would give you a dance you'll never forget, if you agree to no touching, and that you'll drive me to the jailhouse when I'm done."

He snorted, and his eyes heated. "You're a stripper?"

"No, I'm a dancer, and I won't be shucking my clothes," she clarified, amazed that she had forgotten that one important fact.

"Dance in your bra, and I'll do it," he said, and his eyes darkened more.

Twyla gnawed her lower lip and thought about it. She'd worn her sports bra to dance before. Yeah the one she had on was a little skimpier, but she definitely needed him to help her. She was on her own here, and had to figure out something. "I'll do it, but I want you to mouth the words. No touching," she said firmly, and waited until she heard him repeat them.

Ryan would probably kill her if he found out, but he wouldn't find out. She wasn't about to tell him. But she was going to get him out of jail come hell or almost-naked breasts. The man opened the door wider, and Twyla went back inside the even mustier back office. She held her breath until she reached the front. Hopping up on the bar, she scrambled up to her feet, and unbuttoned her shirt.

"Find some music for me," she said sliding the shirt off of her shoulders.

***

Ryan paced the jail cell again, and shoved a hand through his hair as he made the turn to do it again. He was sure he'd almost worn the concrete down between the door and the wall, he'd walked it so many times now. He needed to figure out how the hell he was going to get out of here. He had to get to Houston and see about his mother, his wallet was in his damned truck, and Heather had his cell phone. If that wasn't bad enough, he had to be in a cell next to Zack who taunted and threatened every five minutes.

At least he wasn't in that cell with him. Ryan felt for sure they would be having round two of their 'discussion about Twyla' with their fists. No matter how many times Ryan told Zack that he was sorry, that he had only been trying to work the situation out himself before telling him, Zack didn't believe him. It wasn't the truth anyway. He never planned on telling Zack at all. Because he wanted to save Twyla the embarrassment and harassment that would follow. In the process he'd bought himself an endless supply of both from her brother.

"When I get out of here, I'm going to finish what I started," Zack growled, standing at the bars with his teeth bared, and his face pressed to the bars.

"I'll be ready for you, buddy," Ryan growled, finally tired of ignoring him. Putting up with him wasn't shutting him up, and neither were the guards who had to hear Zack taunting him. This podunk little county jail they'd brought them to was small, and words echoed through the hallway. He knew, because he'd heard them talking about some pictures or something they'd found in Jared Wilkins' trailer.

"Bring it on, pussy," Zack spat and Ryan snapped.

He stormed the bars and put his nose to Zack's. "When my ribs heal, I'll show you what a pussy is, punk. I'm tired of this shit, and your mouth! My fucking mother is dead or dying, and because of you, I'm stuck in this jail cell! I owe you a good ass whipping."

Zack just stood there killing him with his glare, and Ryan had enough of that too. His hand shot through the bars and grabbed the back of Zack's hair, jerking his head back, before quickly slamming his forehead into the metal bars, hoping that would knock some sense into his former best friend.

Zack howled and staggered back rubbing his

forehead while he cursed a blue streak. "That's just a taste, buddy. You want more you know where to find me."

Ryan gave him one more heated glare then huffed out a breath. He walked to the single cot against the other wall and plopped down. He looked up when a guard appeared at the door, and Ryan thought he was about to get more bogus charges leveled against him, because of what he'd just done, but the guard didn't look pissed.

The officer shoved his keys into the door then held it open. "You're out."

"Really?" Ryan asked with surprise, as he shoved up to his feet and almost ran for the door. He was getting the hell out of there before the man changed his mind, or discovered he'd made a mistake. Ryan didn't know who was responsible for springing him, but he wasn't asking questions. He walked very swiftly to the door at the end of the hallway to wait for the guard.

He heard Zack yelling behind him, "What about me?!? When am I getting out?" Ryan bit back a laugh when the guard told Zack he wasn't getting out.

But Ryan wasn't going to believe he was getting out either, until he was beyond this final door. Anything could happen. The way his luck was running, the odds that something *would* happen were too good. He had no idea who would bail him out, and not Zack. An angel, that's who. This had to be a gift from on-high, because Ryan certainly didn't deserve to be bailed out after his stupidity. Maybe the judge had dropped the charges. That would be the ultimate gift. But that wasn't likely. Someone must've put up his bail money.

He'd had plenty of time to cool off and think about it sitting in that cell. Ryan realized he should have just let the police deal with Jared Wilkins. From what he'd overheard while he was in that cell, it sounded to him like they were going to take care of the slimy bastard anyway. If he had just waited a day or two, he probably wouldn't be here.

Ryan had just been so pissed after hearing what happened to Twyla. After seeing her laying in that hospital bed, he was not in his right mind. All he wanted at that minute was to feel Jared's throat under his hands, while he squeezed the life out of him. He's damned lucky he hadn't done that, or he definitely wouldn't be getting out of here tonight. Or ever.

The guard finally settled Zack down and came to open the door. As he walked through the door, Ryan felt like a heavy lead apron was removed from his shoulders. He closed his eyes and took a deep breath of freedom. When he opened them again, white blonde hair caught his attention, and his eyes met Twyla's across the room, where she sat beside a very greasy looking man. She unfolded her arms and stood, then glanced back at the grease monkey. He stood and smiled with a tooth about every mile in his mouth.

He stood, and strangely shook her hand. "Thanks for the dance, Daisy. I'll be coming to see you at the Cowgirl."

Her eyes darted to Ryan then back to the man. She held out her hand. "Keys, please, Larry. Thanks for driving. Do you need me to call a cab for you?"

"No, I've got it. Called a friend to come get me," he replied with a wink and a wheezy chuckle, as he dropped Ryan's keys in her hand. The man's eyes took a tour of her body, and Ryan's fists clenched at his sides. He held himself back, but just barely. The last thing he needed was more trouble tonight.

He stomped across the lobby to stand beside her. "Get me the hell out of here," he growled, then flashes of her in that hospital bed made his stomach lurch up to his throat. "And what the hell are you doing out of bed?!?"

This woman didn't have a lick of sense. She was on death's door in the hospital this morning, and tonight? She was consorting with greasy wrench monkeys like they were friends.

"I came to save *your* crazy ass," she said folding her arms over her chest. She glanced at Larry, and forced a smile. "Thanks for your help, Larry." He walked off and her angry gaze swung back to Ryan. She held out his keys to him. "If you want to get out of here, get your ass in gear. If not, I'll get the two grand plus I just paid to spring you back."

Ryan snatched the keys from her. "Since when do you have two thousand dollars? I thought you were broke," he asked snidely.

"I'm a resourceful *woman*, Ryan," she said smartly. "I can take care of myself, and help you when you get stupid, which is often."

Twyla turned to push through the front door, and Ryan followed her as she double-timed it down the steps and strode across the lot toward his truck. He caught up to walk beside her, and said, "I'll drop you off at your apartment. I've got to get to Houston." They stopped at the truck, and he unlocked the doors. When he hopped inside, Twyla was already in the passenger seat buckling her belt. "I'm going with you," she said firmly, and Ryan's hand stilled on the keys in the ignition, as his gaze flew to her.

"No, you're not. You need to be in bed taking care of yourself, or having someone take care of you. You were in bad shape this morning."

She looked surprised for a second. "You came to the hospital?"

"Your daddy didn't tell you?" he asked, anger tightening his chest.

"The only thing my daddy told me was that I was coming back home with him and mama. After I told him that wasn't happening, he got pissed. When he delivered my new television as a peace offering, mama wouldn't let him say much."

"Well, I was there," Ryan grumbled as he cranked the truck. "And you're going home, because you're not in any shape to be up on your feet." Ryan was surprised that Twyla had an argument with her parents. Usually when Mr. Taylor spoke, it was law in that family. In the fourteen years he'd been around them, he'd never heard either Zack or Twyla argue with him when he laid down the law.

"Ryan?" Twyla said sweetly, and he looked over at her. "You're gonna learn just like my daddy did this afternoon. Nobody is telling me what to do anymore. I'll do what I damned well please, and go where I want. And I want to go to Houston with you. I know you're going because something happened with your mother. I'm not letting you go alone. If your stepdaddy gives you grief, I can get to your mother, where you can't." She slammed her back against the seat and looked out the window. "Since my arm is busted, I don't have anything better to do for the next two weeks."

Stunned, Ryan's head spun toward her. "What the hell do you know about my stepfather?" he demanded.

Her eyes slid back to his. "I know that he uses your mother as a punching bag, and you tried to stop him. That's why you wound up living with us."

Ryan hadn't ever talked to her about that situation. Zack was the only one who knew. And he'd evidently spread that private information to his family. Another thing he owed his former best friend an ass whipping for. "I don't want to talk about it. And you're not going with me. I can handle this alone."

"What about the restraining order? You want to end up in jail again?"

Ryan was flabbergasted. It sounded like Zack had told Twyla everything about his family issues. Some friend he was. "I'm not going to jail again," he ground out as he backed the truck out of the parking spot and slammed it into first gear.

"If you go there, you'll lose your cool and you know it. Just like you did today, especially if your mother is in bad shape. If your stepfather is there, you'll go to jail just by just showing up there. I can at least help you keep your calm, and maybe get close to your mother to see how she's doing, where you can't."

"I don't want your help."

The situation was probably ugly, and exposing Twyla to that kind of ugly would probably scar her for life. When that kind of ugly rubbed off on you, it never came off. It sure hadn't with him. His memories affected everything he did, how he handled situations.

A prime example was how he'd tried to handle Twyla, and screwed everything up by overreacting when he found her working at that bar. If Ryan hadn't known exactly the kind of men that frequented those kind of places, men like his stepfather who thought of women as objects there only for pleasure and service, and remembered the consequences of a woman hooking up with a man like that, Ryan might not have reacted so badly. But he knew too well. And his mother did too, because that's where she'd met his stepfather, while she was working at one of those places because it was good, easy money.

Because Ryan had those experiences, he would probably react the same way the next time too, and Twyla would get pissed at him again. It was just a part of him now, so that was yet another reason he was no good for the woman sitting beside him. Never would be.

"And I didn't want your help either," Twyla said softly, dropping her hand on his arm. "But because you cared about me, you came when you thought I was in trouble. The way you went about helping was all wrong, but you tried. I appreciate that, and now it's my turn to help you." She squeezed his forearm, and the warmth of her palm seeped into his body to melt some of the coldness. The fact that she was speaking now without anger in her tone made him feel better too. Maybe she was on her way to forgiving him for being such an ass in how he went about trying to help her. "It's what families do for each other, Ryan. Let me help you."

Well, her family wasn't his anymore, but at least he hadn't lost the most important member. Twyla was still in his court. Evidently she still cared about him. If he refused her help, that could change. "Okay, thank you."

Besides, having Twyla there with him might make the fact that he was sure his mother was dead this time easier to bear. At least maybe he wouldn't feel as alone as he thought he would when he lost the last relative he had in the world.

CHAPTER EIGHTEEN

Ryan squeezed Twyla's hand so tight he knew he had to be restricting the blood flow to her fingers, but he couldn't turn loose. Thank God, he'd brought her with him, or he'd probably be going off the deep end right now. His heart was squeezed just as tightly in his chest by fear, as he waited for the Chaplain to come into the family conference room at the hospital where they'd been led when Ryan announced himself at the reception desk downstairs.

He closed his eyes and sent up a silent prayer. *Lord, if she's with you, she's probably better off. If she's not, please help her have the strength to leave that bastard. If he killed her, please help me put justice in your hands, and not kill him myself.*

The door opened and Ryan's eyes flew up. Twyla's thumb stroked the area between his thumb and forefinger soothingly, as a man dressed in black except for a white tab color, with peaceful blue eyes walked into the room holding a folder. He smiled, but it didn't reach his eyes, as he sat down in the chair beside him. Before he even opened his mouth, Ryan knew. His heart knew, his soul knew. Hell before he even walked into this room, the hospital, he knew.

Why was it a shock then when the words rolled out of the man's mouth, warbled and as if in slow motion? "I'm so sorry, son. Your mother went to be with the Lord this morning. She's at peace now." He put his hand over Ryan's other hand that rested on his knee.

The words finally registered in Ryan's brain, and a rumble started in his chest. He felt strange. Numb, not in control of his body. His legs started shaking first, then his torso, and finally his arms. That feeling worked up to his face, and a roar exploded from him that had to be heard down the hall. He squeezed his eyes tight, and bore down against the incredible pain that shot through his chest. His heart felt like it was splitting in two.

As hard as he'd tried, Ryan had failed to save her. He could barely breathe, and was fighting hard to hold back another roar. Instead he felt wet heat track down his face in a torrent, and turned his head to the side, sucking in shallow breaths trying to get back his control. It was Twyla's hand that gripped his tightly now, her soothing words he heard as she stroked his hair, his face. Her voice choked up, trembling, she said, "Ryan, let it out, baby. I'm here for you. I'm so sorry." She kissed his cheek, then his temple, and he turned his face toward her.

Oh thank, God, she was there for him, he thought, as he turned to her and pulled her into his arms, her warmth comforting, her whispered words soothing, as she cried with him. Ryan buried his face in her shoulder, sucking from her strength, because he needed it. If he let her go, he felt like he'd probably shatter into a million pieces. Twyla's arms were the only thing holding those pieces together right then.

The priest's hand dropped on his shoulder

and squeezed. "I know you'll help your sister through this," the priest said.

Twyla squeezed Ryan tight once more then leaned away and kissed him, before she slid her arm around his shoulders as he turned back toward the clergyman. He sucked a few gulping breaths, then blew the last one out. "This isn't my sister, sir. Twyla is ah, my...friend." Twyla's fingers dug into his shoulder, and Ryan put his hand on her knee.

Twyla never had been his sister. He'd been stupid to ever pretend that he felt that way about her. She was a lot of things to him, his friend, his lover and his rock. But she had never been his sister, or anything close to it. Twyla had always been there for him, even when he treated her like crap. He didn't deserve her. Had never done anything to deserve her. He loved her, but considering her family's hatred of him now, he could never tell her. He wasn't going to make her choose between her family and him. And right now, he had more than enough to deal with.

The priest looked confused for a minute, then cleared his throat. "I wasn't talking about Twyla, son. I was talking about Mary, your sister."

Ryan swallowed hard, and shook his head trying to clear it. He knew there was some kind of communication gap going on between him and the kind, older man. Maybe he was going senile or something, or misunderstood the situation. He had Ryan confused with someone else.

"Sir, Ryan doesn't have a sister," Twyla finally supplied, and squeezed his shoulder again.

"I'm afraid he does. Mary is with the Department of Family Services, since your stepfather is in jail pending his murder trial. They asked me to find out what you'd like to do."

"Do?" Ryan finally croaked, his brain stuck in neutral.

"Yes, do you want her to go into foster care, or are you going to assume responsibility for her upbringing now?"

Ryan's blood drained down to his toes as he looked at Twyla. Her face was white too, and she looked as stunned as he felt, but he gathered up his senses. "She's coming with me, of course," he said rawly. Good God, he had a sister he had never met. "Um, how old is she?" When it came out, the question sounded dumb to him too.

The priest's wiry gray brows lifted, and he smiled. A real smile, one that lit up his eyes so they twinkled. "Why Miss Mary is twelve. She had her birthday two weeks ago according to her. And she got a pony named Boney from her mother, because that's how he looked when she got him."

Ryan did some mental math. It had been twelve years since he'd seen his mother. She hadn't looked pregnant then, but she had to have been. With what the priest just said, she must've been about three months along. And that bastard had beat her then too. Pregnant with his child. Rage carried every drop of blood in his body to his head and it felt like it would explode. He was on the verge of exploding. Going to that jail, dragging that bastard out of that cell and saving the taxpayers a lot of money. But Twyla squeezed his arm, and Ryan managed to contain himself. "Where, um, do they live?" he asked.

"You don't know?" the pastor asked kindly.

"No sir, it's a long story, but I haven't seen my mother in over twelve years."

The priest's smile faded, and his eyes filled with anger. "Your stepfather?"

"Yes, sir," Ryan replied with a heavy sigh.

"I'm a Christian, but I think that man needs a pound of what he did to your mother for so many years, before he's put to death. The devil will be glad to meet him, that is for certain. And I know the Good Lord isn't going to let him escape the swift sword of justice for what he did."

Anger shot back up to his throat to choke him, but Ryan forced it down. He had to know, because his prayer from earlier wasn't going to cover it, if it were the case. He would go straight down to that jail and drag the bastard out and kill him. "Did he hit, Mary?"

The priest looked down at the folder in his lap. "According to the police, that is why the murder occurred. Your mother was protecting Mary, and your father pushed her. She fell and her head hit a brick on the edge of the hearth…"

"That man is not and never has been my father," Ryan corrected angrily. "My father wasn't much better, but he did not hit my mother."

"Oh, I'm sorry. Well, your stepfather then." The priest opened up the folder, and pulled out some documents. "Here is your mother's death certificate, and the police report. You'll need to decide on the arrangements for her. I can help with that, if you need me to do that."

Ryan looked down at the cream colored paper with the official seal, and emotion burned his eyes again. He sucked in a shuddering breath. "I'd like some help. I need to find a church, and choose a c-c—' Ryan bit his lower lip, and handed the papers to Twyla. He got up from the chair and left the room to walk down the hall blindly, as tears poured down his face. He found the men's room, and pushed inside then walked to the sink to lean over it. His fingers bit into the cold porcelain, as he fought to keep from throwing up.

He felt sick everywhere, in his stomach, his heart, his soul. Bitter regret burned through him. If his mother had just listened to him, moved out when he asked her to, gotten away from that bastard, she would still be alive. If he'd have tried a little harder to convince her to leave with him that day. But she had asked him to leave, begged him to leave. Said it would only make things worse for her if he stayed, or if he came back.

Shortly thereafter he had gotten the restraining order with his stepfather's name on it. As long as she stayed with Clarence James, Ryan couldn't see her. He'd also gotten an assault charge, that the judge had reduced down to disorderly conduct due to the circumstances.

The door swung open then closed, but Ryan

didn't look that way. He didn't want anyone to see him like this. His insides felt like someone had sliced them up with razor blades. He now had a sister to think about, and had no idea what he was going to do. He didn't have a house, his life wasn't stable enough for a child. Hell, he'd been a tumbleweed for too many years. And then there was his now fucked up career. There was no way he could go back to it. How would he support a child, give her what she needed. He wouldn't have an income.

Fear like he'd never known in his life gripped him. His fingers dug deeper into the bowl of the sink, until the tips went numb, as numb as his frozen mind.

"Ryan, I'm going to help you through this. We'll figure it out together, you've just got to stay with me," Twyla said in a raw whisper. "I know you're hurting, but we've got to make plans. I asked the pastor to give us a couple of days to figure things out."

"Good," Ryan croaked, knowing a couple of centuries wouldn't give him time to figure this out.

"The first thing we're going to do is go out to that farm where they lived, and check it out, see if it's anywhere you or Mary could live. If it's not, we'll figure something else out."

"Don't have the address," he said with a shuddering breath. He didn't want to go to the place where his mother lived with that man, where she died. How could he live there?

"I have it. It's on the death certificate. Let's go get something to eat, then go out there."

"It's too late tonight. I need a shower and some sleep. Let's get a hotel, and go in the morning," Ryan said, as he stood and wobbled on his feet.

"Yeah, that's probably a better idea." Twyla put her arm around his waist and threw his arm over her shoulder to lead him out of the bathroom. Her quiet steadiness kept him on his feet, and putting one in front of the other. Ryan was just out of it. He had no idea when he wouldn't feel like this again. Like he was floating in a cloud, and without a whisper of wind to carry it anywhere.

Twyla led Ryan through the hospital, out the door and the fresh air revived him just a little bit. He had no idea what time it was. If he had to guess it was nearly two or three in the morning. She walked him to the truck and he tried to get his hand in his pocket three times, before he succeeded in grabbing his truck keys. His hand shook so badly, he couldn't get them into the lock, so Twyla finally took them from him and unlocked the door.

"Ryan, I want to say I'll drive, but I don't know how to drive a stick. Maybe we should just take a cab," she suggested, stepping between him and the truck door to put her hand on his chest. "You're not in any condition to drive."

He just stared at her beautiful upturned face, her kind caring eyes and wondered how in the hell he'd gotten so damned lucky to have her in his life. Right now, he could be walking around in a daze, not knowing where to go, because he couldn't form a coherent thought, much less decisions. "Thanks for being here, Twy."

She smiled, and put her hand on his face. "Wouldn't want to be anywhere else. You need me, and I'm here," she said and shrugged. "It's what friends do."

The warmth of her palm felt good on his skin, and her faint scent drifted to his nose, waking up his senses a little. Ryan lifted his hand to her face to stroke his thumb over her soft cheek. "Have I told you how beautiful you are and what an amazing woman you've become? And how damned thankful I am to have you for a friend?"

The feelings that gushed up inside of Ryan were almost overwhelming. It was so much, he fought saying the words on the tip of his tongue. He was emotional, and those words wouldn't do a damned thing but complicate matters between them right now. Ryan needed this peace between them, and he needed a friend. He needed to hang on tight to the last one he had.

He stared into her eyes, as he lowered his mouth toward hers. He brushed his mouth over hers and darts of fire shot through him, but he pulled back.

Twyla sighed, and hugged him, laying her cheek on his chest. "I'm glad you're my friend too, Ryan." She pushed back. "Can you drive now?"

"Yeah, I can drive." He stepped aside and helped her get up in the truck, then climbed inside beside her. And now they were friends. Why didn't that feel any better than surrogate siblings? Because

Ryan wanted more.

To his surprise, Twyla didn't scoot over to the passenger door, she straddled the gear shift in the center of the seat. She waited until he was settled, then put her hand on his knee. "I'm going to watch you, so I can learn to drive a stick."

"You don't know how?" he asked in shock.

"No, my truck is automatic."

Ryan smiled at her, and shut the door. He cranked the truck and looked at her again. "Well, as soon as things settle down, I'll take you out in the country and show you how to drive a stick—" He stopped, because he realized how stupid his statement was. She wouldn't be around when things settled down. Once he had a grip on things, she would go back to Dallas, and he would most likely be here. Raising his sister Mary. He was a single father now, had huge responsibilities that he didn't have twenty-four hours ago.

Some little twelve-year-old he'd never met was going to be depending on him to keep his shit together and take care of her, provide for her, love her. Fate had a sense of humor choosing him for that chore. Ryan was about as unsettled as a man could get. But that was about to change. It would have to, because he didn't have a damned bit of choice in the matter. His stepfather hadn't only taken his mother from him, he'd saddled him with a child that wasn't his own to raise.

The weight of it all slammed down on his shoulders and they sank a few inches. Ryan let out a shuddering sigh, as he leaned his arms on the steering wheel and slumped over it trying to get a grip on the rage that consumed him again.

Twyla's hand rubbed the circles between his shoulder blades, and tension eased a little, but not enough. "Why did this have to happen now?" he asked, feeling like he was the single resident in his own little world where nobody else had the same fucked up problems as he did. Alone.

"It happened because it was supposed to happen, Ryan," Twyla's even, comforting voice inched tension inside of him down another notch. "Maybe this happening got you away from the rodeo before you wound up crippled from a horse falling on you during a ride," she suggested. "Or maybe it stopped Mary from growing up damaged and choosing a man just like your stepfather to be with, because it's all she knew. You can't question His plan, baby. You just have to roll with it, and try to enjoy the ride. It can be a good thing if you decide it's going to be a good thing."

The thought that his mysterious new sister Mary could've wound up with someone just like Clarence James, that she would choose someone like him, because it was all she knew made his stomach roll. "You know why I was so hard on you when I first got to Dallas and found you dancing at that bar? Why I was so freaked out?"

"Because you're a control freak like my brother?" Twyla suggested, and he heard the anger and frustration in her tone now.

Ryan lifted and turned toward her to take her shoulders in his hands. He knew he was holding her tighter than necessary, but Ryan couldn't help it. He had to make her understand.

"No, it was because I was afraid that would happen to you too. When Clarence wasn't beating my mother, he hung out in places like that, used the women there and the alcohol to get himself worked up, so when he came home he used my mother to work off the head of steam he'd built there. With his fists and by raping her if necessary, if she didn't feel like having sex with a drunk, horny bastard who wanted to use her."

"Why the hell did you go to those places then with my brother?" Twyla asked softly, with confusion in her tone.

"I don't know why I went. Those women weren't women I lov—" Ryan cleared his throat, and sucked the words back in on a breath. "I didn't care about those women. I wasn't scared they'd end up leaving one night with a man like Clarence, then be in the morgue the next morning like my mother. If that happened to you, I—I" His throat closed up, and he forced it back open. "I always knew if she stayed with him, he'd kill her. And it killed me not to be able to convince her to leave. To have to sit back and wait for it to happen."

"I'm sorry, Ryan," Twyla said, her voice a little hoarse. "This is not your fault. What happened to your mother is not your fault. You tried to help her, but you can't help someone unless they want that help."

"I wanted to help you, but you're right, I didn't do it right, because of this. Twy, you're better than that. The world is a big place, and you are beautiful and talented. You don't have to cheapen yourself like that, or risk getting attacked by a man like Clarence James or J-jared Wilkins." His last words came out on an exhausted breath, as he pulled her into his arms and hugged her. "If something like that happened to you, I'd die," Ryan mumbled into her hair, his throat closing up again, but he managed to squeeze out, "I was so damned scared it would."

Twyla pushed back from him, and put her hands on his shoulders. "Look at me Ryan. This is important." He lifted his eyes to hers, and saw fierce determination there.

"I'm going to tell you this both for myself, and for your new little sister." She took a deep breath, and hesitated a moment, then let it out. "You can't put us in a glass bubble and set us on a shelf then send us off into the world and expect us to know how to take care of ourselves. Without experiencing life, we don't know how to deal with it when we *are* in those situations. I know both you and Zack did what you did with good intentions, but you didn't do me any favors. If I hadn't had Heather to get me up to speed on things, I probably would have wound up with one of those men. The school of hard knocks has taught her valuable life lessons that serve her well. Because she was allowed to take those knocks, she knows how to avoid them in the future.

Does that make sense to you?"

Ryan didn't like it, but her words made perfect sense to him. Too much sense. And it also meant when she went back to Dallas, she'd probably be dancing in that bar again. And he'd be here. He had not a right in the world asking, but he knew he had to. "Twyla, will you please, *please* stop working at the Cowgirl? I'd go crazy here thinking about you dancing there, while I'm stuck here. It about drove me nuts, when I was away two weeks on tour."

She sighed, shook her head, then turned to sit with her arms folded over her chest. "I'll think about it."

That was better than nothing, he guessed. He would keep trying to convince her. He had two weeks left to do that. Ryan sat straight in the seat and put the truck in gear. "I think I saw a hotel down the street."

CHAPTER NINETEEN

Ryan slapped his credit card and driver's license down on the counter at the only hotel with rooms available for the night. It wasn't night anymore, it was now almost four a.m. and he was on the very last ounce of energy he had left.

The woman slid them off the counter, and smiled. "Double or King room?" she asked as she typed his information into the computer.

He glanced at Twyla who looked as tired as he did. "Double, please."

"King," Twyla said at the same time, and their eyes met. She slid her arm through his and repeated herself. "We'll take a King. Top floor if you have it."

The woman punched keys on her computer, then smiled. "We do, the last one, but it's by the elevator."

"That's fine," Twyla said not breaking eye contact with him.

"You sure?" he mouthed, and she nodded. Ryan's heart leapt and his body tried to react, it really did, but there just wasn't anything left in his tank. He almost wanted double beds, because if Twyla expected anything, he was going to sorely disappoint her. He was wrung out. Done.

She squeezed his arm, and grabbed the room keys the clerk placed on the counter. "Have a good night's rest," she said, handing Ryan his cards back.

He put them in his wallet, and put his arm

around Twyla to walk to the elevator. After pushing the button, he said, "Twy—I ah, don't have the energy to, ah…"

She laughed. "You think I don't know that? I want to hold you. Think you have the energy for that?"

Cuddling? Ryan didn't know if he did or not. He'd never slept with a woman, just to sleep with a woman. But if it was in Twyla's arms, he would definitely give it a try. "My eyes are going to be closed before my head hits the pillow, but we can give it a try," he said giving her shoulders a squeeze.

It would be another memory with her to store up. One he could drag out after she left when he was lonely. His heart stopped for a second at the thought, then beat out of control for a few seconds, before it resumed a steady rhythm, when he reminded himself he didn't need to get attached to her. Life would go on after she left, and he had a helluva lot of things to take care of between now and then. That's where his focus needed to be, not on panicking that he'd miss her so much he didn't know how good that life would be when she left. There were a lot more memories to make, before she left. And twelve-years-worth before that. The time he'd spent as a member of her family would be something he'd never forget. He didn't know where he'd be today if they hadn't taken him in. Made him one of their own. Ryan would always be grateful. Even though they hated him now, Ryan would never forget them or what they'd done for him.

They taught him to be a man. A caring man. And showed him how a family was supposed to be, something he could carry over into creating a good family life for Mary.

The thought of his new sister, and his tiredness sent emotion up to clog his throat as he stepped out of the elevator. He squeezed Twyla tighter as he walked with her to the door across the hall from the elevator. She slid the key into the door, and they went inside.

Twyla went to the bathroom, while Ryan shucked his clothes. He staggered to the bed, the pillow calling him like a snake charmer's flute, and he hadn't lied, sleep claimed him before his head even rested good on the pillow.

The next morning, Ryan woke up in what felt like a warm, snuggly cocoon. He felt better than he had in years, had slept better. Then reality slapped him in his face when he realized where he was. His good mood flew right out through that crack in the black-out curtains where the sun shone in so brightly. That light woke him up to the reality of why he was laying in this strange bed. His eyes fell to the blond hair covering his chest, the soft snores of the softer woman whose delicious curves were suctioned to his side like saran wrap.

His mother was dead, and he had a sister to raise.

His chest tightened, and he bit his lower lip to keep from wailing and waking Twyla. That wail filled his eyes and they burned like a bitch. He batted them, and turned his head to the side and sucked in a deep breath. He blew it out slowly and tried to force his body to relax. Twyla rustled beside him, then a warm kiss landed on his shoulder.

"Morning," she mumbled sleepily shoving her hair out of her face. Her bright blue eyes met his and heat shot through him. She smiled up at him, that sleepy smile he'd seen plenty of times, while he stayed at her parents ranch. This time though, he let it work its magic inside of him to heat places he'd never let it travel before. His blood surged to his dick and it went rock hard against her thigh that was draped over him. The feel of her soft skin was making matters worse. He squirmed, trying to put space between them, but her thigh clamped down and her arms tightened over his chest.

"Ut uh," Twyla said, grinning up at him, as she rubbed her calf against his suggestively. "You're rested now, and have no excuse."

He had plenty of excuses, starting with those complications he thought about. And all of the things he had to get done today, face today. But there was no way in hell he wasn't going to take the opportunity to make up to her for the last time. When Twyla Taylor left Houston, she was going to remember him fondly. Not as the rude asshole who had rough, kinky sex with her for her first time. He owed it to her, and to himself. Memories.

Ryan pulled her into his arms, and gently covered her mouth with his. She sighed, her calf pressed harder against his, and she slid her hand down his chest, over his abs, leaving a trail of fire, until her hand closed over his cock. Ryan's body stiffened and he gasped, as electricity shot through his balls, zipped down his legs to his toes. Her fingers loosened, she smoothed her palm along his length then gently cupped his balls. Ryan's heart took a trip around his chest, and he moaned. Pulling her closer, he fought the urge to roll her over and plant his aching cock inside of her body, as memories of how incredible she had felt last time soaked his brain.

Slow, he coached himself. This time it was about loving her right. Showing her how it could be with a man who wasn't in a hurry to reach the end. He rolled her onto her back, her hand released him, and he kissed her deeper.

Ryan smoothed his hand over her stomach and buried his hand between her legs. Twyla was already soaking wet and ready, and he bit back a groan as he spread her dew, before massaging it into her clit. Her body jerked, she gasped, and Ryan's dick swelled against her thigh. He loved those damned sounds she made. Her little whimpers and moans drove him out of his mind. He wanted to hear more of them. Ryan wanted her to be so lost in what he was making her feel, she screamed it to the world. Lifting his mouth from hers, Ryan kissed the corner of her mouth, the underside of her jaw, then slowly worked to her earlobe. When he sucked it into his mouth, and nipped it, she moaned low in her throat.

His balls tightened, and he tongued the shell

of her ear. "I love that sound," he whispered hotly in her ear, and she shivered. "I want to hear you make that sound when I put my cock inside of you."

"Oh, God, Ryan...yes," she whispered, her fingers digging into his shoulder, as he kissed the pounding pulse at the side of her throat. He stopped there to suck her sweet skin into his mouth, and she whimpered, as a tremor rocked her.

Licking his way downward, Ryan dipped his tongue into the crevice at her collarbone. He shifted his body as he kissed across her chest, under her chin, where he stopped to lick that stubborn little notch he loved, because he couldn't resist. She sucked in a sharp breath, and shoved her hands into his hair. She cradled his head in her grasp, as he kissed his way down to the valley between her breasts. Her nipples were rigid and begging for his mouth. And Twyla's back arched them toward him, as if that was exactly what she wanted too.

The tiny little mewls she made as he licked the underside of her breast egged him on, and made him harder if that was possible. He dragged his tongue slowly upward over the erect peak, and she moaned louder. He stopped, hovered above her breast and just breathed, making her anticipate how good his mouth was going to feel on her. Remember.

Those mewls started again, this time of protest, as her fingers dug into his scalp. "Please," she whispered. "Suck me, Ryan."

He laid beside her and reached for her hand to gently pry it away from his head. He laced his fingers with hers, and held their hands by her ear. Cupping her right breast, he lowered his mouth to her body. His thumb brushed over her nipple, as he worshiped the perfect right mound with his lips, teeth and tongue, and those mewls started again. Squeezing his hand tight, she wailed as a tremor shook her body. He released her breath with a pop, and smiled against her skin. "Did you just come, baby?"

"Mhmm..." was her garbled reply, as another tremor rocked her.

"Good, it's time for another one, then," he said with a laugh.

Her eyes flew open, and she sat up. "No, I want you inside of me."

"Nah, patience, baby. I've only kissed about a third of your deliciousness. I have lots more to sample, before it's time for that." He laughed when she rolled her eyes and slammed back against the pile of pillows under her head. "When hotel security knocks at the door, because someone thinks you're dying, I'll be done."

Ryan scooted to the end of the bed and she squealed when he grabbed her ankles to pull her toward the end of the huge bed. He lifted her left leg, and licked her instep. She giggled, and tried to yank her leg back, but he held her tight. He placed an open mouth kiss on the arch and sucked it, while he smoothed his hand up her calf to her inner thigh, then made a pass back up her calf, dragging a throaty moan from her.

He kissed his way to her ankle, and repeated

the process, getting closer and closer to her wet pink folds, with his fingers. He watched them quiver as if anticipating his touch, her body open and close, as he worked his way closer there. At her knee, he kissed the inside, then gently laid her leg on the bed. Her eyes flew open, and she growled. It was so damned cute, Ryan laughed. "Patience, baby. I'll get there," he said as he lifted her right leg, and kissed her instep.

He tongued it, and she laughed, then moaned when he sucked it. The sound danced along his spine to settle in his balls. He followed the same process as he had on the other leg, but didn't stop when he reached her knee, he slid his tongue up her inner thigh, and Twyla groaned loudly. "Suck me, Ryan," she begged. "Please make me come. I love it when you make me come."

"Touch your breasts, and I will," he said as he pushed her knees wider. "Help me make you come, Twy. You know what feels good. Have you touched yourself before?" he asked, because he was damned curious. She'd come awfully damned fast when he had simply sucked her breasts.

"Yes," she moaned as she covered her breasts with her hands. She sucked in a sharp breath, and turned her head to the side, as she rolled them in her fingers.

Because he was a man, he had to ask. "Did you think about me, baby?"

"Yes, only you," she admitted on a hot released breath.

That fact made his heart dance in his chest.

This woman was his. Would always be his, no matter where she was or who she was with, she would think of him.

But that was little consolation that another man would be making love to her while she thought of him. His heart skidded to a stop, and melted, dripping slowly down to his toes. If he didn't do something, she would leave him very shortly, and he knew she wasn't going to wait around for him to fix things with her family. He didn't think he could even if he tried.

Twyla would go on with her life without him. She might want him, love him even, but Twyla had a new life now. Her days of waiting for him to come around were over.

She leaned up on her elbows, and looked down at him with impatient blue eyes. "You fall asleep down there?" He laughed, and she laid back down to fondle her breasts.

Ryan settled between her legs and leaned closer to inhale her unique scent. He wanted to remember it, have it imprinted on his mind. He didn't ever want to forget it. He knew he'd taste her sweetness on his mouth every time he closed his eyes and thought about her. Laying out his tongue, he made a slow pass up her folds. Her breath hissed out like a balloon losing air, and her hands shot to the cover to fist it.

Her flavor spread over his taste buds to filter though his body and he moaned, closed his eyes and savored it. Leaning in, he circled her clit and Twyla made a garbled sound in her throat. Her lips quivered, and he felt her inner muscles clenching and releasing under his palms that rested on her lower abdomen. She was damned close, one nip, or suck and she'd probably shatter. Ryan's body was telling him it was time to move things faster too. He nibbled the bud, then pinched his lips over it and sucked in a slow steady rhythm. Her body jerked, she screamed then her fists dragged the comforter to her sides, as she wailed his name and her body vibrated. On the last tremor, she sighed, and Ryan kissed his way up her right thigh, across her belly to her navel. He swiped his tongue inside, and she giggled, swatting at his head.

Ryan knelt over her, and said, "Roll over on your stomach, baby. I want to see your beautiful ass when I fuck you." That would also give him better position to go deeper, and make her come with him inside of her. God, to feel her body sucking him deeper inside, feel her come again around his cock would be incredible. Twyla rolled and laid flat. "Get up on your knees, he said slapping her ass a little, which got him a whimper.

A delicious thrill shot through him. He could explore all kinds of things with Twyla. She didn't know what sex was, he was teaching her, and she trusted him. Teaching her what he liked, and learning what she liked would be an adventure. But a short-lived one he reminded himself. She would be leaving soon.

"Fuck," he muttered as he positioned himself

behind her.

"What?" Twyla turned her head to ask. "Did I do something wrong?"

Ryan massaged her ass cheeks with his hands. No she didn't do a damned thing wrong. She was perfect, and as much as he wanted her, she would never be his forever.

But she was his at this moment, and he was going to try and gorge himself. Get his fill of her delicious body. Enough to last him a lifetime. Because by being banned from the Taylor family now, he knew he'd never have her that long. If they knew he was having her now, they'd probably drag him out to the field and string him up in a tree.

"Ryan?" she asked with concern.

"Yeah, baby. I'm sorry, just got lost for a minute." He reached between them, and raked up her moisture with his finger, then slathered it on her anus. A tremor shook her body, and she whimpered when he circled it. He would love to shove his dick in that tight hole, but knew it wasn't the time for it. Maybe he'd have time before she left town.

And maybe Boney the Pony would sprout wings and fly out of his pen at that ranch. The odds were the same. Once they left this room, the odds were they wouldn't have sex again. He was going to be busy. Up to his eyeballs in chores and repairs. He had a feeling as lazy as Clarence James was, he hadn't done a damned thing with the ranch for years.

So Ryan was determined to milk every ounce of pleasure out of this time that he could, and give it too. He grabbed his cock and situated it at her opening, then spread her legs wider. He leaned over her, reached around her waist and found her clit with his fingers. He slid his cock halfway into her body. He gritted his teeth, fighting for control of the orgasm building in his balls as her wet heat pulsated around him.

He rubbed her nub between his thumb and forefinger and she gasped, rotated her hips with his hand. Her body opened and relaxed so she could take a little more of him. Ryan waited for his body to settle, because the urge to just shove himself inside of her was strong. This was going to be a test in his control for sure. Right now he just wanted to pound himself in her body until he found release, but he was determined to get her there again first.

With every rotation of his fingers on her body, her hips took wider circles in response, her back arched lower, she stretched so her ass was higher, and he went deeper, until he was buried to the hilt in her sweet, wet heat. Small tremors of her inner muscles were his first clue she was almost there, but then she clamped down on him, and Ryan moaned. Twyla bit down on the pillow and her muffled scream and frantic pants came in time with her muscles.

Ryan's control snapped and he leaned behind her, grabbed her ass, and slid out of her, before he slammed back in, the incredible suction of her body dragging his orgasm closer to the end of his cock. Twyla lifted her ass, pushed back toward him, and his fingers dug into her flesh, as he pounded into her.

The sweet slapping sounds as he entered and left her wet heat inched his orgasm closer. Blood pounded in his ears, his heart floated out of chest, tremors worked through him, then like a floodgate opening he roared his release as his body filled hers in wave after hot wave. Weak, and his body washed in endorphins, Ryan collapsed beside her and pulled Twyla into his arms. He kissed her hair, and pulled her tighter, as emotion choked him.

Ryan didn't have any fucking idea how he was ever going to let her go.

CHAPTER TWENTY

Twyla dipped her sponge in the bucket of soapy water again, and moved on to the next section of nasty, smoke-stained wallpaper. She was only halfway through and she probably smelled like the wall had before she started cleaning it. She had to get done and showered before two o'clock when the social worker would be bringing Mary home.

They'd both been working their asses off since they got here, after the short service at the church for Mrs. James the day before yesterday. She had been buried in a small graveyard behind the church. It wasn't too far from here, maybe ten miles, so Ryan and Mary could visit her grave if they felt like it.

Ryan had made it through the service okay, even kissed his mother's cheek before they closed the coffin, but when the casket was lowered, he had a meltdown. Twyla was so damned glad she had come here with him. The amount of emotional stress, on top of the work needing to be done to make this place livable was more than two people could handle. She had no idea how Ryan would have done it alone.

For two days now, she'd been working with Ryan to make it a home, instead of a dirty flophouse, which is what it looked like before he'd taken out his hammer and saw, and she'd broken out the broom and cleaning supplies.

The first thing she'd done was take peroxide

to the blood stains by the hearth. When Ryan first walked into the house that sight had him on his knees having a breakdown, and Twyla couldn't blame him. This house had a very bad vibe to it, and they needed to change that. Mary deserved a home filled with love and light. Something she'd probably never had before, and so did Ryan. Ripping down the old, drab drapes and opening the windows had helped, but now they had to either replace them with blinds or new curtains, because it was hotter than hades in the house. Ryan was out back working on the old air conditioning unit, hoping he could save it by adding a little Freon. Or at least helping it limp along until he could buy a new unit.

According to him, most of his savings had been invested in a rough stock herd with her brother Zack. Bucking bulls that were being kept at Cord and Dean Dixon's ranch. He didn't have enough left in his savings to pay someone to do the repairs. He had enough to buy supplies to do it himself, but it would take him forever.

Twyla suggested he sell either Dean, Cord or her brother his share of the stock, but he said he was in too deep, and Zack probably wouldn't agree to anything he suggested. They weren't on speaking terms. Because of her.

Twyla's lower lip trembled and she bit it. Zack was hardheaded and could hold a damned grudge a long time, Twyla knew that firsthand. He was as stubborn as a mule, but he and Ryan had been friends a helluva long time, and Ryan needed him right now. Zack should be here, hammering right alongside him.

If Zack were in the same situation, Ryan would be there for him. She was going to talk to her brother. Set things straight. Ryan didn't know it, but this morning she'd also used his phone to call their rodeo friends. Lucky, a bull-rider friend in their circle, said he would talk to the others, but he thought they could probably come out Thursday morning, as long as they made it back by Saturday morning to ride. Something good was happening. The next circuit stop was in Houston. The guys could stay longer, help more.

Ryan needed to call the admin office and quit, but when she mentioned it he had walked off. She knew it was killing him to have to give up riding, but he had to realize he couldn't continue. He had a child now. But Twyla wasn't going to push him. Ryan would do it soon, she was sure. When he was ready and had resolved himself to that fact.

Twyla heard a whistle and spun on her knees. Ryan stood there wiping his forehead with a bandana. "It looks amazing in here, baby."

"I'm not done yet. How's the a/c?"

"Given up the ghost. There's no patching it, the compressor is gone." His eyes narrowed, and a muscle worked in his jaw. "There's no telling how long they've lived here without air. We need to go buy some fans to get the air moving."

"I think Coop used to do a/c work with his dad," Twyla suggested. Coop Wiley was a bronc rider now, but before he went pro, he also worked in his father's air conditioning and refrigeration company. Cowboys helped their own, so she knew if he couldn't fix the unit, he could get one at a discount. His family was three hours from Houston, but they could go pick it up if needed.

"I don't want the guys out here," Ryan said shortly as he walked through the archway into the kitchen. Twyla followed him, because this is something he needed to bend on.

He needed help, and stubbornness wasn't going to get that for him. "Ryan, I've already invited them out here. They'll be here tomorrow, and can stay til Saturday morning."

He spun toward her to shout loudly, "I *said* I don't want them here!"

Twyla's head rocked back and she flinched. Ryan had never raised his voice to her before, and she couldn't say she liked it.

Ryan's shocked face went white, and he ran over to pull her against his chest. A groan rumbled through his chest, then his voice low and tortured, he said, "I'm so sorry for shouting, baby. It will never happen again."

"Ryan, it's not like I've never been yelled at before. I didn't appreciate it, but don't be so dramatic." Twyla pushed against his chest, but he wouldn't let her go. "Ryan, let me go. I have to finish the walls."

"No, kiss me," he said his hand going into her hair to tilt her head back, before his mouth covered hers, tasting salty. His kiss held an edge of desperation, a tone of remorse, but nothing remotely like love. "Tell me you don't hate me, Twy," he whispered as his lips brushed hers a final time.

"I could never hate you, Ryan. I've loved you too long," she said with frustration, stepping back from him. This man was a basket case. His emotions were so close to the edge these days, that he would end up falling apart when the social worker got here. That would never do. Mary would get upset, and the social worker might not leave her. "But don't yell at me again, or I'll leave. And you need to take a break. Go out to the barn and mess around, do something other than work. You need to pull yourself together, because when Mary and that social worker get here falling apart is not an option. Got that?"

He didn't look relieved, he looked more frustrated as she turned and walked out of the room. She picked up the sponge from the bucket, and angrily scrubbed a nasty spot on the wall. An hour more and she would be done. One hour and she could take a shower and get her own self together, so she could help him keep it together.

Twyla only hoped that by the time she left next week, he'd have a better handle on things. On himself. Mary needed him to be strong, and the man who had just kissed her, the man he'd become since they'd come to this house—that was it. This house was making him act this way, and no amount of cleaning was going to change that. This house held too many memories for him to be happy here.

She dropped the sponge in the bucket, then ran into the kitchen. Ryan was leaned over the chipped porcelain sink with his head bent. The faucet was running, so Twyla ran over there and shut it off. The old well pump didn't take kindly to running for long stretches, and she wanted a shower. She put her hand to his cheek and turned his face toward hers. He wouldn't meet her eyes, because he was crying. He pulled his face away and turned away.

"Ryan look at me. I understand," she said calmly. "I know what's going on with you."

His head spun and he fixed his angry tortured eyes on her face. "How the hell could you know? You've never lived it Twy—this place is killing me one minute at a time. Every time I turn a corner, I see him hitting my mama. I never lived here, but I lived it, before I left home."

Twyla slipped her arms around his waist and hugged him. "I think it would do both you and Mary to start fresh somewhere else."

"That can't happen. I'm stuck here, because I'm poor. I've worked my ass off since I was too young to work, and this is what I've earned." He snorted, then shook his head. "Oh and a bunch of bucking bulls I have no use for, and can't do a damned thing with."

Twyla eased back and her arms fell to her sides. "Ryan, if you want my help, I'm here to help. If you want to have a pity party, you do it by yourself. Yeah, this sucks, but unless we work together to figure something out, I'm spinning my wheels. This is your life, not mine. I have my new life back in Dallas. You need to find yours." She turned toward the archway. "I'll call Heather to come and get me."

She took one step then a sound like that a wounded animal would make turned into a fierce roar. "Noo*ooo*!! Ryan grabbed her shoulders and spun her around. He dropped to his knees in front of her. "Please don't leave, Twyla. I'm so sorry, baby. I lo—" he swallowed a couple of times. "I promise I'll stop feeling sorry for myself." He hugged her knees and his shoulders shook. "I just feel so overwhelmed with all this. I'm trying, fuck I really am."

Twyla dropped to her knees and hugged his shoulders. "Try harder." Ryan nodded against her shoulder, and she kissed his temple. "Because in two hours you're going to be what amounts to a new daddy. That little girl will fall apart if you do. She has to be as torn up as you are."

"I know," he choked out. "She'll probably be scared here too. I don't know what that bastard is charged with, or if he'll get out. If he does, he'll come back here and I'll kill him. I swear I'll kill him."

Twyla pushed back from him. "So call and find out what he's charged with. You have the right to do that."

"I can't today. I'm going to take a walk, then get ready. " He pushed up to his feet, and Twyla stood. Ryan pulled her to his chest again, and Twyla slipped her arms around his waist.

"Then do it tomorrow. We don't have to solve the world's problems, or yours, in one day. The guys want to come and help, Ryan. Will you accept their help? Even if you don't stay here, you'll need to fix it up to sell it."

"The bastard owns it, there's no way he's going to let me sell it. We're stuck here."

Twyla sighed and put her hand on his ravaged face. "Things will work out, just take a breath and that walk. Have faith."

Ryan nodded then turned his face to kiss her palm. "Thanks for talking me off the ledge, Twyla. I really don't know what I'd do if you weren't here."

One side of her mouth kicked up. "Keep your cool, and march on. I'll be right there beside you, cowboy."

Two hours later, Twyla pulled her only pair of jeans on. The same pair she'd washed nightly with Ryan's, before they headed back to the hotel. They needed to go shopping soon, but they were conserving money for building supplies, and the fricking hotel. They couldn't stay here though. There were only two bedrooms in the house, Mary's that had a dingy little single bed in it, and his mother's. She'd slept in there with Clarence. There is no way she was going to even suggest they stay in that room. And the furniture in the living room was ratty and cigarette burned. It smelled just like the walls had before she cleaned them. Clarence must've been a chain-smoker is all she could figure.

She wished like hell she had that twenty-five-hundred dollars she'd wasted on bail money for him.

Twyla could do a lot with that money right now. According to Heather, the charges against Ryan had been dropped the afternoon after she'd bailed him out. Zack was out on bail too, her parents had put it up, but his assault charge against Ryan was still pending. That was a relief, but she hoped her brother got off too. She was mad at Zack right now, but she did not want him to have a criminal record. Because of her.

If she hadn't put herself in the stupid position with Jared Wilkins, none of them would be in this fix. But they were here, and needed to deal with that too. She also wanted to call and find out what was happening with the charges against Jared. She hoped that bastard rotted in prison.

Twyla was pulling her hair into a ponytail when Ryan walked in with a towel wrapped around his trim hips. He heaved a breath but when their eyes met in the mirror on the dresser he smiled. It was the first smile she'd seen on his face since before they'd gotten to Houston.

His eyes heated and he dropped the towel, standing there naked as a jaybird, seeming proud of himself. Twyla couldn't help but drink him in. Ryan was a beautiful man, wide shoulders, firm pecs, washboard abs and dayum, he was happy to see her. The sad part was Ryan Easter knew it, and knew that she thought so too. Pasting on a smug smile, she repeated the same words to him she had that day in Heather's kitchen, as she fixed her eyes on his dick. "Well cowboy, I'm sure that little sprout satisfies those buckle bunnies just fine, but I'm used to um, more mature men."

Twyla's teasing words had the desired effect. Ryan's smile faded, and he looked a little insulted but then a determined look filled his eyes as he stalked her and she backed up against the dresser. He put his palms down on either side of her, trapping her there. Twyla leaned back, and the intensity in his blue eyes scorched her. "I don't seem to remember you complaining about my sprout when I had it shoved up inside your—"

Twyla gasped and put her fingers over his mouth. She clicked her tongue. "We're gonna have little ears in the house. You need to watch your mouth."

His eyes fell to her lips. "I'd rather watch yours when it's wrapped around my—*sprout.*"

Twyla bit back a laugh, but slapped her palm over his mouth. He nipped it and she yelped, then gasped when Ryan shoved his hips into her hard. His rock hard cock hit her right where she would love it to be. Wanted it to be right now, if they weren't expecting visitors.

"And the only little thing in this house will be those ears," he growled, pressing himself harder against her. "As for mature men. I'm the *only* man you're gonna be trying on for size, got that, Daisy?"

Her eyes widened, and she wondered if he knew what he'd just said. "Ryan…I…ah."

Twyla didn't know what to say.

As it turned out she didn't have to say

anything, because Ryan swooped down to claim her lips in a kiss she felt all the way down to her toes. He leaned in, pressed himself tighter to her body. Twyla moaned, circling her hips against him, and Ryan forced her mouth open with his tongue then courted hers to dance.

This man was so damned confusing, Twyla gave up on figuring out what was going on with him. She just slid her arms around his neck and kissed him back. She had two weeks to drink her fill of Ryan Easter, and before she left this ranch, she would be full of him. Ready to savor these moments for the rest of her life. This man was the Ryan she'd always dreamed of having hold her, kiss her just like he was kissing her. The only thing missing were the words she given up on him ever uttering. And wasn't that too damned bad for both of them?

The flagging screen door rattled as someone opened it then knocked on the wooden front door. "Oh my God, they're here," Twyla said, panicking as she slid her body from under his. "Get dressed! I'll stall them. Hurry!"

Twyla straightened her shirt and tucked it into her jeans as she ran for the door. When she opened it, there stood the prettiest blue-eyed blonde girl Twyla had ever seen. Well, she wasn't a girl really, she was almost a teenager. The only resemblance between her and Ryan were their penetrating blue eyes. Mary's were sad and afraid and it almost ripped Twyla's heart out.

She realized she was gawking and forced her

eyes to the woman standing behind Mary. With a smile, she stepped back and waved them inside. "Come in. Ryan will be out in just a minute," she said, trying to stop the nervous quiver in her voice.

The social worker held Mary's shoulders, as she stepped inside. Her eyes immediately tracked around the house. Twyla knew she was judging, even though she tried to make it appear she was admiring. "Um, nice place," she said with a polite, but cool smile.

"We've been fixing it up. It was a mess," Twyla said, wiping her sweaty palms on her jeans, her own eyes moving around the room trying to see it through the social worker's eyes. It wasn't fancy, but Twyla could attest it was now clean.

"Would you like some sweet tea? I made some earlier."

"Miss Nell, I want to go see Boney Pony. He's out in the barn," Mary said timidly, before she cast her eyes back down at the chipped pink polish on her toenails, as she wiggled them in her worn flip flops.

"I'll take you out there when Ryan gets in here so he and Miss Nell can talk."

That would probably be better anyway. Twyla wouldn't stick her foot in her mouth with this woman and make the situation worse. She hoped Ryan didn't either.

She looked at Mary, when the silence lengthened. "I've been feeding Boney for you. You might have to change his name," Twyla said with a laugh. "He's getting a little pudgy, since you haven't been here to ride him." The pony was big, but not large enough for her. Her legs would drag the ground, so she hadn't ridden him. Well that and he had hoof problems she had to treat. He hadn't ever been trimmed, Twyla didn't think. The farrier agreed when he came out to take care of him.

Without lifting her eyes, Mary mumbled, "I don't ride him. I don't have a saddle."

Shock rocked Twyla for a second. What adult bought a kid a horse, and didn't get them a saddle? That was pretty damned cruel in her opinion. And so was the fact the damned horse had been underfed for so long his ribs were showing. That is the only reason his name fit.

Twyla's saddle didn't fit Tango anymore. Yeah, it was her lucky saddle, but Randy was right. It wasn't very lucky if she wasn't winning, and it didn't fit her horse right. She needed a new one anyway. "Well, I have one you can have. It's special. I won it barrel racing. It doesn't fit my horse anymore, but I think it might fit Boney."

The girls eyes shot up then, and she smiled. "Really?" she asked with awe in her tone.

Twyla returned her smile. "Yep, but it's in Dallas, so I'll have to go get it for you."

Her face fell, and Twyla wanted to shove Ryan in the truck right then to drive to Dallas to get the damned saddle. Ryan walked in looking handsome as sin in his spit-shined boots, freshly washed faded Wranglers and black t-shirt. He smiled that smile that always hit her in the gut and stuck his hand out to Nell, and she shook it.

"I'm Ryan Easter, um," his eyes darted to Mary who was staring at him with the same awe in her expression she'd had over the saddle. "I'm Mary's brother."

Mary's expression was also the same expression Twyla imagined she'd worn when she first met Ryan. When she fell in love with him ten years ago out by the bonfire at her parent's ranch. Her heart wiggled in her chest remembering how young they were. And how damned handsome he was even then. She could imagine just how the little girl was feeling.

"You're my brother?" Mary asked, her eyes widening.

"Yes, ma'am, I am," he said with a grin, ruffling her hair like he would a five-year-old. And like a teenager she harrumphed and ran her fingers through her hair until she thought it was straight.

"I'm not a ma'am and don't do that!" she said sassily, jerking a laugh from Ryan.

Twyla saw that the little girl wasn't kidding, she was winding up to blast her new brother. She quickly put her arm around Mary's shoulders. "I think Mary and I are going out to the barn to visit Boney. Y'all have a nice talk."

Twyla stepped around Nell to open the door, and quickly ushered Mary outside. Twyla knew that kid's attitude, because it mirrored hers at that age. Her mouth got her into trouble often, and Twyla knew that would be the case with Mary too if they didn't get out of there. Ryan Easter was going to have both hands full with his new sister, and Twyla would love to be a fly on the wall to watch the fireworks.

But she wouldn't be that fly. She would be in Dallas living her new life, while Ryan figured out his. Sadness tried to steal her good mood, but she pushed it away.

Heather's words came back to shore her up. *Don't give up your dreams for a man.* Well Heather had never been in love with a man like Ryan Easter, but she was right, Twyla wasn't going to do that. She was going back to Dallas to learn cowboy mounted shooting just like she planned, and she was going to live her life. Just the way she wanted to live it. And nobody was going to tell her differently. And from all appearances Ryan wasn't going to try and convince her to stay by uttering the words that would change everything.

She pasted on a smile, when they reached the barn. "Girlfriend, we've got to get you some boots. If Boney steps on your toes, you're going out of luck."

Twyla watched Mary's face wilt when she heard Boney whinny for her at the fence. She had to know what was wrong now. Had she said something to upset her? Walking on eggshells wasn't going to cut it. She stopped walking and turned Mary to face her.

"Why are you frowning?" her damned lower

lip trembled and those blueberry eyes filled.

She pulled her into her arms and hugged her tight. "What's wrong?"

Her voice was barely above a hoarse whisper, when she said, "Daddy was going to give away Boney. That's why him and Mama were fighting."

Twyla hugged her tighter, and rocked her, as she fought her own tears. "Boney isn't going anywhere, baby. Your brother loves horses. He won't make you get rid of him."

"But if my Daddy comes back—"

"He's not coming back," Twyla cut her off. "Your brother is going to make sure he stays right where he belongs and that's not here with y'all." Twyla could only hope her words would prove true.

Tomorrow morning, Ryan was going to make that call if she had to make it for him.

CHAPTER TWENTY-ONE

"What do you mean you can't find his case? It's James, Clarence James," Ryan said impatiently, his heart pounding in his chest. The prosecutor's office not being able to find the file on his stepfather was scaring the shit out of him. What if they'd turned him loose and he was on his way here? His eyes shot to Mary, who was in the kitchen making fricking cookies with Twyla. Lord knew how that would turn out.

The last thing he'd eaten that Twyla made was rock hard biscuits she'd surprised him with one morning at the ranch. The thought had been good, but the biscuits, not so much. He'd choked one down, because at seventeen she had been so proud of herself. He only survived by chasing it with a gallon of coffee, but he hadn't forgotten Twyla's cooking skills. After that, he ran when he saw her in the kitchen at the ranch. But at least Twyla was trying to distract Mary so he could make this call.

"Hold, please," the frustrated woman on the other end of the line said, but she didn't wait for him to respond. Elevator music grated on his nerves while he waited not so patiently. Ryan held three more minutes, and was just about to hang up when a man came on the line.

"Mr. Easter?"

"Yes, who's this?" Ryan had been talking to a damned woman, and he wanted her back because he had a few things to say to her for keeping him on hold so long, and giving him the run around.

"This is Robert Miley, the prosecutor on Mr. James case. You are his stepson is that correct?"

"Yes, he is my stepfather." Saying those words left a bitter taste on his tongue, but Ryan pushed on because surely this man could tell him where the hell Clarence was. "What are the charges against him, and when will it go to trial?"

"I'm afraid it won't sir. You see we didn't have next of kin information for Mr. James, so I'm glad you called..." There was a long pause and Ryan wanted to reach through the phone and choke the information out of the man, before he finally cleared his throat and said, "I regret to inform you that your stepfather was found hanged in his cell yesterday morning. The death seems suspicious in nature, so it is under investigation. If you give me your number, I'll call you when we find out anything." Ryan was too stunned to think, then his shock turned into elation so great he still couldn't speak.

"Mr. Easter, are you there?"

Ryan finally caught his breath, and sucked in a deep lungful of sweet oxygen, then it came out on a whoop so loud his voice echoed off the living room walls. He pressed the button to disconnect the call, and yelled again. Twyla and Mary came running into the room to look at him like he'd lost his mind.

He got choked up. "The Lord works in mysterious ways," Ryan said his voice trembling.

"Yes, He does. He improved your mood. That is a miracle for sure," Twyla replied with a grin.

Ryan saw the confusion on Mary's face, and knew this wasn't a conversation to have in front of her. He'd tell her later, but right now he needed to tell Twyla or bust. "Darlin' can you run out and check to make sure Boney Pony has enough water? I thought the bucket was empty when I was out there earlier."

Mary hesitated a minute, but then she turned and walked to the front door. Once it closed, Ryan put his hands at Twyla's waist and lifted her up. She put her hands on his shoulders and laughed as he spun her around and around.

"Put me down and tell me what the hell has you so excited!" She protested, wiggling out of his grasp.

He sat her down, then held her face in his hands. "Clarence James will never be bothering anyone else ever again. That bastard is dead, d-e-a-d, and may the devil take his evil ass. Someone gave him exactly what he deserved," Ryan threw back his head and his laughter rang in his ears.

When he finished laughing he was weak from it. He staggered to the sofa and sat down. "When are the boys coming over? I think this calls for a celebration. We need to build a bonfire and burn every stick of nasty furniture in this house, and his clothes. Ryan looked at Twyla again, felt his lips twitch and threw his head back against the sofa and laughed again. Fuck, everything in here. Burn the damned house, we'll build another one."

"I think it will be therapeutic, don't you?"

Twyla asked with a smile, as she walked over to him. "Sleeping on the floor and all. I hear it's good for your back. Maybe you should leave it at the furniture and clothes, because you won't have a roof over your head."

Ryan grabbed her and pulled her down on his lap and wrapped his arms around her. "I'm never letting you go baby, you're my good luck charm."

Twyla's eyes glossed over and she looked away, but he didn't miss the tremble in her chin. He grabbed it and turned her face back toward him. His smile fled and his eyebrows slammed down over his eyes. "What's wrong?"

She didn't respond, she just shook her head and got up off of his lap. Without a word, he watched her walk into the kitchen. Ryan got up to follow her in there. She was going to tell him what was wrong with her. She was leaning over the sink with her head bent, and he walked over to her and put his hands on her hips and his chin on her shoulder. "Tell me what's wrong, Twy."

Suddenly, she turned in his arms and put her hands on his shoulders. "If you can't figure it out, I'm not telling you. This one is for you to figure out, Ryan. I've given you enough clues. Ten-years-worth of clues," Twyla squeezed out and ran into the living room. He saw her swipe his cell phone off the end table, before she ran toward the front door, leaving him standing there dumbfounded. He played back the previous minutes in his mind and their conversation, and what he'd said finally dawned on him.

I'm never letting you go baby, you're my good luck charm.

Ryan blew out a breath, and laid his head on the back of the sofa. He didn't want to let her go ever. When she wasn't with him, he felt lost. Ryan Easter was in love with Twyla Taylor, no ifs, ands or buts about it. Had been for years. Twyla meant more to him than his next breath. And she loved him. She'd said so, over and over. Had shown him over and over what it could be like between them. And it was damned good.

"So why the hell are you letting her go, dumbass?" he asked himself and sat up to put his forearms on his knees. He dropped his head and laced his fingers together. "Because her parents hate me now. Her brother hates me. Told me to stay away from them and her."

"When have you ever listened to anyone who told you what to do?" A chill raced down Ryan's spine and he looked up to look around the empty room for the voice he'd just heard in his head. It wasn't his own, it kind of sounded like his mother's. The weirdest sensation floated over his skin, a quick buzzing over every nerve, and then it was gone.

Ryan shoved up to his feet and looked over his shoulder as he almost sprinted toward the front door. He kept running toward the barn. Ryan didn't stop until he spotted a shiny blonde head duck into a stall. He stopped at the barn door and cupped his hands to his mouth to shout, "Twyla Taylor! Get your beautiful ass out here, cowgirl. I have something to stay to you!"

He was going to shout it to the world, just as soon as he found her. He thought for sure she would've come out when he yelled, but she didn't. He walked into the barn and to the stall he'd seen her enter. Opening the door wider, he looked inside and saw Mary sitting on a bale of hay in the corner. Her head was bent and her shoulders shook.

"Mary, what's wrong?" Ryan asked walking inside to kneel beside her.

"She's gone," she said on a whisper. Her hand shot out and she handed him his cell phone. "You made her leave, because you're a dumb man. How can you not love her? Can't you see how great she is? I love her!"

"Where did she go, Mary?" he asked frantically, his heart sinking to his toes. "I am a dumb man, but I'm about to get a lot smarter, baby."

"Heather is picking her up down the road."

"Down the road!?!" he yelled and Mary flinched, covering her head with her hands.

Ryan knelt back down beside her and pulled her trembling body to him. His voice shook as he said, "Mary, I will never hit you, or hurt you. I swear to you on our mother's grave. That will never happen to you again as long as I live…I promise."

Heather was in Dallas. That was a three hour drive, so Twyla had a lot of walking to do, unless they arranged to meet somewhere. He could probably catch her walking on the main roads. "Do you know where they were meeting?"

"She only said down the road," she mumbled into his chest, then sniffed. He thought she was sniffing up her tears, but she sat back and said. "Do you smell smoke?"

Ryan lifted up to sniff, and sure enough something was burning. He walked to the barn door and bright orange flames shot up through the roof through thick black smoke. The whole left side of the house was on fire. The side where the kitchen was located.

"Oh my gosh, it's the cookies!" Mary shouted as she sprinted past him out of the barn running toward the house.

"Mary, no!" he yelled, running behind her. That little girl was track star fast as she pumped her arms in time with her colt-like legs that reminded him of Twyla's. His feet stumbled, but he pushed on after her. "Mary, stop!"

A sharp pain sliced through his side, but he ignored it. "Mary, please!" he yelled, as he focused on putting one foot in front of the other without putting one of those feet into the rutted holes pitting the path to the house. Mary seemed to be zoned in on the house though. As she reached the yard, a figure darted out and caught her around the waist. They rolled several times, ending up under a shade tree near the house. Relief washed through Ryan as he staggered over to the tree and dropped to his knees.

Twyla held Mary to her to her chest and rocked her as she cried, but she didn't look at him.

Ryan dragged in a breath finally, managed to croak, "Thank you."

"I wasn't far down the road and I smelled the smoke and remembered I left the cookies in the oven. I'm so sorry, Ryan," Twyla said in a shaky voice. "I didn't mean to burn your house down. Did you call the fire department?"

"Nope, not going to," he replied with a smile, as he sat on his butt and propped his arm on his knee to watch.

"Ryan, your house is burning down. Don't you think you should call the fire department?" Twyla asked incredulously glancing back at the crackling pile of tinder that was the old farm house.

"Nah, you were right, baby. This is therapeutic," he said with a smile. He tilted his head up to watch the flames licking the eaves of the house, curling over to ignite more of the roof.

More frantic, her voice rose an octave, as she repeated, "Ryan, have your lost your ever loving mind? *Your* house is on fire! It's yours and Mary's now. *Call 9-1-1!*"

Ryan shrugged. "You're not inside, I'm not inside and Mary isn't inside. That's all that matters. That house is not mine, it's Clarence James house." After a loud pop, and a lot of creaking, Ryan flinched when the roof collapsed sending sparks into the air. Ryan tsked, then his eyes glided to hers a he said, "You need to have faith that everything will work out just fine, baby." Twyla had given him that faith with her quiet, steady support. "Too bad the boys are gonna miss the bonfire though."

Twyla, pushed Mary off of her lap and crawled over to him. She grabbed his chin and twisted his face to hers. "Who the hell are you?"

Ryan leaned forward and kissed her. "I'm the man who loves you, sweetheart. You are all I need. Not this house, not the rodeo, nothing other than you. If I've got you, I'm the luckiest bastard on earth." Ryan pushed the heartfelt words past the knot in his throat. "Today has been the best day of my life, baby. Thank you for coming back."

Twyla's eyebrows slammed down over her eyes. "Good Lord, Ryan, I'm calling an ambulance, because something is wrong with you. Did you inhale smoke?"

He laughed. "Are you asking me what I'm smoking, darlin'? Ryan's lips twitched, and he threw his head back and laughed. "I'm just high on life." He sobered and looked back at her. "You've given me a new lease on life, Twyla. I don't know how this can possibly work out, because your family hates me now, but I'm going to try to make it work. I owe them an apology, and I just hope they'll listen. I have faith, and you. That's all I need."

A loud whoosh preceded a blast of heat, before the house that evil built collapsed inward and fell in upon itself. Ryan felt like the last vestiges of his anger and frustration collapse with it.

Burn in hell, Clarence James, he thought, as Twyla put her hand on his shoulder and squeezed. He looked back at her. "I love you, Twyla Taylor."

He leaned over and kissed her cheek. "I want to love you for the rest of my life, but we have a long row to hoe, sweetheart."

"Well, I've loved you half of my life. I evidently like hoeing," she said with a smile against his lips. "We'll get there together, after we figure out where you're going to live now."

"Where we're going to live," he corrected, nipping her lower lip.

Two weeks later, with the on and off help of Lucky, Coop, Tucker and a few more of their rodeo buddies, the remnants of what was Clarence James' house had been razed. The boys had also driven to Dallas to drag Twyla and Ryan's trailers back to Houston, and stopped by her apartment to grab Twyla's stuff too. The trailers were their temporary home until he could figure out how he was going to build a replacement for them. They had joined them at the end, and cut a door between, so Mary would have her own space. It wasn't comfortable, but it was home because Twyla and Mary were here with him.

The ground was now cleared all the way to the back of the twenty acre tract, except for the ramshackle barn that was Boney Pony and Tango's home for now. Ryan's next hurdle turned his blood to ice water in his veins. Breaking that damned pony that Twyla promised Mary she could keep. That pony was a mean bastard. Definitely meaner than any of the broncs he'd ridden on the circuit. He'd almost rather buy her a horse, but he knew he couldn't right now. And Tango was too hot for an inexperienced rider.

And Boney Pony was too hot for him.

With a groan, Ryan headed back to the barn where he saw Twyla and Mary feeding the pony carrots, stroking his forelock, spoiling the damned pony rotten. It was no wonder the animal was mean, the two girls coddled him terribly. And it wasn't any wonder that the now fat black pony hated Ryan, because he didn't.

This would be his third try to get on Boney's back. And this time he was going to do it. Either Ryan would be broken today, or that pony would. He was tired of messing around. When a professional saddle bronc rider couldn't break a damned pony, it was a sad day. Today was a happy day. Every day had been happy since he finally found his balls and admitted his love to Twyla. Whatever happened at her parent's house this weekend, Ryan had already told her he was not letting her go. He would keep trying to make peace with her family until it happened.

And as soon as he managed that, Ryan was asking her daddy for her hand.

Yeah, it was old-fashioned, but it was what Ryan felt was respectful. He owed Mr. Taylor a lot, and that's how he was going to do things. If that man decided he wouldn't forgive Ryan, he and Twyla would live out here in sin for the rest of their lives.

And damned if he didn't love sinning with that woman.

His eyes landed on her delicious rear end in the faded jean shorts with the ragged fringe at the hem. Paired with her cowboy boots, she was just lickable. He wanted to push her into that old barn, find a haystack and make love to her until neither of them could walk.

But he had things to do first. Riding that pony.

Ryan walked into the barn and hefted Twyla's saddle onto his shoulder, then walked back out to the catch pen. Twyla and Mary looked away from the pony to smile at him, Ryan could swear the pony bared his teeth, but not to smile. He wanted to sink those teeth into Ryan's shoulder if he turned his back on him. His penny-colored eyes issued a challenge that Ryan was about to accept. He dropped the saddle and halter on the ground by the fence, so he could climb inside the pen. "Hand me the saddle," he said and Twyla picked it up and hefted it over the fence.

She handed him the halter and rope reins. "Ryan, honey, we can wait until next week to do this. I know your ankle is still sore."

"My ankle is fine. Me and this pony are coming to an understanding today."

"Don't hurt Boney, Ry," Mary said firmly crossing her arms over her chest.

Don't hurt Boney? Boney had kicked his ass three times now, and Mary hadn't worried about him. The last time resulted in an almost-sprained ankle, and who had she run to when he was thrown? The damned pony.

"You wanna ride this pony or not, kid?"

"I want to ride him, but I don't want you to hurt him," she said sticking out her stubborn chin. The resemblance between Twyla and his little sister in both appearance and attitude was remarkable. Fate was a funny thing, saddling him with two difficult women to give him hell on a daily basis was just the ultimate twist. And his heart twisted in his chest. He wouldn't have it any other way. He knew Mary would grow up to be just like Twyla. Strong and determined. That is exactly how he wanted her to be.

Ryan hefted the saddle onto his shoulder again, then leaned over the top fence rail for a quick kiss from Twyla. "Wish me luck."

"I'm your lucky charm, so get your ass in the saddle. But don't get hurt!"

"Yes, ma'am," he said with a laugh and a tip of his hat.

Ryan edged his way over to the pony, and kept his eye on his hind legs, as he threw the saddle over his back. The pony shifted and stomped, snorted a few times, but didn't throw the saddle off and run around the ring this time. Progress. He didn't tie the saddle down yet, he just left it there for the pony to get used to it while he put on the halter, and clipped on the reins.

"Remember he likes to hold in air," Twyla said with a laugh, and Ryan frowned.

"Oh, I remember." The first attempt had ended with him under the pony's belly and the two girls sitting on the ground outside of the fence laughing their butts off at him. Ryan secured the saddle, waited a minute, then slapped the horse's belly. Boney neighed, swished his long tail to slap Ryan in the back, but his belly deflated.

Ryan tested the saddle to ensure it was tight, then picked up the reins and led Boney to the center of the arena, so he didn't try to brush him off against the fence rail like the last time. He didn't want to give the pony the opportunity to finish the job of breaking his ankle.

No, he was wise to all of this animal's tricks now. Like stopping short and throwing him over his head, as in attempt number two, which ended up with him flat on his back in the dust with the horse staring down at him in victory. Ryan was the one who would be victorious today, and Mary was going to have a pony to ride.

Ryan held the saddle, and put his foot in the stirrup, but he stopped to take a deep breath and compose himself. He knew as soon as his ass hit the saddle he better be ready to ride. Adrenaline surged through him, the same feeling he had when he rode wild broncs in the arena came over him, and Ryan hefted himself up. He threw his leg over Boney's back, and like he expected, before he could get his foot in the right stirrup, the pony bucked, danced around from side to side, then squatted. Knowing his next move, Ryan's legs tightened on his sides as he jumped. All four feet left the ground, then Ryan gritted his teeth against the jarring impact when they landed back on the ground.

I'm riding you, bitch, he thought, as his fist tightened on the reins. Give me your best shot. My ass is glued in this saddle today. Ryan's fist tightened on the reins as the pony headed for the rail at a sprint. Ut uh, not today he thought, turning him by bending his neck to the left. The pony ran along the rail, and Ryan held on for dear life. Surprisingly, he only kicked once on the second circuit, then on the third he snorted, and slowed his pace a little. Ryan patted the pony's neck. "Good boy," he said, and the horse snorted again and slowed to a walk.

"You did it, Ry!" Mary squealed over at the fence, and pride shot through him.

He smiled over at her, and just that fast taking his eye off the ball cost him. The pony's neck bent to the left, and his teeth clamped on Ryan's calf.

"*Fuck!*" Ryan squealed, his voice a couple of octaves higher than normal, as he jerked the reins. Boney bucked, then took a hard right, before Ryan could get his balance again. He felt himself flying, and tucked to keep from breaking something. He rolled three times, before he stopped in a heap at the center of the ring.

Embarrassment heated his face, as Ryan got to his feet and brushed off his ass, then his chaps. He saw his hat on the ground near the rail with the crown smashed flat to the brim. Anger surged through him as he walked over there and snatched it up to dust it off. He put his fist inside and punched it back out.

"Damned pony," he grumbled, as he spun

back to go in for round two of the day. He stopped short when he saw Mary stroking the pony's neck. Hugging him, and him nuzzling the side of her face. Women, he thought as he started toward them. Mary stepped back and bent to take the reins in her hand. Ryan stopped again, but held his body tense ready to intervene if necessary. That pony was damned mean, and totally unpredictable. Mary grabbed the horn and gingerly watched Boney, as she put her left foot in the stirrup. The pony stood perfectly still for her, which was an amazing thing in itself.

"It's okay, Boney. I want us to have fun together," she cooed, as she slowly lifted herself up, then eased her leg over his back. The pony swished his tail, but it was fly swatting swish, not an angry swish. He shifted his weight on his feet, but it wasn't in preparing to kick out.

Mary eased her butt down into the well of the saddle, then inserted her right foot into the stirrup and smiled. Thank God she had the boots on that Twyla had found for her at the thrift store. At least if she fell off her feet wouldn't get stomped on and her toes broken. Just her skull he thought, and his body lurched forward. But Mary clucked to the pony and his ears perked up. Ryan saw her nudge him with her knee, and the pony moved.

Mary giggled. "Good boy, that's it. Let's ride, boy. Teach me to ride."

Twyla had been working with her, and teaching her, but as far as he knew this was the first time Mary had been up in her life. Fear was a vise that squeezed his heart in his chest as he watched her move the pony along the rail.

"You're doing good, Mary," Twyla said calmly as she passed her at the rail. "That's it baby, keep your center of balance in the saddle."

And didn't that just beat all? A twelve-year-old girl had just shown up a seasoned professional rodeoer. Sometimes life didn't make a damned bit of sense. But if the end result was what you wanted it to be, what the hell did it matter? The smile on Mary's face made losing his dignity very worthwhile.

CHAPTER TWENTY-TWO

Ryan was as nervous as he'd ever been in his life, but Twyla's fingers laced through his was a lifeline as he walked through the front door of the Taylor home. This was the most important day of his life, and he definitely needed to bring his A game, and as much backup as he could gather, if he was going to get Mr. Taylor to listen to him.

His life depended on that. Twyla would never be his for real, forever, unless he managed it. Yeah, she would stay with him. She loved him, against all odds, but it would never be the same until he put his ring on her finger. He knew she wanted that. He did too. Badly. That ring would tell the world that she was his. That he was hers. And with her family's blessing, they could live the life they wanted to live. The way they wanted to live it. Together.

The part that made him most nervous about this family meeting that Twyla had called, was the fact that Zack was going to be there. He hadn't seen his best friend since they were in jail together. Ryan knew that Zack would blame him for that too. It was just the way he was. Hardheaded, opinionated and usually put upon. But he could be one of the most caring men you've ever met in your life too. He was the one who had dragged Ryan to his house after school the day he told him he was running away from home, because his new stepfather was an asshole.

That day he'd become a part of the Taylor

family. They had taken him in without question, after his mother gave her permission for him to live with them. And thank God she had, or he would never have become who he was today. He probably would be in prison for killing Clarence. This family had saved him. And because of his choice not to tell them about what Twyla was up to he had hurt them, let them down.

This situation was all his damned fault, and he felt damned bad about it. But he wasn't going to let their anger or warning to stay away keep him from what he needed to do.

When have you ever listened to anyone who told you what to do?

Those mysterious words replayed in his mind, and a chill skirted down his spine to settle at the base. Whoever kept repeating that to him, was definitely doing him a favor. Those words had played over and over in his mind since he'd heard them in the farmhouse. They gave him determination, because they were right on the mark. Everything Ryan wanted in life he'd gone after, until Twyla. Her he'd backed off from, because of the debt he owed her family.

Her brother made sure he was reminded of that debt, but usually in subtle ways.

Now that Ryan thought about it, Zack had to know how he felt about Twyla. Those subtle warnings were to keep him away from her too. The warnings he'd given other men who showed an interest in Twyla weren't so subtle. Ryan was thankful for those though, because it kept Twyla from getting attached to someone else. It kept her there for him. Even though what Zack had done to her wasn't fair, Ryan didn't fault him for it.

He'd done the same thing for years, but for different reasons.

He released her hand to put his arm around her shoulders. She smiled up at him and the impact hit him right in the gut. He was so damned lucky. "I love you, Daisy," Ryan said gruffly, before he stopped to give her a quick but potent kiss.

"I love you too, cowboy," she said tightening her arm around his waist.

Together they walked into the living room, and the Taylors were already assembled. None of them looked happy about being there. Mr. Taylor's eyes burned a hole in him from his seat in the large chair by the fireplace. Zack and his mother sat on opposite ends of the sofa, so the only place left for he and Twyla to sit was the loveseat.

Ryan forced a smile, but not a single one returned it. Twyla stroked his side in silent, but steady support as he led her to the loveseat. They sat down, and she put her hand on his knee. Again the silent support. God, he loved her. That gave him the courage to say, "I came here to say I'm sorry, Mr. and Mrs. Taylor." His eyes bounced over to Zack who had a look on his face that said he'd love nothing better than to personally escort Ryan out of the house. He sucked in a breath. "I'm sorry, Zack."

"You certainly are you sorry sonofa—"

Cowgirl Crazy

"Zack!" Mrs. Taylor shouted, giving him a warning look.

"What exactly are you sorry for, Ryan?" Mr. Taylor asked, with an edge of anger in his tone. Mrs. Taylor shot him a look too, and he left it at that. Ryan knew he had a lot more to say, because it was right there on his face.

"I'm sorry for not telling you what Twyla was doing in Dallas, before she got hurt doing it. That was wrong of me. I thought I could fix things before they got out of hand, but—" he stopped to swallow down the knot of emotion that choked him. "But I was wrong."

"Damned straight you were," Mr. Taylor said with a snort. "You left it to her friend to tell us what was going on. We probably still wouldn't know if she hadn't ."

The words settled in Twyla's brain, and stunned her. Her gaze swung to her daddy, and she shook her head. "Wait. Are you telling me that Heather is the one who told you I'd been dancing at the Cowgirl?"

"That's right. She came to the hospital, before *he*," her daddy's lip curled, and his eyes pinned Ryan. "Before he got there and let the cat out of the bag. You should be ashamed."

Anger surged up to choke her. Twyla shot to her feet, and pulled away when Ryan's hand clamped down on her forearm. "Well, I'm not daddy. The only damned thing I'm ashamed of is how you and Zack acted when you found out. How you're treating

Ryan now. It's not Ryan's fault I was dancing, and it certainly not his fault I continued even after he tried to get me to stop. I'm a grown woman, and I make those decisions."

"You were raised better, Twyla," her mother said with a shake in her voice.

"I was raised by the best two parents a girl could ever have. That's why you should have faith that I will make the right decisions for myself. They might not be what you'd decide, but you don't get to decide for me anymore. You've done your job, raised me to be a good, caring person, now let me be that. If I make a mistake, then I have to deal with that too. I'm an adult now." Twyla ran out of steam, so she sat back on the loveseat beside Ryan.

He slipped his arm around the back of her shoulders, and she felt his body tense. "Mr. and Mrs. Taylor there's more…"

"Lord help us," Twyla's mother muttered, covering her mouth with her hand. Zack growled, and her daddy sat up straighter in his chair.

Ryan's eyes met her daddy's and he swallowed hard. "I'm in love with your daughter sir. I don't deserve her, but she loves me too. We want to make a life together, and I'd appreciate your blessing."

Her daddy's face turned a shade of red she'd never seen before. Almost purple, and Twyla knew if she didn't say something, this was going to hell in a handbasket right before her eyes. She stood again. "I do love him, Daddy. This is one of those adult decisions I was talking about. You can get red in the face all you want, and rant all you want, but Ryan and I are going to be together whether you approve or not. The choice you do have is whether you want me in your life or not from here on out. If you do, you'll accept him back in the family. He hasn't done a damned thing wrong, or slighted any of you." Twyla slowly moved to each one giving them a meaningful glare, then her eyes swung to Ryan, who looked so proud of her he was about to burst with it. This next part wasn't true, but they didn't know that. It would help her win her case, and that is what she was determined to do here. This idiocy had to stop.

"Ryan only did what I asked him to do. He voiced his opinion on what I was doing, he didn't like it a bit either. But let me make up my own mind. I'd ask you to do the same."

"You sure have got a lot to say lately, lit—" her daddy stopped and his mouth formed an O, then he cleared his throat. "Twyla Renee."

Her heart lurched in her chest. She loved it when her daddy called her little girl, but it had to take on a different meaning now. A show of affection, instead of domination.

"Daddy, I will *always* be your little girl. That will never change. What has changed is I'm no longer a little girl. I'm all grown up, and thanks to you I know right from wrong." Her eyes slowly moved from person to person, before they settled back on her daddy. "What this family is doing to Ryan Easter is just wrong. You've shunned him," she said waving a hand at her father. Her eyes swung to Zack, who sat there in brooding silence with his body language saying he wasn't listening. "And you've bankrupted your best friend." Her eyes left her brother to meet her mother's gaze. "And you have judged him, mama. You may not have voiced it, but I see it in your eyes when you look at him. He sees it too and it hurts, because you are all as close to family as this man has ever had, will ever have. You should love him as much as I do, and I know you do. He's as much a part of this family as I am. Are you going to shun me too, cut me from the herd, because you think I made the wrong decision by dancing at the Cowgirl?"

She folded her arms over her chest to wait for an answer. Bodies squirmed, faces ticked and fists clenched, but not a single one of them said a word. "I need an answer now. If you cut Ryan, you cut me too. We'll leave and you'll n—nev" Twyla sucked up the emotion that shot to her eyes on a deep breath, and blew it out. "You'll never see us again, if that's the way you want it. Never see the grandchildren we might have, or the one you've already gotten by osmosis."

Her daddy shot to his feet and roared, "*What?!?*"

She laughed, because she couldn't help it. "I'm not pregnant, daddy, and there's no hidden baby." His breath escaped like a deflating balloon as he collapsed back in the chair. "But Ryan has a sister he didn't know about, and since his mother and stepfather are dead..." Twyla stopped when her mother gasped as her eyes flew to Ryan, her father's face paled, and her brother just looked shocked. "That's right, that's what *we've* been dealing with. *Real life problems*, not made up drama over things that don't amount to a hill of beans." Twyla let the silence linger before she drove home her final point. "The house he had to raise his sister in burned down. We're living in our trailers on the property, until we can do better. Our money is pretty doggone slim right now because neither of us has an income, and we now have an extra mouth to feed. But you know what? We're both happier than we've ever been in our lives. And that should make you happy if you love us. If you hold onto your grudge, and don't want us around? We'll still be happy, which is more than I can say for you." Twyla plopped back down on the sofa and breathed a sigh of relief. She'd said her peace, now it was up to her family to decide what they were going to do.

Her mother was the first to break the silence. "Ryan, I'm so sorry about your mother, honey. Was it your..."

Ryan's body tensed beside her, his eyes welled up, and he nodded.

"Ooh, I see. I'm so sorry, honey." Hope sprang and grew inside of Twyla when her mother got up and walked over to Ryan to put her arms around his neck. He hugged her back tightly. Finally, they separated and she sniffled, as she walked back to the sofa and sat down.

Next her daddy rose, and Twyla held her

breath as he walked to stand before Ryan. He studied him a minute then stuck out his hand, and Ryan took it. "I'm sorry for treating you poorly, son. I don't have any excuse except I treasure my daughter, and want what's best for her. I think you're best for her." He looked at Twyla and chuckled. "You're gonna have your hands full though. I hope you know what you're biting off."

"I know exactly what I'm buying into, Mr. Taylor, and I want a lifetime of it from your daughter. I wouldn't have her any other way. Thank you, sir." Her daddy gave her a long searching look, then nodded before he walked back to his chair.

Zack hadn't said a word, he'd barely moved. Twyla knew he was going to be the toughest nut to crack, and if it took her cracking his to get him to come around, that's what she was going to do. She pinned him with a hot glare and lifted her brow, letting her eyes do the talking.

They had a standoff between them for long minutes, then he finally broke. Zack pushed up off of the sofa and walked over to Ryan to grudgingly stick out his hand. Ryan stared at it a moment, looked up into Zack's hard blue eyes, but he didn't take his hand. He stood up, and they were nose to nose. A position they'd been in a lot lately. "You're my damned brother, and I expected a helluva lot better from you," Ryan grated, his voice emotional.

"And you're my damned brother, and I expected you to tell me Twyla was working in a strip club, before she ended up in the hospital, because some asshole took advantage of her. And I also didn't expect you to make time with her yourself."

"You're not blind. You know I've been in love with her for years, but you've run interference every single time. I appreciate what you and your family have done for me, but I didn't think you did it so I was indebted to you. If that's the case, tell me how much I owe you and I'll work twenty-four hours a day to pay it back. I love your damned sister, but not like a sister. I want her to be my wife, and you'll just have to deal with having me for a real brother, asshole."

"I'll deal with it. And you'll just have to deal with me being a permanent fixture in your life too. I'll be watching you, *brother*. You fuck my sister over and I'll mess you up," Zack growled.

"You fuck my wife over, and you'll deal with me too," Ryan shot back. "Oh, and if you are so worried about your sister being taken care of, I suggest you put your money where your mouth is. Buy out my share of the rough stock herd, so I can build her a house."

"*Fine*!" Zack hissed through his teeth.

"Fine!" Ryan spat back. They glared at each other a moment longer, then Zack's lips twitched, before he pulled Ryan into a man hug and pounded him on the back.

Twyla just watched the interaction in awe of how Neanderthal the apology was between the two men she loved. Whatever, it worked, and they were hugging. At least they weren't fighting, even though that's exactly what it sounded like.

Before Zack released him, he growled in his ear. "Take care of her, dude."

Ryan sucked in a breath. "I will. I promise."

Twyla stood up and tapped Ryan on the shoulder, and he separated from Zack to face her. Zack stood at his side. She folded her arms, and tilted her head. "Um, have y'all forgotten one small detail here?"

Ryan looked at Zack then they glanced at her parents, before looking back her way. "I don't think so?" he said.

"Y'all have married us off, everyone has agreed here but me. I don't remember anyone asking me, yet."

"Holy shit," Ryan said his eyebrows shooting up to his hairline. He grabbed her hand in his then sank to his knees. "Twyla Renee Taylor," he looked down a moment and breathed, seeming to gather himself, then looked back up at her. "I love you more than I thought I could ever love a cowgirl who has driven me slap damned crazy for a decade. You are my lucky charm, baby, and my life goes to hell every time you're not in it. Would you please do me the honor of marrying me?"

Don't give up your dreams for a man.

Heather's words played through her mind. Well, she was following Heather's advice. Twyla wasn't giving up her dream, she was going to live it. This man was her dream, had been her dream since she was a teenager. "Yes, I will. But that obey thing has definitely got to be removed from our vows. I hope you know that ain't ever gonna happen," she said with a grin.

Her brother snorted, her mother giggled and her father guffawed from his chair by the fireplace.

Ryan didn't look one bit surprised.

ABOUT THE AUTHOR

Becky McGraw is a married mother of three adult children, and a Southern girl by birth and the grace of God, ya'll. She resides in South Texas with her husband and dog Abby. A jack of many trades in her life, Becky has been an optician, a beautician, a legal secretary, a senior project manager for an aviation management consulting firm, which took her all over the United States, a real estate broker, and now a graphic artist, web designer and writer.

She knows just enough about a variety of topics to make her dangerous, and her romance novels interesting and varied. Being a graphic artist is a good thing for her, too, because she creates her own cover art, along with writing the novels.

Becky has been an avid reader of romance novels since she was a teenager, and has been known to read up to four novels of that genre a week, much to the dismay of her husband, and the delight of e-book sellers.

She has been writing fictional short stories and novels for fun, as well as technical copy for her jobs for many years. She was a member of the Writer's Guild on AOL during her last venture into writing romance, as well as a founding member and treasurer of the first online chapter of the Romance Writers of America, From the Heart Romance Writers. Currently, she is a member of both organizations.

You can contact Becky McGraw at
beckymcgrawbooks@gmail.com
Please 'Like' Becky on her Facebook fan page at
www.facebook.com/beckymcgrawbooks and visit her
website at www.beckymcgraw.com

Printed in Great Britain
by Amazon.co.uk, Ltd.,
Marston Gate.